Also by Matthew Reilly

CONTEST
TEMPLE
HOVER CAR RACER
THE TOURNAMENT
TROLL MOUNTAIN
THE GREAT ZOO OF CHINA
THE SECRET RUNNERS OF NEW YORK

Scarecrow
ICE STATION
AREA 7
SCARECROW
HELL ISLAND
SCARECROW AND THE ARMY OF THIEVES

Jack West Jr
THE SEVEN ANCIENT WONDERS
THE SIX SACRED STONES
THE FIVE GREATEST WARRIORS
THE FOUR LEGENDARY KINGDOMS
THE THREE SECRET CITIES
THE TWO LOST MOUNTAINS

MATTHEW REILLY

THE ONE IMPOSSIBLE LABYRINTH

MATTHEW REILLY

THE ONE IMPOSSIBLE LABYRINTH

MACMILLAN
Pan Macmillan Australia

This is a work of fiction. Characters, institutions and organisations mentioned in this novel are either the product of the author's imagination or, if real, used fictitiously without any intent to describe actual conduct.

Pan Macmillan acknowledges the Traditional Custodian of country throughout Australia and their connections to lands, waters and communities. We pay our respect to Elders past and present and extend that respect to all Aboriginal and Torres Strait Islander peoples today. We honour more than sixty thousand years of storytelling, art and culture.

First published 2021 in Macmillan by Pan Macmillan Australia Pty Ltd
1 Market Street, Sydney, New South Wales, Australia, 2000

A catalogue record for this book is available from the National Library of Australia

Typeset in 11/14 pt Sabon by Post Pre-press Group
Printed by IVE

The images on page 56 are from Getty Images
All other internal illustrations and endpapers by IRONGAV

The author and the publisher have made every effort to contact copyright holders for material used in this book. Any person or organisation that may have been overlooked should contact the publisher.

The paper in this book is FSC® certified. FSC® promotes environmentally responsible, socially beneficial and economically viable management of the world's forests.

This one is for all of my
loyal readers.
You'll soon see why!

Sometimes what people think is your greatest weakness
can actually be your greatest strength.

JACK WEST JR

A man's reach should exceed his grasp.

ROBERT BROWNING

PREVIOUSLY . . .

At the end of *The Two Lost Mountains* the fate of all life in the universe hung in the balance.

A dozen cities around the world lay silent, their populations gripped by the mysterious sleep of **SPHINX**'s Siren bells.

A wild battle was fought at the entrance to the Supreme Labyrinth as **JACK WEST JR** and his friends blasted their way through thousands of bronzemen guarding the Labyrinth's entrances.

At the very last moment, using a side-turned ejection seat, Jack managed to get inside the Labyrinth with **ZOE**, **LILY** and **EASTON**.

Now, with **THE OMEGA EVENT**—the collapse of the universe— only three days away, everything depends on what happens inside the Labyrinth.

If someone sits on a fabled **THRONE** inside the Labyrinth, the collapse of the universe will be prevented, all life will be saved, and that person will rule the world.

But if no-one sits on the throne in time, the entire universe will stop expanding and rush inward, crushing itself and extinguishing all life in a mighty instantaneous singularity.

AT THE LABYRINTH

Five separate groups entered the Supreme Labyrinth.

Team 1, 24 hours ago: **SPHINX** and **CARDINAL MENDOZA**, escorted by three **KNIGHTS OF THE GOLDEN EIGHT** and eight cannibal **VANDALS**.

Team 2, 24 hours ago: **BROTHER EZEKIEL** and five of his monks from the Order of the Omega.

Team 3, 12 hours ago: **DION** and three **SQUIRES OF THE GOLDEN EIGHT**, coming to assist Sphinx.

Team 4, ten minutes ago: **GENERAL RASTOR** and seven of his fanatically loyal Serbian commandos.

Team 5, right now: **JACK, ZOE, LILY** and **EASTON**, plus four **PALEMEN** (bronzemen splashed with pale blue paint who obey Easton because of the ring of command that he wears).

JACK'S PEOPLE

The Two Lost Mountains ended with Jack's larger team split into four subgroups:

SUBGROUP 1: THE FOUR IN THE LABYRINTH
JACK and his group at the Labyrinth.

SUBGROUP 2: EN ROUTE TO ITALY
IOLANTHE and her former mentor, the Jesuit named **BERTIE**, headed to Italy with **NOBODY BLACK** in search of the **BLUE BELL**—the long-lost Siren bell capable of undoing the sleep—and someone named 'Albano's Emissary'.

SUBGROUP 3: ON THE BATTLEFIELD
During the battle outside the Supreme Labyrinth, **ALBY CALVIN,**

ALOYSIUS KNIGHT and RUFUS ejected out of Rufus's Sukhoi Su-37 just as it was overwhelmed by bronzemen.

Where they landed is as yet unknown.

SKY MONSTER was last seen inside the smashed remains of a C-5 Super Galaxy cargo plane that he had deliberately crashed onto the battlefield as part of Jack's Russian Doll plan.

SUBGROUP 4: THE ROYAL HUNTERS

When Jack and the others had headed off from Cairo International Airport for the Labyrinth, POOH BEAR and STRETCH had departed from Cairo with SISTER LYNDA FADEL and the ear/bell specialist DR TRACY SMITH, to find out where the royal families of the world would go in advance of the Omega Event.

We rejoin our story inside the Supreme Labyrinth . . .

FIRST TEST OF WORTH

ENTERING THE LABYRINTH

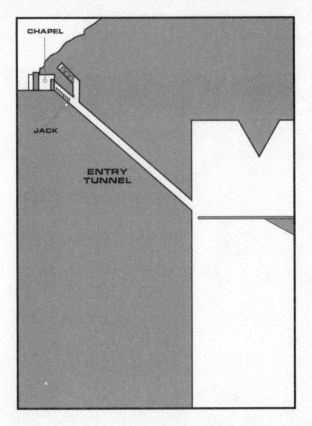

Initiation is much more than a communication of knowledge.
It involves not only knowing the hieroglyphic code . . . but also
demonstrating that one is worthy of this knowledge.

THE SECRET HISTORY OF
HERMES TRISMEGISTUS
FLORIAN EBELING
(CORNELL UNIVERSITY PRESS, 2011)

Holding a glowstick above his head, Jack West Jr stood at the top of a long square-sided tunnel that plunged into darkness.

Lily and Zoe stood beside him, while Easton and his four pale-men stood at the rear.

They all peered down the entry tunnel.

It descended at a steep angle, with broad steps going all the way down its length and walls of solid stone.

A dim orange glow could be seen at the bottom end, two hundred metres away: a small square of light.

And then they heard them.

Distant sounds, coming from down there.

Screams. Shouts. Gunfire.

The sounds of battle.

Amid the gunshots and shouts, a voice wailed, '*Kill me! Oh God, please kill me!*'

'What the hell are we walking into?' Zoe breathed.

'The final battle in a winner-takes-all war,' Jack said. 'Let's move.'

He edged down the tunnel, leading with his glowstick and Desert Eagle pistol—

—when with a shrill squeal a small red figure sprang out of a wide shaft in the ceiling, landing on Jack's shoulders and quickly trying *to bite his face off.*

Jack caught the attacker at the last instant, grabbing the short man by the throat as they both fell back onto the steps in a jumbled heap.

As Jack desperately held him at bay, the little man snapped and snarled savagely—his red tattooed face a vision from a horror movie—his sharpened fangs, filed to deadly points, clamping together inches away from Jack's nose.

Jack leaned back, his eyes widening in revulsion and . . . recognition.

He'd seen a man like this once before.

In the Underworld.

Hades's sinister jester, Mephisto.

The one who had toyed with minotaurs before he killed them for the entertainment of the royal guests.

The one who had stowed aboard Jack's plane when Jack had departed from the Underworld after the Great Games and who had tried to murder Jack while he slept.

But Jack had turned the tables and caused Mephisto to be sucked horrendously out through one of the plane's windows, killing him.

This little bastard looked exactly like Mephisto: short in stature but lean and muscled, with tattooed red skin that was spiked in places with horns that had been surgically implanted subdermally.

And like Mephisto, the little fucker could fight.

He produced a short curved blade that Jack caught as it came rushing at his throat.

And those teeth, razor sharp and slashing in a manner that was more animal than human—

Boom!

The little man's head snapped back in a burst of blood, blown almost completely off his shoulders, as Zoe fired her pistol from point-blank range.

The attacker's body, its fingernails still clinging to Jack's jacket, went limp and Jack kicked it off him.

'Goddamn,' he gasped. 'A nasty little welcoming party Sphinx must have left behind.'

Lily slid to Jack's side. 'Are you okay?'

'Yeah. Just some scratches.'

Zoe looked distastefully at the dead attacker. 'Who the hell is this? *What* the hell is this?'

She hadn't been at the Underworld for the Great Games.

Jack said, 'He looks like that jester from the Underworld. Mephisto.'

'He is Vandal,' Easton said, appearing beside them.

'A Vandal?' Lily said. 'Like the ones who sacked Rome in the fifth century?'

'Yes,' Easton said.

Jack said, 'Sister Lynda mentioned Vandals once. She said Sphinx brought some to Novodevichy Convent in Moscow when he came for the Siren bells.'

Easton said, 'Vandals are small warrior race. Fearsome and fierce, like rabid dogs. Use teeth in combat. Eat flesh. But Vandals very rare now. Only the richest royals keep them.'

'Like Hades kept Mephisto?' Lily said.

Easton nodded.

Zoe said, 'As I recall, Sister Lynda mentioned Sphinx had eight of them.'

'Seven now,' Jack said.

He frowned in thought. 'Speaking of numbers, we need to take stock. Figure out who's here and when they arrived.'

He ticked off each group on his fingers: 'Okay. Sphinx got here first, twenty-four hours ago, presumably accompanied by his advisors and military muscle. He's a whole day ahead of us.'

Zoe nodded. 'Second were the Omega monks led by Brother Ezekiel. We saw their crashed jet outside.'

'Third was Dion, with some Squires of the Golden Eight. We overheard Sphinx ordering him to come here from Mont Blanc to help. And finally, Rastor and us.'

Lily said, 'We're behind again—'

A loud noise from the low end of the entry tunnel cut her off.

An explosion.

Jack spun instinctively, ready to run, but he caught himself.

He didn't want to rush around inside this place. Who knew what traps and snares lay in it.

He looked at the tunnel around them.

Its stone steps stretched from wall to wall.

Lowering his glowstick closer to the ground, he noted that one of the steps was *not* cut from stone.

It was made of some kind of metal. It shone dully.

'A shining stair,' Jack said softly. 'Lily. You translated some of those phrases on Imhotep's skull before. What was it you said about a shining stair?'

Lily looked at the mummified skull in her pack, the head of the Egyptian architect and thinker, Imhotep, covered in tattoos:

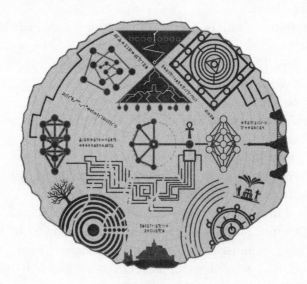

She read one set of Thoth glyphs on it.

'These markings say, *Once you pass the shining stair, there is no going back.*'

Jack frowned. 'It's a threshold of some ki—'

'Captain Jack,' Easton interrupted a little urgently.

'Yes?'

'One more thing about Vandals. Mephisto was unusual Vandal. Lived alone. Killed his partner as joke. Usually Vandals work in pairs.'

Jack spun, alarmed. 'Wait, what?'

He snapped to look up at the dark recess in the roof of the tunnel above them just as a second Vandal came leaping out of it, teeth bared, knife raised and shrieking in animal rage!

The small red-faced assassin slammed down on top of Jack and the two of them went tumbling down the stairs, bouncing on the metal step—

—and instantly an ominous groaning sound came from within the recess in the ceiling.

The sound of stone grinding against stone.

Booby trap.

Lily and Zoe looked up at the noise, while Easton dived to help Jack.

The diminutive Vandal was a ball of ferocious energy. Knife in hand, it hissed fiercely as it leapt at Easton, only to be caught in mid-leap, literally snatched out of the air by—one of Easton's palemen.

It was the paleman whose eyeless metal face had been scratched as it had rolled under the lowering stone slab closing off the Labyrinth, leaving a curved mark that resembled a crooked smile.

The emotionless automaton held the writhing Vandal three feet off the ground with one robotic hand. Its grip was vice-like.

'Kill it,' Easton commanded.

The paleman obeyed immediately, squeezing its fist, breaking the Vandal's neck with a sharp crack, killing the little assassin. It dropped the corpse to the floor.

Jack clambered to his feet, looking from the dead Vandal to the paleman with the scratched smile.

'Thanks, Smiley,' he said.

The grinding sound from within the recess above them grew louder.

'I think I just crossed the shining stair and triggered a trap. We need to move. Go! *Go!*'

They bolted.

They were thirty metres down the tunnel when a massive cube-shaped stone dropped out of the recess into the tunnel—filling the square-shaped passageway perfectly—and began to slide down it after them.

Down the tunnel they bounded, running for all they were worth.

Jack led the way, eyeing the square-shaped opening at the bottom.

It still glowed with dim light. As he came closer to it, he saw that it was actually a full-sized doorway.

The others raced down the tunnel with him, while behind them the big square stone rumbled as it slid, grinding against the steps, gradually gaining speed.

The thing was huge.

It must've weighed thirty tons. And it filled the tunnel completely.

Imhotep had been right: once you crossed the shining stair, there was no going back.

Jack reached the doorway at the bottom end of the tunnel and he stopped with a lurch.

'Uh-oh . . .'

Zoe arrived at his side. 'What's the hold-up—oh my.'

Jack stole a glance back at the thirty-ton stone block sliding down the tunnel behind them. 'We got a serious problem.'

The problem: their tunnel just *ended*.

The staircase simply stopped, its bottommost step dropping away to nothing but thin air, leaving them standing on a small ledge cut into a colossal underground cliff overlooking a larger cavern . . .

. . . in which a wild battle was already taking place, with bullets flying and grenades exploding . . .

. . . all while the sliding stone accelerated down the stairs behind them, coming to hurl them off the cliff.

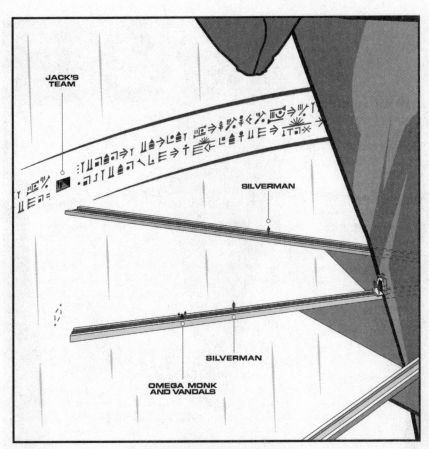

**JACK'S ENTRY TUNNEL
AND BRIDGE**

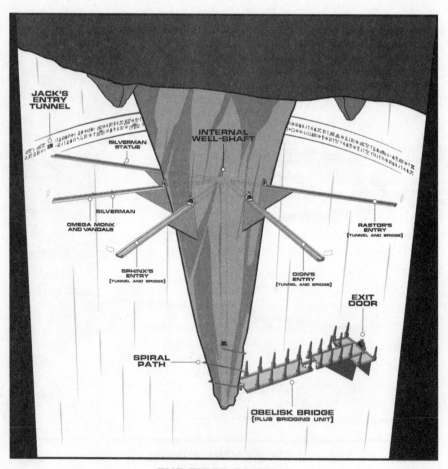

THE FIRST CAVERN

Jack figured he had about twenty seconds.

First, he took in the enormous cavern.

It was unlike anything he had ever seen before.

Its walls, bridges and other surfaces were made of three substances: rough uneven rock, smooth concrete-like greystone and a burnished bronze-coloured metal.

Jack and his team were high up on one side of a gigantic abyss that plummeted away into fathomless darkness.

The main feature of this space was a colossal stalactite hanging from the ceiling that was the size of a fifteen-storey skyscraper.

Up at the top, where it was widest, this upside-down skyscraper appeared to be made mostly of natural rock. But as it stretched downward and became narrower, it was fashioned from the two added-on materials: metal and greystone.

Five bridges—superlong and made of the strange bronze metal and sporting low gutters—radiated like spokes on a wheel from the upper reaches of the skyscraper.

Each bridge was aimed at one of five entry tunnels—all identical to Jack's—that opened onto the vast space.

Only the bridges didn't reach *all the way* to the entry tunnels.

They ended six feet short of them and about six feet *below* them.

Jack looked down at the wide gap of empty space between him and the tip of the half-bridge facing him.

The intention of the gap was clear: it was designed to stop anyone from jumping *back* to the entry tunnel after they had leapt across—

Jack froze.

There was someone on his half-bridge.

Right in its middle, blocking the way.

Wait, no, it wasn't a person.

It was a statue. A stone statue, tall and man-shaped.

But then the statue began to shudder, as if it were cracking from within, and suddenly its outer shell of stone fell away in many tiny flakes to reveal a figure previously encased inside it.

A silverman.

One of the elite automaton guards, one level higher than the bronzemen.

And this one stood guard halfway along the bridge, barring the way.

'We are *so* not in Kansas anymore,' Lily whispered.

'Jack . . .' Zoe urged.

The big sliding stone was grinding down the entry tunnel behind them, gathering speed.

Jack's mind raced.

This was all happening too fast.

He wanted to know more about this place before he jumped across onto some guttered half-bridge with a silverman on it, but the sliding stone bearing down on them was making the decision for him.

He was processing all of this when a hideous scream from nearby made him turn.

'*Somebody kill me!*' It was the same voice they'd heard before.

Jack spun to his right and saw the source of the cry over on the next half-bridge.

It was an Omega monk.

Jack swallowed in horror at what he saw.

The lone Omega monk was lying on his back on the half-bridge . . . only his guttered bridge was *filled* to knee-height with solidified greystone and the monk lay half encased in the cement-like substance.

He must have fallen into the greystone when it had been in liquid form, for his hands, waist and mid-section were sealed in it while his head was above it.

Only that wasn't the horrific part.

The horrific part was the pair of Vandals currently crouched over him and taking slashing bloody bites out of his exposed face and shoulders.

They were eating him alive.

'Please Lord, kill me!'

Jack stared in horror. Sphinx must have left more Vandals at the other entrances.

Near the two feasting Vandals stood another silverman, the one evidently assigned to guard that bridge. It stood *on* the greystone, not in it, and it just remained there impassively, doing nothing about the gruesome cannibalism taking place in front of it.

'This is messed up,' Lily said.

'*Jack* . . .' Zoe said again.

The huge sliding stone behind them was moving fast and almost on them.

'Lily, Zoe, quickly, jump across, now,' Jack ordered. 'Onto the half-bridge. We'll follow behind you.'

The two women leapt out from the open mouth of the entry tunnel, flying briefly across the gap above the abyss, before landing on the metal bridge in identical crouches.

Jack checked on the sliding stone. It kept rumbling down the entry tunnel.

Easton went next, with his palemen.

Then it was Jack's turn.

The oncoming sliding stone was only a few feet away when Jack jumped, launching himself from the mouth of the tunnel, out over the void—

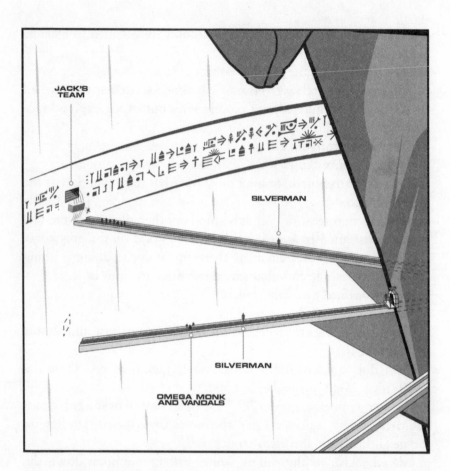

—just as the sliding stone came roaring out of the tunnel behind him, flew off the edge and dropped away into the abyss.

Jack landed on his stomach on the half-bridge. Lily and Zoe hauled him up.

'There's no going back now,' Lily said.

'No,' Jack agreed.

From his position at the end of the half-bridge, he looked out over the cavern.

And spotted what he was looking for.

The exit.

Far below them, level with the bottom tip of the upside-down skyscraper, was a striking ultra-long bridge decorated with an avenue of obelisks.

This obelisk bridge led to the only apparent exit from the cavern: a high decorative arch framing a tunnel that burrowed into the wall down there. But there was a problem with that bridge.

It was broken in the middle.

Someone—probably Sphinx—had blasted away a segment in its centre, presumably to prevent later arrivals from crossing it.

But the strategy hadn't completely worked.

For Jack could see something *on* the obelisk bridge, spanning the exploded-open gap.

A military bridging unit: a long plank of telescoping carbon fibre that had been laid over the gap.

Then, abruptly, Jack saw a group of eight tiny figures emerge at a sprint from the bottom tip of the skyscraper and run out across the bridge *and* the bridging unit.

He recognised their leader instantly. It was hard not to, he was such a huge man.

It was General Garthon Rastor.

Rastor.

The insane yet brilliant royal general. The man who had murdered Jack's mother at the Falling Temple in Jerusalem. The man who wanted to see the Omega Event happen and watch the universe end.

Rastor and his forces had arrived at the Supreme Labyrinth shortly before Jack's team had.

As Jack had been charging through the ranks of bronzemen outside, Rastor had been entering the Labyrinth through another gate and he was now about ten minutes ahead of Jack and already at the exit.

As if sensing Jack's presence, Rastor turned and looked up at him.

He gave Jack a mock salute and then, with the help of his men, kicked the bridging unit off the broken bridge and into the abyss.

The obelisk bridge now had a fifteen-foot gaping void in it.

'Son of a bitch, as if this wasn't hard enough,' Jack whispered.

'I think it's about to get harder,' Zoe said.

She jerked her chin at their feet and Jack saw a rush of flowing water wash over his boots and begin to pool at the end of their guttered entry bridge.

He hadn't noticed it before, but the knee-high gutters of this metal half-bridge extended not just down its sides, but also across its end, making the whole hundred-metre bridge essentially a super-long *tray*.

'Water?' Lily said, confused.

'Not just water,' Jack said. He nodded at the bridge beside theirs, the one with the Omega monk embedded in a shallow layer of grey-stone being eaten by the Vandals.

He then looked straight up . . .

. . . and saw some inverted mini-pyramids sticking out from the ceiling of the cavern directly above their half-bridge.

'I'm guessing that some greystone pellets are about to drop out of those little pyramids up there and into this water and turn it solid,' he said. 'We have to get past this silver guy before that happens or else we're gonna end up like that monk.'

Their guttered bridge was filling quickly.

The water was pouring out of a spout at its far end, positioned above a trapezoidal stone doorway set into the upside-down skyscraper.

The steady flow funnelled down the length of the half-bridge, passing the feet of the silverman, before pooling around Jack and the others at the end.

'What do we do?' Lily said. 'I don't think that silverman's gonna just let us pass.'

Jack glanced over at the Omega monk being torn apart by the Vandals . . .

. . . at the exact moment that one of the Vandals looked up from its gorging and spotted him and his group.

The Vandal froze . . . and grinned.

Its mouth was smeared with blood and flesh.

'Why, hello, hello, hello!' it called in a shrill voice.

'New meat!' the second one squealed in delight as it also saw them.

Like hyenas that had spotted fresh prey, the two Vandals leapt away from the monk and nimbly swung hand-over-hand down the length of their bridge—gripping its gutter with their finger-tips and thus skirting the silverman on it—heading for the central skyscraper.

'Oh, shit . . .' Jack said, seeing them go.

His mind was reeling, once again trying to keep up.

Not only did he have his own bridge to traverse—a bridge that was filling with water, water that would soon become greystone that would solidify over his group's feet—he also had his own silverman to get past.

And now the two Vandals were on their way over.

Keep calm, he thought. *Keep calm.*

Break down each step, then figure out your plan.

Okay.

First step: get past this silverman.

Jack drew his pistol. It still had a clip full of specially-tipped rounds in it: bullets with shavings from the sword, Excalibur, that Easton had painstakingly attached.

'Okay,' Jack said. 'Zoe. You, me and the palemen are gonna take on this silverman and distract him. While we do that, Lily and Easton, you're going to get past him by hanging from the gutter of this bridge like those Vandals just did.'

'But Dad . . .' Lily protested.

'No, kiddo, this is how we have to do things in here. If we get held up in any way, Zoe, Easton and I will play decoy for you. We keep the traps and the other players busy while you move on to the next stage of the maze. Then, hopefully, we catch up.'

'What if you don't catch up?'

Jack gave her a look. 'Then you'll have to go on alone. Easton? If past experience is any guide, as soon as we get close to that silver dude, he's going to come alive and be very hard to handle. Can you order your boys to take him on?'

Easton pointed to three of his palemen: 'You three. If that silverman moves, attack him.'

In a corner of his mind, Jack wondered why Easton hadn't ordered all four of the palemen to do this.

Then Easton addressed the fourth and last paleman, the one with the smile-shaped scratch on its metal face, Smiley.

'You,' Easton said softly, 'protect *him and her.*'

And Easton pointed at Jack and Zoe.

He had just given them a bodyguard.

Then Jack stepped forward and, as expected, the silverman raised its head, coming alive, and the first three palemen charged at it and the battle commenced.

As soon as the palemen charged, Jack raised his Desert Eagle and fired it at the silverman's head.

The shot hit the chrome automaton right in the forehead, causing its head to snap back briefly.

But then the creature's head just rose again.

As its eyeless face glared back at Jack, he saw that the bullet impact had left a tiny indentation in its metal brow, but the shot hadn't dropped the silverman.

'Damn.'

He knew from prior experience that his special bullets 'killed' a bronzeman with a direct shot to the head.

But this was a silverman and they were more advanced than the bronzemen; better fighters, with tougher skin, harder to kill. Clearly, one special bullet to its head wasn't enough.

Zoe joined in with some shots of her own and their booming rounds pinged off the shiny chrome head, kicking up sparks.

While their bullets didn't penetrate the silverman's head, their barrage of gunfire did knock its head around, which enabled the three palemen to get in close and launch themselves at it.

'Lily! Easton!' Jack called. 'Go now!'

Lily and Easton quickly climbed over the gutter of the bridge and, hanging by their fingers, moved hand-over-hand down its length while the palemen fought the silverman.

The three palemen battled the silverman, grabbing its arms and struggling with it as Jack and Zoe kept firing and the water kept trickling down the bridge, steadily filling it.

Lily and Easton worked their way down the gutter. Once they were past the fighting, they swung back up onto the bridge, now only twenty metres from the doorway set into the central skyscraper.

Once she was back up on the bridge, Lily looked hesitantly at Jack.

'Keep going!' Jack called. 'We'll catch up!'

With reluctant nods, Lily and Easton dashed into the doorway at the end of the bridge, passing two tall man-shaped stone statues that flanked it.

Jack and Zoe were still separated from that doorway by the fight between the three palemen and the silverman, when suddenly the silverman threw one of the palemen off the bridge and he went plummeting into the abyss.

'No!' Zoe shouted, just as Jack got a clear line at the silverman and fired a round right *into* the indentation his very first shot had made.

This had an effect.

The silverman went instantly still, suddenly freezing, as if its power had been shut off.

It dropped to a kneeling position in the ankle-deep water, its head bowing, its arms falling limp.

Jack saw the opening and said to Zoe, 'Go! Get past it!'

Guarded by Smiley, the two of them edged around the fallen silverman, their feet splashing in the shallow water, followed by the other two palemen.

They now had a clear path to the doorway set into the skyscraper.

'Great work!' Jack said. 'Now, let's—'

Plop.

Plop.

Jack turned . . .

. . . in time to see the leftover ripples from two greystone pellets that had dropped into the water.

Then he spotted a third pellet drop from one of the mini-pyramids in the ceiling and, with a *plop*, splash into the rising shin-deep water on the bridge.

'Run!' he yelled to Zoe. 'Get off the bridge! Before the water hardens into stone!'

Jack and Zoe bolted up the length of the bridge, sloshing through the water, accompanied by their three remaining palemen, leaving the silverman behind them, still frozen on its knees in the water.

The water around their feet began to darken, turning grey and then black: the telltale sign that it would soon turn to stone.

As he ran, Jack saw the trapezoidal doorway up ahead, with the two stone statues on either side of it.

He, Zoe and the three palemen reached the end of the bridge and jumped through the doorway, over a low rim and under the water spout, into the skyscraper . . .

. . . just as all the water that filled the length of the bridge turned to stone, solidifying around the kneeling silverman.

And then the silverman raised its head.

It isn't dead, Jack thought ominously.

It tried to stand. But it couldn't. Its knees and feet were embedded in the cement-like greystone.

'It's trapped in the stone,' Zoe breathed.

'Thank God,' Jack said. 'That's one less threat to deal with. We deserve a break.'

Which was precisely when, with a loud crunching sound, the silverman wrenched its feet out of the solidified greystone, stood up and turned to face them . . .

. . . and started striding after them . . .

. . . at the exact moment that the two stone 'statues' on either side of their doorway began to crack open from within as silvermen inside them awoke.

'Shit!' Jack called. 'Run! We can't stop!'

With the original silverman advancing up the long bridge and the two new ones smashing out of their stone shells, Jack, Zoe and the three palemen dashed inside the doorway to the skyscraper, chasing after Lily and Easton.

A day earlier.

Sphinx gazed out over the same vast space from the mouth of his entry tunnel.

The gigantic cavern was silent.

There were no screams, no fighting.

He was unhurried.

For he hadn't triggered the sliding stone in his tunnel: he knew from Imhotep's instructions—kept by his advisor, Cardinal Mendoza—to step over the booby-trapped metal stair, not on it.

He was joined at the tunnel's mouth by Cardinal Mendoza, his three Knights and the eight Vandals he had brought along.

He eyed the walls of the cavern.

Deeply carved glyphs ringed the space, level with all five entry tunnels.

'My Vandal friends,' he said. 'Lie in wait in some of these tunnels. Feast on whoever enters through them.'

He released four of his Vandals and they climbed like monkeys around the curving wall to two of the other tunnels, using the deep glyphs as handholds.

Sphinx himself then jumped across to his bridge, the middle one of the five, defended by its own silverman. He was followed by his people.

As the silverman registered their presence, it stood fully erect and stepped forward to block them, only for Sphinx to hold up his Ring of Command.

The silverman immediately went still, bowing its head to the man bearing the Emperor's ring.

Sphinx strode past it, across the bridge and through the ancient trapezoidal doorway leading into the inverted skyscraper.

PRESENT

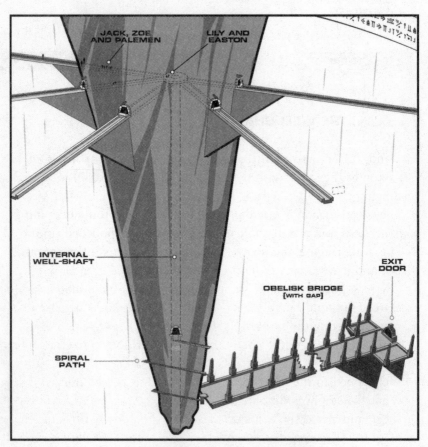

THE INTERNAL WELL-SHAFT

THE WELL-SHAFT

Lily and Easton arrived at the core of the upside-down skyscraper.

Easton lit the space with the beam of his pistol's barrel-mounted flashlight.

They were inside a circular chamber with five tunnels coming together at it and a well-shaft in the middle of its polished floor.

The wall ringing the space was made of a mix of stone and metal, and it was *covered* with engraved runes and glyphs.

Lily saw ancient images she had seen before: including one of the Great Pyramid being hit by a shaft of light from the sun and another depicting the symbol of the Machine.

'This is where the five entry tunnels and bridges converge,' she said. 'And the only way to go is down.'

She stepped to the edge of the well-shaft and peered into it.

What she saw was dizzying.

Sheer and perfectly vertical, the shaft shot down through the spine of the skyscraper before it ended at a hole at the very bottom that opened onto nothing but the yawning abyss.

The shaft must have been sixty metres deep.

Whoever had passed through here earlier had affixed some faded yellow glowsticks to its wall. From Lily's vantage point at the upper rim, they got smaller and smaller as they receded downward.

By the light of the glowsticks, she could see a vertical line of ancient ladder-like hand-rungs cut into one side of the shaft, leading down to a doorway cut into the wall about forty metres below.

'Looks like there's a side exit down there,' she said. 'I guess we climb—'

Easton was bowled over, crash-tackled from behind by a streaking blur.

Lily whirled to see him go sprawling to the ground, almost sliding into the shaft.

Easton sat up—

—to find himself staring into the snarling, blood-smeared face of a Vandal.

Lily spun just as the second Vandal from the other bridge sprang out from its tunnel and leapt at her with its fangs bared.

Lily caught the leaping man, pivoted and hip-tossed him right into the well-shaft.

She landed at the shaft's edge and watched as the Vandal fell down it, screaming, before—

—the falling figure was *sliced* into multiple pieces as he fell through some kind of crisscrossing wire array that Lily hadn't seen when she'd looked down the shaft before.

'What the hell?'

And then she realised what it was. It was—

The grunts of Easton's struggle with the other Vandal made her spin and she rushed to his aid.

The Vandal was on top of Easton, slashing maniacally with its clawed fingernails, but Easton managed to reach up and jam his pistol—complete with its barrel-mounted flashlight—into the little man's fanged mouth and he fired, blowing out the back of his skull.

The Vandal dropped to the floor, limp, dead.

'Vandals,' he gasped. 'Very nasty.'

'Sure are,' Lily said. 'A quick tip, Easton: *don't fall*. There's something crisscrossing the shaft below the side exit, an ancient kind of wire, some sort of filament. I saw it once before, at the headquarters of the Knights of the Golden Eight; they had a hand-held weapon made of that filament. It's wickedly sharp. Dion used it to cut off Alby's hand.'

Easton nodded.

'Let's go,' Lily said.

And into the well-shaft they went.

<<<<<<<< **24 HOURS** EARLIER <<<<<<<<<<<<<<<<<<<<<<<<<<<

Tethered to a rope gripped by two of his Knights at the top of the same well-shaft, Sphinx climbed slowly and carefully down it, high above the drop and the glistening web of fila-ment wires spanning it.

Another Knight had already made his way down the shaft, attaching yellow glowsticks to the wall to light his boss's way.

Sphinx stepped easily into the side exit and continued onward.

>>>>> **PRESENT** >>>>>>>>>>>>>>>>>>>>>>>

Lily and Easton were in the well-shaft when Jack arrived at its top with Zoe, Smiley and the two other palemen.

Jack peered into the shaft and saw Lily and Easton halfway down it, using the hand-rungs to descend.

He glanced behind him: the original silverman was striding down the tunnel in pursuit, flanked by the two new ones.

'Jack, go. Help Lily,' Zoe urged. 'I'll give you a head start and follow right behind you.'

Then she levelled her gun back at the tunnel, took aim, and waited.

Jack didn't have time to argue so he just started down the shaft with Smiley.

He hustled down its slick wall, gripping the ancient hand-rungs.

He peered downward . . .

. . . to see Lily and Easton step into the side exit, safe and away.

A second later, he heard gunshots from above.

Blam!-Blam!-Blam!-Blam!-Blam!-Blam!

Up in the chamber at the top of the well-shaft, Zoe opened fire on the first approaching silverman while her pair of palemen launched themselves at the other two.

Her gunshots boomed in the tight space as the automatons grappled with each other.

One of the palemen was battling the first silverman next to the edge of the shaft when Zoe leaned in and double-tapped the silverman through the same spot in the head at point-blank range, causing the silverman to suddenly freeze . . . and sway . . . and topple into the well-shaft.

Zoe had time to dive to the edge of the shaft and yell, 'Jack! Look out!'

Down in the shaft, Jack snapped up at the shout.

And saw a silverman falling right at him!

Suddenly, a strong metal hand—Smiley's—pulled Jack aside and the falling silverman whistled past, missing Jack by inches—before plummeting further down the shaft.

Jack hadn't seen the web of filament wires.

Which was why his eyes widened in shock when he saw the silverman hit them.

One second, the silverman was falling, the next, it was falling *in pieces*, pieces that tumbled away into the abyss below.

Jack hurried downward, arriving at the side exit.

Now that he was closer, he could see the crisscrossing filament wires spanning the shaft.

They resembled fishing line: thin, taut and glistening.

Fresh blood dripped off them. He didn't know it, but it was the blood of the Vandal that Lily had hurled down the shaft a minute earlier.

Filament wire, he thought.

It had taken two shots with his specially-tipped bullets just to slow one silverman.

But these filament wires—left here by the same intelligence that had designed and built this Labyrinth—had cut through a silverman as if he had been made of tissue paper.

'Zoe! Get down here! We gotta get out of this place!'

Above him, Zoe slithered into the well-shaft while her two palemen grappled with the last two silvermen.

Suddenly, a muffled explosion boomed from somewhere and the walls around Jack shook.

It felt like an earthquake.

'*Dad!*' Lily's voice called. '*Get outside!*'

Jack hurried down a short stone passageway beyond the side exit, toward a doorway at its end and stepped out onto a tiny ledge overlooking the cavern . . .

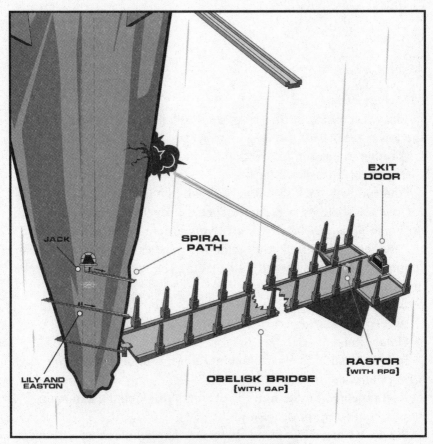

**THE SPIRALLING PATH
AND THE EXIT BRIDGE**

. . . where he stopped.

He was standing at the top of a spiralling path that wound down the lower reaches of the upside-down stalactite-skyscraper.

Another explosion boomed.

The skyscraper shook again.

And suddenly Jack saw Rastor down by the exit, wearing a tactical vest and holding a Predator rocket-propelled grenade launcher on his shoulder, *firing RPGs up at the upside-down skyscraper!*

Another RPG struck the giant rock tower, causing a burst of fragments to rain outward and making the entire structure shake and shudder.

And then there came an awful noise.

A deep, resonating cracking.

Craaaaaaack!

It came from high above Jack as, all of a sudden, the whole skyscraper lurched dramatically.

Zoe appeared beside him, breathing hard. 'What's happening?'

Jack looked up in dismay.

'Rastor's firing RPGs at this stalactite. This whole thing is about to fall away from the ceiling. We have to get off it before it drops. Run!'

24 HOURS EARLIER

With the colossal inverted skyscraper looming behind him, Sphinx strode across the long obelisk-lined bridge with his entourage.

Once they were all across it, he heard them.

Ezekiel and his five Omega monks had entered the Labyrinth and were crossing their upper entry bridge.

Sphinx turned to his most senior Knight, Jaeger Sechs. 'The Omega monks are here! Blow the bridge behind us!'

Jaeger Sechs—Knight Six—laid an explosive pack on the bridge and detonated it.

The blast echoed throughout the cavern, creating a billowing cloud of smoke . . .

. . . and suddenly out of that cloud fell a fifteen-foot section of the bridge. It dropped away into the abyss.

Sphinx raced out through the exit, penetrating deeper into the maze.

Trailing Sphinx by only a matter of minutes, Brother Ezekiel and his Omega monks came to the broken obelisk bridge.

But they'd anticipated Sphinx's defensive measures and come prepared: they'd brought a carbon-fibre bridging unit with them and now they extended it across the void Sphinx had created.

They crossed the obelisk bridge and dashed further into the Supreme Labyrinth, chasing Sphinx.

12 HOURS EARLIER

Twelve hours ago.

Dion raced across the same bridging unit, flanked by his three armed Squires, desperate to catch up to Sphinx and give him help.

PRESENT

Rastor watched as Jack bolted down the spiralling staircase that ringed the lower half of the skyscraper, followed by Zoe and Smiley.

He could see Lily and Easton ahead of Jack, two storeys further down the same staircase.

What Jack's people hadn't seen yet was the stone slab lowering into the exit doorway immediately behind Rastor.

As Rastor knew, each maze had to be overcome within a day—or one rotation of the Earth, as Imhotep's instructions had put it— before it was sealed off.

The slab behind him was doing precisely that and it was almost fully closed.

Rastor fired another grenade up at the skyscraper and it rocked again . . .

. . . and with the crunching sound of breaking stone, the great upside-down tower began to peel away from the ceiling.

Rastor grinned.

There was no stopping it now.

The skyscraper would fall.

His work here was done.

It was time to go. He had to get out before the slab in the exit doorway closed completely.

He also didn't want to be anywhere near the obelisk bridge when the skyscraper fell—it might take the whole damn bridge with it.

He nodded to his men—seven grey-masked Serbian commandos— and they all hustled out through the exit, under the lowering slab of stone.

Lily and Easton arrived at the bridge at a sprint and raced out onto it, dashing between its high stone obelisks.

Each of the obelisks was huge, easily forty feet tall, and they ran in pairs down the length of the bridge, creating a striking avenue.

Lily and Easton came to the jagged void in the bridge's middle. Two obelisks stood at its edge like posts for a missing gate.

Lily bit her lip in thought. 'Easton, you got any grenades on you?'

Easton pulled one from his belt and handed it to her.

'Step back,' she said as she lay the grenade at the base of the left-hand obelisk, pulled the pin and stepped back.

Bang!

A short sharp blast detonated at the bottom of the giant obelisk, blowing a chunk of stone out of it, and . . .

. . . the obelisk toppled toward the void.

And Easton realised what Lily's plan was: she was trying to use the fallen obelisk to create a bridge across the gap.

He was smiling at her ingenuity when the obelisk slammed down against the opposite edge of the broken bridge.

Only it fell slightly askew—not perfectly across the void—and to Easton's horror it teetered on the opposite edge for a moment before it rolled off and dropped away into the abyss.

'Damn it!' Lily shouted.

'Lily!' a voice called and she spun to see Jack, Zoe and Smiley running at full speed off the spiralling path onto the obelisk bridge.

'What's going on!' Jack called.

'Kinda busy here!' she shouted back. 'Easton, quick, have you got another grenade?'

Easton did. He handed it to her.

Lily dashed over to the remaining right-hand obelisk, set the grenade at its base and pulled its pin.

This was their last chance.

If this obelisk didn't fall and land cleanly across the void, they had no way to get across it.

It was all or nothing now.

Bang!

The grenade detonated. The obelisk fell . . .

. . . and slammed into place across the gap, so that it now lay horizontally across the void like a fallen tree across a creek bed.

'Let's go.' Lily danced across the fallen obelisk, high above the abyss.

Easton went next.

Jack and Smiley didn't stop running as they came to the fallen obelisk and raced out across it, closely followed by Zoe.

Jack and Smiley leapt off the end of the horizontal obelisk onto the intact far section of the exit bridge.

When it happened.

The gigantic upside-down skyscraper of stone fell away from the ceiling of the cavern.

It was a momentous event, shocking in its sheer scale.

Weakened by the repeated impacts of Rastor's rocket-propelled grenades, the great mass of stone—millions of tons of it, an awesomely heavy thing—tore away from the ceiling and fell.

It looked like it dropped in slow motion, but that was an illusion created by its size.

It dropped at an angle, tilting as it fell.

Standing on the far section of the exit bridge beside Lily, Easton and Smiley, Jack turned to look up at the sight.

It filled his vision.

His last two palemen, the other two silvermen, even that dying Omega monk embedded in the greystone on his bridge would all be taken down into the darkness with the great stalactite.

Then Jack glanced down . . .

. . . to see Zoe still running across the horizontal obelisk, with maybe seven feet to go.

It might as well have been a mile.

For as the gigantic inverted skyscraper of stone fell, it took the horizontal obelisk with it and in the blink of eye, Zoe was gone.

Jack lunged forward, diving for the edge of the bridge.

'Zoe!' he shouted.

But it was no use.

In that final terrifying split second, their eyes met and, for Jack, everything really did slow.

He saw the terror in his wife's eyes, the horrific realisation that she wasn't going to make it across and there wasn't a damn thing anyone could do about it.

She was going to die.

And in the infinity of that moment, Jack saw the years they had spent at each other's side.

Studying together under Wizard at Trinity College.

Seeing her at that meeting of nations in County Kerry, Ireland, in 1996, just after Lily had been born.

The time she and Lily had coloured the tips of their hair in matching hot pink.

Morning coffees, just Zoe and him, on the porch of their desert farm in Australia.

The time Zoe had attended the careers day at Lily's school dressed in full combat uniform.

Her gorgeous Irish blue eyes.

The freckles on her nose.

Her beautiful smile.

And then she fell out of his sight, along with the obelisk, replaced by the immense bulk of the skyscraper rushing by in front of Jack with a tremendous *whoosh*.

It was only blind luck that Jack and the others weren't taken down as well, but they were just out of range as the tower streaked by.

Then the skyscraper was gone, disappearing into the abyss below, blocking Jack's view of the falling figure of Zoe, and as he lay there looking down into the abyss, his horror was complete.

His beloved wife was dead.

Jack was numb with shock.

Two sets of hands grabbed him by his jacket's collar, lifted him to his feet and hauled him away from the edge.

He heard Lily: 'Dad! You can't stay here! The exit's closing!'

Easton manoeuvred himself under Jack's shoulder and supported him as Jack staggered, dizzy with grief, away from the edge of the broken bridge.

The enormous cavern behind them—now robbed of the hanging skyscraper that had been its centrepiece—yawned glaringly empty.

The only evidence that anything had been here before were the five square entry tunnels arrayed around the cavern's walls high up near the ceiling.

Jack let Easton and Smiley half-carry him while Lily guided them underneath a lowering slab of stone.

Then the slab closed with a resounding boom and Jack was enveloped by darkness.

THE SECRET
ROYAL WORLD

THE BATTLEFIELD, THE BELL
AND THE ROYAL BANKER

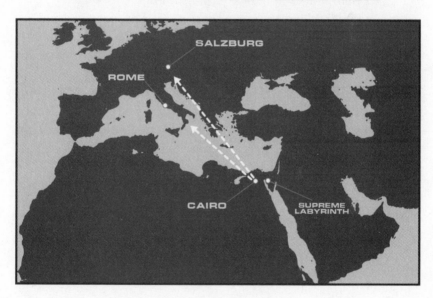

Follow the money.

ALL THE PRESIDENT'S MEN
SCREENPLAY BY WILLIAM GOLDMAN

ALBY, ALOYSIUS AND RUFUS
OUTSIDE THE GATES TO THE SUPREME
LABYRINTH
26 DECEMBER, 0903 HOURS

The second ejection seat from Aloysius Knight's Sukhoi Su-37 came slamming down against the side of the low brown mountain that covered the five entrances to the Supreme Labyrinth.

Huddled together on the seat were Aloysius, his pilot Rufus and Alby Calvin—having shot skyward out of the Sukhoi just before it had been overwhelmed by bronzemen.

Even though it had a parachute, the seat landed hard, and as it hit the side of the mountain, the impact sent the three men on it scattering: Aloysius and Alby tumbled down the rocky hill, while Rufus was thrown onto a nearby ledge.

Alby was knocked out cold. He slumped to the dusty ground.

Beside him, Aloysius blinked, concussed, seeing stars. He tried to shake it off—

'Freeze, motherfucker,' a hard voice commanded.

Aloysius looked up to see a Knight of the Golden Eight—Jaeger Zwei, Hunter Two—and some men standing with him gripping Steyr AUG assault rifles aimed at his face.

Aloysius didn't know Zwei, didn't know about his three encounters with Jack in Moscow, Jerusalem and here outside the Labyrinth.

Aloysius raised his hands. He glanced surreptitiously around the area, searching for Rufus.

But he couldn't see his loyal pilot anywhere. He wondered if the gentle giant had been knocked out like Alby when he'd been thrown clear of the ejection seat as it landed.

Jaeger Zwei looked over at Alby's immobile body and nodded to his men.

'That's the kid Sphinx told us about. Albert Calvin. He has value. Jaeger Eins gave me special instructions if we found him. We take him with us.'

Zwei turned to Aloysius.

'As for you, asshole, I got no instructions for you, which means you're fucked—'

Zwei cut himself off, his eyes narrowing.

'Wait. I know you. You're Knight. Aloysius Knight, the bounty hunter. You're also the *fucking bastard* who helped West attack our base at Ischia Island. I think Jaeger Eins would love to see you, too. Get a little payback, if you know what I mean.'

And with those words, Aloysius and the unconscious Alby were yanked off the ground and taken to a nearby truck, loaded onto it, and whisked away.

Hiding behind a boulder on his ledge forty metres up the hill, Rufus watched it all happen in helpless dismay.

He saw Jaeger Zwei's truck speed away, heading westward across the smoking, dust-hazed battlefield, winding its way past all the wrecked and ruined vehicles lying on the plain until it came to a C-5 Super Galaxy parked in the distance.

'Damn,' he breathed.

They had Aloysius and Alby.

That Rufus would go after Aloysius was a given. They were buddies for life.

But Rufus also really liked Alby: he was a nice kid, sweet and smart, and they'd bonded during their shared mission to that abandoned Russian spaceport in Libya.

He'd damn well rescue him, too.

★ ★ ★

But he couldn't do anything yet.

For on the desert plain in front of the gates to the Labyrinth, the battle was *still* actually raging, or at least coming to a conclusion.

Sphinx's superior force of bronzemen and humans now ruled the battlefield and the only threat remaining was Rastor's huge four-rotored V-88 Condor.

The massive V-88 was hovering above the right-most gate to the maze, having briefly landed to drop off Rastor and then successfully provide cover for him to enter the Labyrinth.

But now the flying fortress became the sole target of *all* of Sphinx's remaining forces.

Three terrific explosions rang out as the V-88 was hit by a trio of ground-to-air missiles fired from Jaeger Eins's anti-aircraft jeeps.

And that was it for the V-88.

Trailing a plume of black smoke, it wheeled in the air, mortally wounded, and amid the whine of its dying engines, it plunged into the side of the low mountain and exploded in a towering fireball.

Once the Condor was gone, Sphinx's forces quickly reformed and regathered.

The massive army of bronzemen marched in orderly ranks away from the Labyrinth's gates, returning to two more C-5 Super Galaxies out on the plain.

Rufus watched as some Knights of the Golden Eight managed the evacuation. He fiddled with his digital radio scanner and found their frequency.

The intercepted voice of Jaeger Eins came over his earpiece: *'Pack it up, people. There's nothing more we can do here. We need to move to the surface point of the Labyrinth to support Sphinx if he needs us. Mendoza said it's somewhere underneath the Red Horizon Star-4.'*

After a time, the C-5 Super Galaxies took off and flew away to the west, leaving the dusty plain in front of the five gates to the Labyrinth empty.

Nothing moved.

All that remained on the barren desert plain were the vestiges of the enormous battle that had been fought here.

The remains of the V-88 lay smouldering on the low hill while the crumpled fuselage of Sphinx's equally large quadcopter had crashed in front of another gate.

The Super Galaxy that Sky Monster had flown in as cover for Jack's Hercules rested nose-down in the sand, unmoving and veiled in dust.

Closer to the Labyrinth, Jack's Hercules lay amid a heap of bronzemen, many of them tangled in its landing gear. His crashed troop truck was similarly enmeshed in twisted automatons.

Some of the bronzemen moved, waving their arms, but they were hopelessly pinned beneath the heavy vehicles.

The final element of Jack's Russian Doll plan—a vehicle within a vehicle within a vehicle—was parked outside the left-most gate of the Labyrinth beside an overturned jeep: his motorcycle-with-sidecar—

Movement.

Rufus sprang back.

A figure was stepping tentatively out of the broken Super Galaxy.

It was a man, a bearded man, staring in mute shock at the carnage all around him.

'Sky Monster . . .' Rufus gasped to himself.

Rufus broke cover and ran out onto the empty battlefield, calling out to his fellow pilot.

Sky Monster heard him and when he saw Rufus running up, he smiled.

They clasped hands and Rufus said, 'Jack got inside the maze, but the Golden Knights just took Aloysius and Alby. I heard their leader say they were taking them to the Red Horizon Star-4, which is apparently near some surface point to the Labyrinth.'

Sky Monster frowned.

'Zoe mentioned something like that once. It was in a note she found in the Pope's study at the Vatican: the fourth red horizon star. But none of us know what it refers to.'

'Oh, I know what it is,' Rufus said.

'You do? What?'

'The Horizon Stars are a fleet of oil rigs owned by the Horizon Oil Company out of Russia,' Rufus said. 'Aloysius and I did some protective work for Horizon a few years back. Defended a couple of their rigs off the African coast from pirates. The rigs that the company designate as "red" are the ones that drill in the Red Sea. Red Horizon Star-4 is the company's fourth rig in the Red Sea.'

Sky Monster blanched. 'That's some seriously helpful knowledge you got there, Rufus. You can hang with us anytime.'

As he said this, Sky Monster turned and watched their rivals' Super Galaxy planes become tiny dots in the sky heading west . . . in the direction of the Red Sea.

'And it looks like that's exactly where the bad guys are headed with Aloysius and Alby,' he said. 'Well, what are we waiting for, Rufus, let's go after our friends. And maybe in the process, find out exactly what this surface point to the Labyrinth is.'

The two pilots hopped onto the only vehicle in the area that still worked: Jack's abandoned motorcycle-with-sidecar.

The bike kicked up sand and gravel as it peeled away from the gates of the Labyrinth, leaving the ruined battlefield behind it as it raced westward toward the Red Sea coast.

WORLDWIDE
26 DECEMBER

In the hours after Jack entered the Supreme Labyrinth and the various players left the battlefield outside its gates, Sphinx's forces moved steadily around the world, ringing Siren bells and putting more major cities to sleep.

Sweeping across the United States: Boston, Chicago, Dallas, Houston.

In Central and South America: Mexico City, Panama City, Rio de Janeiro.

Europe: Zurich, Geneva, Lyon and Marseille. Munich, Vienna, Budapest.

Asia: Hong Kong, Macau, Taipei, Manila, Jakarta.

And Africa: Tangiers, Lagos, Nairobi.

They were all deliberate, calculated sweeps from city to city, designed to silence the power centres of each region.

People cowered in terror, fearing that their metropolis might be next.

The entire internet was shut down. Television signals had been hacked using the Emergency Broadcast Satellite System so that every single TV set in the world showed the same sinister phrase:

**YOU
WILL
WAKE
AS
SLAVES**

Various military forces around the world also made sudden moves.

Sensing opportunity, the armies of Brazil, Thailand and Venezuela seized all the government offices in their countries.

A Chinese strike force quickly stormed Taiwan, only to see both the local population and their own men drop as a bell was rung over Taipei shortly after.

And an entire Russian aircraft carrier group sailed from the Persian Gulf to the Red Sea.

The Russian government said the manoeuvre was simply to protect some Russian-owned oil rigs located in the northern half of the sea.

Western military observers—those who were still awake— labelled it an opportunistic play by Russia to use the current crisis of the sleeping cities to seize control of the Suez Canal, something Russia had long desired.

But those in the secret royal world knew differently.

Aware of Sphinx's historic mission at the Supreme Labyrinth at a location somewhere in or near Egypt, they also knew that the Russian military—and all its nuclear missiles and hardware—was commanded by officers loyal to him.

And since they now knew that the Supreme Labyrinth was somewhere near there, they saw the arrival of the Russian carrier group in the Red Sea as a move in preparation for Sphinx's glorious emergence from the maze as the undisputed ruler of the planet.

In the United States, with the internet and the airwaves down, rumours flew among the citizens hiding in towns and suburbs.

There were reports that the President had been whisked away by car, through a tunnel, to a secret location near Washington, D.C.

This was after everyone at Andrews Air Force Base—the home of *Air Force One*—had been struck down by the ringing of the Siren bell in D.C. earlier. Unable to get to his plane, the President had had to go to his secure location by car.

The consensus among those who knew about such things was that the President had gone to the massive underground facility close to Camp David known as Raven Rock.

IOLANTHE, NOBODY AND BERTIE
THE PAPAL PALACE OF CASTEL GANDOLFO
20 KM OUTSIDE ROME, ITALY
26 DECEMBER, 1745 HOURS

Mounted on a lush tree-covered hill overlooking a gorgeous crater lake, the Papal Palace of Castel Gandolfo is one of the most luxurious, splendid and beautiful palaces in the world.

'Wow, nice,' Professor David 'Nobody' Black said as he flew Iolanthe and Bertie over the palace in a jet they had taken from Cairo International Airport.

While Jack had dashed off to enter the Supreme Labyrinth, Nobody, Iolanthe and Bertie had come here in search of the Blue Bell, or the Orphean Bell as some called it: the lone Siren bell that awoke people from the coma-like sleep caused by the other bells.

They all knew how important this was.

While they might've been able to wake up a few individuals one at a time with Dr Tracy Smith's serum, they knew that whoever found the Blue Bell could use it to wake entire populations from the Siren sleep. It was vital to foiling Sphinx's plan to let millions of people die in their comas before he stepped forward to rule the world.

They had to find the Blue Bell before his people did.

Already Sphinx had put a bunch of cities to sleep with the Siren bells, and even as they flew here, more cities around the world were falling by the hour.

With this in mind, they were following up on a clue to the Blue Bell's location, something Zoe had found at the Vatican among the Pope's personal papers.

Before he had been murdered by Sphinx, the Pope had ordered that the Church's notes regarding the location of the Blue Bell be taken to 'Albano's emissary'.

Referencing those words, Bertie had suggested they come here.

It was just after sunset, but the sky still shone with a lingering orange glow. As they banked low over Castel Gandolfo, Bertie recounted its history.

'Honestly, this palace is remarkably interesting and for several reasons.

'First, for the last five hundred years, it has been the summer residence and vacation home of the Pope, although this practice ended with Pope Francis who didn't like such ostentatious displays of wealth by the Church.

'Secondly, legally speaking, it actually resembles a national embassy. The palace and its grounds are the sovereign territory of the Vatican State.

'Third, it's built on the site of an older palace that was constructed by the Roman emperor, Domitian, in the first century, which itself was built on the site of a much older pagan temple.'

'That's not uncommon,' Iolanthe said. 'New religions have often built their temples on the sites of pre-existing local shrines. The Catholic Church has done that all over the world.'

'True,' Bertie said, 'but Domitian was in a category of his own when it came to stomping on other religions. He was an especially cruel emperor. History has always positioned him firmly in the shadow of his two predecessors: his father, Titus, who built the Colosseum, and his grandfather, Vespasian, the all-conquering military commander.

'Emperor Domitian, on the other hand, is known mainly for being a vicious ruler who harboured a particular hatred for one very influential group in Roman society: the Vestal order. Indeed, this is the source of Domitian's most bizarre achievement. Of all the emperors of ancient Rome, he executed the most Vestal priestesses during his reign.'

'Vestal priestesses,' Nobody said. 'You're talking about the Vestal Virgins, right?'

'Urgh, yes, the *virgins*,' Iolanthe sighed. 'Honestly, the prurient modern world's obsession with the Vestal order's pledge of abstinence is all anyone ever focuses on. They were much more than that.'

'Hey, sorry,' Nobody said.

'Hold on now, I'm not finished,' Bertie said. 'Castel Gandolfo, the summer palace of the Pope, has one other curious claim to fame. It possesses within its walls not one but two state-of-the-art *astronomical observatories*. Look, you can see their domes inside the palace walls.'

Nobody looked down and indeed he could see them. Two modern silver domes—complete with openings for the massive telescopes inside them—were the tallest structures on the site. They could be seen sticking up from the larger cluster of older buildings.

In the copilot's seat beside Nobody, Iolanthe was scanning the wider area around the palace.

She said, 'I can see people lying on the streets, in parks, even on some boats. Looks like the Siren bell that struck Rome also knocked out everyone here.'

Nobody pointed. 'I'll land on that strip of highway over there. Bertie, no offence, your history lesson is wonderful, but tell me again why we're here? Is it because of the palace? Or the nasty virgin-killing emperor?'

'No,' Bertie said. 'It's because of the lake. That crater lake is named Lake Albano and it is where we will find Albano's emissary.'

ENGRAVINGS OF THE ROMAN RUINS
AT LAKE ALBANO
BY LUIGI ROSSINI (1790–1857)

VIEW FACING CRATER WALL

VIEW LOOKING BACK AT LAKE

Twenty minutes later, they arrived at the shore of the lake, far below the enormous papal castle.

They had encountered no resistance at all as the inhabitants of the area had indeed been felled by a Siren bell.

The lake spread out before them, encased by the high, almost vertical walls of the crater.

'Lake Albano is not a natural lake,' Bertie said. 'It's a volcanic crater that's fed by rainfall. This means that, unlike a regular lake, it has no natural outlet for the accumulated rainwater to escape.'

They came to a Roman ruin at the shoreline.

It was a large and complex structure, a square-sided brick building that delved into the forested hillside of the shore.

At its core was a straight sunken stone channel that allowed water to flow from the lake into a tunnel in the rear wall of the ruin. A gloriously high stone arch towered over the whole scene.

The ruin was well preserved and jaw-droppingly beautiful.

'The Romans were very skilled builders, especially when it came to moving water,' Bertie said. 'This lake, like several others in the region, occasionally overflowed the crater's walls and flooded nearby towns. So the Romans constructed an outlet to control the level of the lake and release water when necessary. That's what this ancient structure is. It's called an *emissary*.'

Iolanthe shook her head. 'Albano's emissary isn't a person, it's a Roman ruin.'

'Correct,' Bertie said.

The stonework of the emissary was shot through with dozens of gnarled tree trunks and snaking roots. Through the leafy canopy above it all, they could see the fading orange sky.

It looked like an idyllic grotto from a fairytale.

'It's in amazing condition,' Nobody observed. 'Got to give it to the Romans. They built things to last.'

'I've seen pictures of this place before,' Iolanthe said. 'Old pictures.'

Bertie nodded. 'Luigi Rossini and Giambattista Piranesi did detailed etchings of these ruins. I prefer Rossini's, as they give a clearer image of the incredible masonry, but Piranesi's engravings are quite lovely, too.'

'It all looks like a giant drain,' Nobody said.

'That's exactly what it is,' Bertie said. He indicated the tunnel in the inner wall of the grotto: the sunken channel disappeared into it. A person could fit inside it but it was a tight squeeze.

'That tunnel runs for over a kilometre at a steady descending grade. It was built around 400 B.C.E. It took thousands of slaves six years to excavate it, digging through the crater wall. It was terribly dangerous work—'

'Bertie,' Iolanthe said gently. 'Like Nobody, I love your history lectures, but we're racing to save the world here. What are we going to find?'

'Right, right.' Bertie hurried into the ruin, stepping quickly over the roots and vines, heading for the tunnel.

'The Pope said he sent the Church's notes about the location of the Blue Bell to Albano's emissary. Now, Castel Gandolfo is one of the Church's most secure places. This emissary lies deep beneath it.

'I have heard whispers from some old priests in their dying moments about a vault built within the grounds of Castel Gandolfo, a repository for special secrets of the Church—both valuable and embarrassing—that they do not wish anyone to find. I think the Pope was referring to that vault when he referred to Albano's emissary.'

'What do you think?' Iolanthe asked Nobody.

Nobody assessed the ancient tunnel. Framed by vines and

cracked with age, it looked dark, old and forbidding.

He flicked on his flashlight. 'We need that bell to wake the world, so we don't have a choice. We go in.'

They entered the 2,500-year-old tunnel, their boots splashing through fetid ankle-deep water, their flashlight beams sabring through the gloom.

Rats scurried in the shadows. Mould covered the Roman brickwork.

And then, about four hundred metres in, they came to an old iron gate set into the right-hand wall.

Behind it was a modern steel door, obviously heavy and seriously reinforced. It had rubber around its edges to create a seal.

The steel door stood ajar, propped open by a middle-aged priest lying slumped on the ground in the doorway, asleep.

'He must have been standing here when the Siren bell rang,' Nobody said.

They stepped over the sleeping body and entered the subterranean vault.

It was a modestly sized chamber. Its two side walls were lined with glass display cases containing ancient objects and treasures.

Iolanthe saw an old iron nail in one.

A plate on its glass panel read: CLAVUS EX CRUCIFIXIONEM CHRISTUS.

Iolanthe translated: '"Nail from the crucifixion of the Christ." Whoa.'

A large stone sarcophagus covered in hieroglyphics lay in front of the far third wall. It was easily the largest item in the vault.

Iolanthe read the glyphs on it. 'Good God. This is *Khufu*'s coffin. From the Great Pyramid. This is one of archaeology's greatest treasures that has supposedly never been found.'

'The Church also had the uraeus from the Great Sphinx at the Vatican,' Nobody said. 'They sure had a keen interest in ancient Egypt.'

'Sun cult,' Iolanthe said.

A reading desk sat in the middle of the space and on it, laid out side by side, were two ancient Roman scrolls.

Bertie scanned the first one.

'What's it say?' Nobody asked.

Bertie's eyes raced back and forth as he read the text. 'It's a record from the Emperor Domitian. He says, "Even under torture, the Vestals would not divulge the location of the waking bell. The *virgo maximus*"—that's the head of the Vestal order—"would not tell me even when I had her sisters killed in front of her. So I had her executed, too."'

Nobody said, 'He sure hated those Vestals.'

'As only an ignorant emperor could,' Iolanthe said. 'He hated the educational advantage they had. For many centuries the Vestal priestesses occupied a very powerful position in Roman society, chiefly because they hoarded in their temple a vast repository of ancient astronomical knowledge, most of it sourced from Egypt. It was easy to dazzle an uneducated populace by predicting an eclipse that you knew was coming. To the regular folk of Rome, the Vestals were almost magical in their wisdom and the Vestals happily encouraged this.'

Nobody said, 'Didn't the Vestals tend to some kind of eternal flame?'

'Yes,' Iolanthe said. 'Inside their temple, the Vestals famously kept alight the sacred flame of Rome. They had convinced the people of Rome that this flame embodied Rome's very essence, its lifeblood, its soul. If the flame went out, Rome would collapse into ruin.

'It was very clever. Not only had they made themselves appear magical by virtue of their advanced knowledge, with the sacred flame they made themselves indispensable to the continued existence of the entire Roman nation.

'Thus the Roman people went to great lengths to keep the Vestals happy. Their virtue was protected. Anyone who deflowered, raped or killed a Vestal forfeited their life. It became a great honour for someone's daughter to be accepted into the order. Naturally, the Vestals had enemies, among them Domitian and the rising Christian movement which for some reason didn't like women with brains.

'When Rome fell to the Vandals in 455 C.E., the Vestals fled their temple and extinguished the sacred flame. Once that flame went out, Rome was no more, which actually only furthered their mythology.'

'Do they exist today?' Nobody said.

'Of course they do,' Iolanthe said. 'Just like the Cult of Amon-Ra became the modern-day Catholic Church, so too did the Vestal order transform. It just changed its name and base of operations every few centuries. Why, you've even met two modern Vestals: Sister Lynda and Dr Tracy Smith.'

'Oh, no way . . .' Nobody said, finally getting it. 'The nuns from Moscow.'

'Correct,' Iolanthe said. 'The current name of the Vestal priest-esses is the Order of Serene Maidens at Novodevichy Convent.'

'Here!' Bertie shouted suddenly, making both Iolanthe and Nobody spin. 'Here it is!'

He was looking at a line on the second scroll.

'What have you got?' Iolanthe asked.

Bertie said, 'It says here:

"The location of the Orphean Bell is inscribed on the Crown of Priam, the most honest man of his time, guardian of the mighty vault at Ilium, trusted keeper of the treasures of the four kings of old."'

Nobody cocked his head. 'Priam? Ilium? Even I know what Ilium is. It's Troy, the site of the Trojan War. Priam was the king of Troy.'

Iolanthe frowned in thought.

She gave Bertie a concerned look. 'The Crown of Priam used to be kept by the King of Land at his hunting retreat on the Welsh coast.'

'What do you mean, *used* to be kept there?'

'It was destroyed, along with some other priceless treasures, in a fire there back in 1871. The royal family kept it quiet for fear of embarrassment. But I do know of a copy.'

'A copy of Priam's Crown?' Nobody said.

'Yes. A statue, to be more precise,' Iolanthe said. She gave Bertie that look again. 'The one at Tenedos Island.'

Bertie went pale. 'I know the one. Yes, that could work.'

'Er, hello?' Nobody said. 'Can you two please stop speaking in code?'

Iolanthe turned to face him. 'Sorry. We all know the story of the Trojan War: how a prince from Troy named Paris ran off to Troy with Helen, the beautiful young wife of the Greek king Menelaus. So the Greeks, led by Agamemnon—'

'—Menelaus's brother—' Bertie added.

'—sailed an armada of a thousand ships to Troy and attacked the city to get Helen back.'

'Sure, I know the story,' Nobody said. 'I also saw the movie with Brad Pitt in it. The Greeks were brutish thugs, while the Trojans were all elegant and refined. Troy's walls were too strong and the war bogged down into a ten-year siege. The Greeks only won by using the most famous trick in history: the Trojan Horse, a big wooden horse, filled with Greek soldiers, that they left outside the gates of Troy and which the Trojans foolishly brought inside.'

'Right,' Iolanthe said. 'That's the traditional story, largely taken from Homer's two books, *The Iliad* and *The Odyssey*. It's also wrong. Priam wasn't a king. He was a banker, the *royal* banker to the four kingdoms, their Master of Coin.

'And that war wasn't about some woman. It was a full-scale raid by some upstart Greek princes trying to steal the treasures held inside the most secure vault of the four legendary kingdoms, the vault of the royal banker at Troy.'

'That's where we have to go now,' Bertie added. 'For it seems that's where we will find the location of the Blue Bell: inscribed on the Crown of Priam, and in that vault is a giant statue of Priam *wearing his crown.*'

'Okay, hold on. You're saying we have *to find the lost city of Troy?*' Nobody said incredulously. 'I thought some strange dude already did that in the 1800s. Schlinkman, or something.'

'Heinrich Schliemann, yes,' Iolanthe said. 'But he was a better self-promoter than he was an archaeologist. He found something, but not the real Troy.'

'All right,' Nobody said. 'Let's cut to the chase. To find the bell, we need to find this Crown of Priam. To find the crown, we need to find Troy, and I'm guessing you know where Troy really is.'

'I do,' Iolanthe said.

'Then let's—'

The sounds of shouts and splashing footfalls cut Nobody off.

'Someone's here.' He dashed to the door—

—to see shadows advancing quickly down the tunnel.

At least twenty people.

'Ms Carnarvon said it was down here,' a man's voice called.

Nobody turned away from the tunnel, thinking fast.

He figured they had about thirty seconds.

'There's too many of them to fight, so we have to hide,' he said. 'This way.'

A few seconds later, a heavily armed Knight of the Golden Eight entered the secret vault inside the Roman emissary, flanked by some Squires and a dozen bronzemen.

The vault was empty.

There was no sign of Iolanthe, Nobody or Bertie.

'We're in the vault,' he said as he scanned the room with a cell phone, as if filming it for someone on the other end of the line.

'*Stop. Turn back to the left,*' a woman's voice said from the phone. It was the voice of Chloe Carnarvon, Iolanthe's old assistant. '*That table in the middle. Show it to me.*'

The Knight obeyed, stepping over to the table and holding his phone over the ancient documents on it.

'*Zoom in on that scroll.*'

He leaned in closer and Chloe read it from wherever she was, translating the Latin aloud.

'*The location of the Orphean Bell . . . the Crown of Priam . . .*'

There was a pause.

'*The Crown of Priam . . .*' Chloe's voice said thoughtfully. '*Historically, it was kept at the Land King's hunting estate in Wales. Grab that scroll. I've been called to Salzburg, so bring the scroll to me there as soon as you can. I need to examine it more closely. I'll call the Hall of Royal Records and get our people there to do some further research about the fate of that crown.*'

The Knight snatched up the Domitian scroll and hustled out of the vault with his team close behind him. And just as quickly as they'd arrived, they were gone.

A few minutes later, as the splashing footsteps of the Knight's team echoed away up the tunnel, the heavy stone lid of Khufu's sarcophagus moved slightly, pushed off from within, and Nobody, Iolanthe and Bertie peered out from inside the priceless stone coffin.

'She knows about Wales,' Nobody said.

'She does.' Iolanthe frowned. 'Chloe was my assistant. She knows almost everything that I do about the secret royal world. But while she may know about the Land King's estate, she may not know about that fire in 1871 or that Priam's crown was destroyed in it.

'We might've just caught a little break. If Chloe has to wait for that scroll in Salzburg, that'll give us a head start, maybe as much as half a day. We go to Troy and find the copy. By the time she discovers the truth about the destruction of the original crown, we will have got the information we need from the copy and be on our way. Come on! We need to hurry. We might have just taken the lead in this race.'

POOH BEAR, STRETCH, SISTER LYNDA AND DR TRACY
AIRSPACE ABOVE AUSTRIA
26–27 DECEMBER

The Airbus A340–200 airliner commenced its descent through the snow-capped peaks of the Austrian Alps.

This, however, was no ordinary airliner.

For one thing, it bore the Egyptian flag on its tail and had ARAB REPUBLIC OF EGYPT written in large letters on its flanks.

It also had four engines, not the usual two, which was unusual for this model of airliner. The extra engines made it capable of speeds and manoeuvres that a regular Airbus A340 could not do.

Finally, on the inside, it was luxurious and high-tech. It had a plush master bedroom, multiple office suites and some of the most sophisticated communications equipment a dictator could buy.

The reason: this plane was the personal aircraft of the President of Egypt.

Only today it wasn't occupied by the Egyptian president. He lay asleep in his bed in Cairo, immobilised by the ringing of a Siren bell there, along with the rest of the city.

No, today his plane was being used by Stretch, Pooh Bear, Sister Lynda Fadel and Dr Tracy Smith.

They had purloined it from Cairo International Airport the previous day and, after an overnight stopover at a U.S. military base not far from Munich that had been struck down by a Siren bell, they'd flown it here as part of the mission they had been assigned by Jack before he had departed for the Supreme Labyrinth.

That mission: to find out where the royal families of the four legendary kingdoms were going in preparation for the Omega Event and what they planned to do after it.

This was why they had flown to the U.S. Army base in Bavaria.

Known as Katterbach Kaserne, like many of the American garrison bases in Germany, it was equipped with some of the world's finest satellite and signals interception equipment, equipment that could scan every secure frequency—military, cellular or otherwise—for radio chatter, in particular, any chatter that mentioned Omega, Sphinx, the kingdoms or royal families.

Because of the Siren bell that had gone off at the base, Stretch strode unchallenged into its comms centre and began the search.

It took a while.

A whole day of waiting and listening, waiting and listening . . . until suddenly the airwaves started pinging with frantic calls: the calls that he'd been hoping to hear.

Stretch gathered everyone in the comms centre.

'Okay,' he said. 'With cities around the world falling asleep and the Omega Event almost here, the royal world is scrambling. A lot of worried rich people are making a lot of calls. Listen to these intercepts I caught.'

He hit play on his console.

Voices on cell phones:

'—*Storm Cellar Protocol has been initialised. Time to batten down the hatches before the big ceremony in the maze and the transition. Hardin put his old buddy, the royal banker Sir John Marren, in charge of the rendezvous operation—*'

'—*Marren has the three master lists. All royal families will receive formal notification from him as to which of the three rendezvous points they are to report to. Don't call him in Geneva. He's busy as hell. His executive secretary, Jennifer Fraser, will call you—*'

'—*We haven't received anything yet—*'

'—*Just got ours. Raven Rock. Flying there now—*'

'—*I heard Sky Kingdom families are being sent to Xian*—'

'—*What if we don't get a call?*—'

'—*Then you must've pissed off Sphinx*—'

'—*There are Siren bells going off all over the world. Sphinx gave them to the Knights of the Golden Eight and those bastards are ringing them everywhere without a fucking care who's still around. I gotta get that call*—'

'—*Zampieri just texted me. He and his family are on their way to Austria*—'

'—*So are we. I received an encrypted message from Sir John's executive secretary thirty minutes ago. He's ordered us to report to the European rendezvous point, Hohensalzburg Fortress. He's on his way there from Geneva right now, to make sure everything is in order before he heads to Raven Rock to manage the overall transition*—'

Stretch stopped the playback and looked at his team.

'I'm sensing a lot of anxiety out there in the secret royal world.'

'The rich and powerful fear nothing more than losing their status,' Sister Lynda said. 'Even with the world falling down around them, they hold on tightly to their money and privileges.'

Pooh Bear said, 'So, who's this royal banker? Who is Sir John Marren?'

Lynda said, 'He is an old friend of Sphinx's and a very powerful ally. They went to boarding school together. Marren is a blue blood of the highest order; his family line goes back centuries. While Sphinx was dispatched to his faraway station as Watcher of the City of Atlas, Marren remained firmly ensconced in the royal world. But he always maintained his friendship with Sphinx, inviting him to royal weddings and the like.

'John Marren is supersmart. Shrewd and cunning. And the ultimate numbers man. If the royal world wants to crash a stock market or bankrupt a country, he's the one who makes it happen. He was actually the banker for the Sea King for many years until he was elevated to the rank of Duke during the Great Games when Jack competed in them. But then, after the previous royal banker was killed in the minotaur uprising at the end of the Games, Marren was named royal banker for all four of the kingdoms.'

Tracy added, 'Hohensalzburg Fortress is a likely place for them to gather. It's long been owned by European royalty.'

'Where is it?'

'Salzburg, Austria. Not far, actually. About halfway between here and Vienna.'

Pooh Bear nodded, thinking. 'Jack's task for us is to find out what the royals are planning to do during and after the Omega Event. This man, it would seem, is integral to those plans. So I have an idea.'

'And what's that?' Lynda asked.

Pooh Bear grinned.

SALZBURG, AUSTRIA

The Austrian town of Salzburg has a long history that is by turns marvellous and amazing, and hideous and awful.

Mozart was born there.

The Sound of Music was filmed there.

For a thousand years to this day, salt has been mined under and around Salzburg in deep labyrinthine mines that run for miles, hence its name Salzburg, or *Salt Castle*.

But it also has a darker side.

It is very close to Adolf Hitler's mountain retreat at Berchtesgaden. The nearby Altaussee salt mine was—infamously—used by the Nazis to store billions of dollars' worth of artwork stolen from museums and collections across Europe. Other mines in the region were used as Nazi weapons facilities and manned by slave labour.

Overlooking the entire Salzburg valley from a perch atop a hill is the Hohensalzburg Fortress.

It is a gigantic medieval castle, with mighty walls and ramparts that cascade down the hill. Constructed in the year 1077, it reputedly sits on its own hidden network of caves and tunnels.

It's more than that, Sir John Marren thought as his Bombardier private jet came in to land at Salzburg Airport and he saw the fortress out the window.

Over the past fifty years, the tunnels and chambers beneath Hohensalzburg Fortress had been reinforced and modernised to accommodate a large number of royal families and their staffs.

It was the perfect place to ride out the Omega Event and prepare for Sphinx's plan to reshape the world with the Siren bells after it.

Speaking of the bells, as Marren's jet touched down on the runway, he saw a few figures lying on the ground near hangars and on the road outside the perimeter fence. Only a handful of cars moved on the streets of Salzburg—the vehicles of royals and their families, arriving.

Marren nodded.

The same Siren bell that had hit Munich and then Vienna had struck Salzburg on the way, precisely for this purpose.

The world did not need to see the many private jets of the secret royal families landing here and gathering at the fortress.

Marren's jet taxied to a private hangar.

Twenty other jets were already parked around it: the usual Gulfstreams and Bombardiers, but also larger planes, the 737s and A340s of the truly ultra-wealthy.

John Marren felt a little self-conscious.

Here he was, the Master of Coin, the royal banker, arriving in Salzburg in a little fucking Bombardier.

In the new world that his old friend, Hardin Lancaster, the Sphinx, would shape after the Omega Event was taken care of, Marren would be a major player, not a mere banker. And when that happened he would make sure he got himself a big fully loaded airliner.

That said, there were still perks to his current position, like the black Maybach limousine with tinted windows that was waiting for his plane at the end of a short red carpet.

A tall, thin driver stood beside it, holding the rear door open.

Marren gathered his things.

He put his laptop, cell phone and some files into a stylish black leather briefcase. It was a custom-made Underwood high-security case. Luxurious and sleek, the briefcase was also bulletproof and fireproof; essentially a portable safe. Even so, Marren cuffed it to his wrist.

For the items in it were important.

Between them, the computer, the phone and the printed documents contained all the financial records and contact details of every member of the secret royal world, including those inside major governments and armed forces.

In the new world order, when key officials were appointed and borders redrawn, this information would be vital.

The royal banker's jet pulled to a halt in front of the Maybach and John Marren strode out of it, gripping his briefcase, and, without missing a step, slid straight into the back of the limousine while the door was closed behind him.

Someone was already there.

Marren was shocked to find himself staring down the barrel of a gun held by a portly bearded man with an eye patch.

'Hello, Sir John,' Pooh Bear said.

Marren whirled to see the tall driver slide into the front seat and look back at him: Stretch.

Pooh Bear said, 'My name is Zahir al Ansar al Abbas. That's Benjamin Cohen. We work with Jack West Jr and we'd like you to come with us.'

Tyres squealing, the limousine sped away.

It raced into a nearby hangar where Marren was bundled into the Egyptian president's A340–200 and before anyone at the airport knew what was going on, the Egyptian plane took off, with the captured royal banker on board.

A MAN NAMED JACK

PART I
ZOE

INSIGNIA OF THE SCIATHÁN FIANNÓGLAIGH AN AIRM
THE SPECIAL OPERATIONS FORCE OF IRELAND

Jack kept a copy of his Message from the Other Side in the small utility box clipped to the side of his helmet.

He knew by heart the section of it that referred to Zoe.

Zoe, my wife, my love, my soulmate. I've never loved anyone else.

You are brilliant, caring and kind. And you never, ever, ever give up.

You were the finest role model Lily could ever have and the best thing is you never even knew you were doing it. A warrior who was forged in Irish special forces, with a brilliant mind sharpened at Trinity College. You were just being you.

I remember one evening watching from the doorway as you read to Lily the poetry of Maya Angelou: 'Phenomenal Woman' and 'Still I Rise'. It was electrifying. Every little girl should have that experience: hearing a woman like you read those poems.

And, oh my God, you're tough! I often recall that time when we were racing around the world chasing the six Ramesean stones and I was waylaid, so you led the team into Africa. And there, single-handedly, you beat that Neetha tribe. Bad. Ass.

And after all that, when I think of you, all I can see is your smile.

Zoe, it's been the honour of my life to be your husband.

I'm so sorry it had to end.

But Zoe would never read it.
She had beaten Jack to the Other Side.

SECOND TEST OF WORTH

THE ENDLESS TUNNEL

Queen Pasiphae [the wife of King Minos] gave birth to Asterion, who was called the Minotaur. He had the face of a bull, but the rest of him was human; and King Minos . . . shut him up and guarded him in the Labyrinth.

BIBLIOTHECA, 2ND CENTURY

'Would you believe it, Ariadne?' said Theseus. 'The Minotaur scarcely defended himself.'

'THE HOUSE OF ASTERION'
JORGE LUIS BORGES

Jack West sat in semi-darkness, his head buried in his hands.

He was in a stone tunnel of some kind, but he didn't care.

He was still thinking about Zoe, taken down into the abyss during the cataclysmic fall of the upside-down skyscraper.

Lily knelt beside him while Smiley stood guard. Rastor had come through here only minutes before and they weren't sure if he was still nearby. Easton edged further down the tunnel, his gun-mounted flashlight raised, seeing where it led.

Lily wrapped an arm around Jack's shoulder. 'Oh, Dad.'

Jack said nothing. He just stared into space, mute with shock.

Lily whispered, 'Dad, we have to keep going.'

Jack said nothing.

When he looked up at her, his eyes were moist with tears.

'Do we? Do we have to?'

Lily was taken aback. She'd never heard him say anything like that before. Ever.

'Of course we do,' she said. 'We have to stop Sphinx. And Rastor and those asshole monks.'

Jack said nothing.

'Dad, look at me.' Lily grabbed his chin and made him face her. 'This sucks, it really does. You loved her, I know. I loved her, too, but she's gone. You knew this could happen. This is why she wrote her note, why we all wrote our notes.'

Jack was still silent.

He just stared blankly back at her.

Lily didn't let up. 'What are you going to do now? *Stop?* Because if that's what you're gonna do, I have to tell you that *I can't.* I won't stop. If you give up, I'll just go on by myself, because someone has to.

'Now, I could give you some bullshit pep talk about Zoe not wanting you to quit, but you're smarter than that, Dad, and we both know it.

'So how about this: you saw what happened to Julius Adamson after the Knights of the Golden Eight killed his brother Lachie in London. Julius got consumed by that loss and because of that, he ended up foolishly confronting the Knights and all he succeeded in doing was getting himself killed. Now, you can't—'

'Hey,' Jack said softly. 'Kiddo. I get it. Thanks. Just give me a moment to process this.'

He pulled his cell phone from his pocket and pulled up a file he wished he'd never have to look at.

Zoe's Message from the Other Side.

It was short, just a couple of paragraphs:

Jack,

I loved you from the moment I met you. Thank you for loving me back, with all my imperfections. That alone made my life worthwhile.

I'll be waiting for you on the other side.

Jack swallowed, blinking back tears.

Then he wiped his eyes, stood up and nodded to Lily. 'All right. We still got a job to do.'

Lily smiled tenderly and gave him a hug.

'Sorry I had to get a little rough with you there.'

'It's okay. I needed it. I won't lie, I'm hurting, but you're right, I can't stop now.'

Jack looked down the tunnel ahead of them.

It was square in shape, with grim stone walls.

Easton came back from the darkness.

'Tunnel runs for approximately a hundred metres,' he said. 'Then it forks. But only one fork remains open and it leads to, well, a difficult place.'

'All right, Easton,' Jack said. 'Lead the way.'

Jack and Lily followed Easton and Smiley down the straight stone-walled tunnel.

There was no sign of Rastor.

After destroying the skyscraper in the entry cavern, he had evidently hurried ahead to catch up to their other rivals in the Labyrinth.

About a hundred metres down the tunnel, just as Easton had said, they came to a fork.

The tunnel continued either straight or ninety degrees to the right.

But the straight section was filled from floor to ceiling with a dense metal door that was covered in Thoth hieroglyphics.

The carved glyphs shone dully under the light of Jack's helmet flashlight.

Lily knew the drill.

She stepped forward, scanned the Thoth runes and translated them:

'Life is rule, Death is life.
You have arrived at this place challenged, so the Emperor's
Way is closed to you.
Now, the Labyrinth performs its role.
In it, as outside it, Life precedes Death.
Ascend the pinnacle of Life or sit in the embrace of Death, it
matters not to Omega.
For to avert the end of all things, you must now defeat the
impossible Labyrinth.'

Lily gazed at the wall of metal blocking the tunnel going straight ahead. 'This must be the Emperor's Route, the shortcut to the end of the Labyrinth.'

Jack scanned it, too. 'But it's been closed off because Sphinx didn't come in here alone and *un*challenged. He has competition, so he has to go the long way and defeat the Labyrinth like the rest of us.'

Lily frowned. 'Any idea what *ascending the pinnacle of Life* and *sitting in the embrace of Death* mean? Not another human sacrifice, I hope.'

'I don't know,' Jack said, concerned. 'Not yet.'

He turned to his right, now the only way they could go.

The tunnel in that direction was shorter. It went for about ten metres before it opened onto a wider space. A gentle breeze blew from there.

Jack ventured down it and stopped at its end.

'Okay, this is interesting,' he breathed.

**THE SIX CHOICES
TO ENTER THE ENDLESS TUNNEL
(FROM JACK'S POINT OF VIEW)**

For the second time that day, Jack found himself standing on a ledge at the mouth of a tunnel overlooking a sheer drop.

This shaft, however, was much narrower than the earlier one—it was only maybe thirty metres across—and Jack's tunnel was situated right up near its flat ceiling. It was rectangular in shape, with sheer sides that dropped away into infinity.

Across the space from Jack, perched above the drop, were six tunnel mouths. Four were on the wall facing him while two were on the side walls.

All six were trapezoidal in shape and beautifully constructed with ornate brickwork. Each had a small stone ledge protruding from it like a balcony.

Ominously, each doorway was flanked by two grey man-shaped statues like the ones they had seen in the first cavern: silvermen covered in greystone.

Even more ominously, the statues that had 'guarded' the third door from the right had been broken open: they looked like eggs that had cracked from within and were now just empty open shells.

Above each tunnel mouth was an image carved into the wall. Each image was contained within a rectangular border and they all looked similar, depicting stylised circles and snakes.

Six lines of hand-rungs ran across the ceiling, originating just above Jack's tunnel and extending out to each of the six tunnel mouths in separate branches, ending about twelve feet above each doorway.

Jack deduced the intent of the chamber instantly.

'You have to climb across the ceiling and drop down to the correct tunnel mouth.'

'Only which one do you choose?' Lily said. 'How can we know which is the correct one?'

Jack thought about that.

He pulled out Imhotep's mummified skull, with its dark dry skin covered in tattoos.

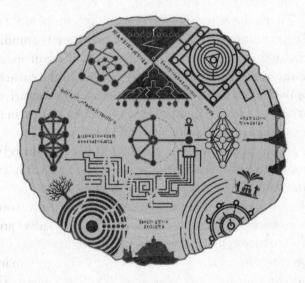

'Lily,' he said, 'can you read the Thoth markings on this skull for me again, please?'

Lily leaned in.

'Sure. They're arrayed all around the skull, in between all the symbols and pictures. They say stuff like: *Move forward or die, for the Labyrinth closes itself: each maze remains open for but one rotation—Once you pass the shining stair, there is no going back—To find the endless tunnel, take the doorway below the image of Ningizzida—In the tunnel, always to take the sinister fork—Speak not in the presence of the gold ones: only in silence may you pass—Look not in their faces, or thine eyes will not see again—Beware the liquid fire.* And lastly, *Life is rule, death is life. But there is no escaping the ultimate choice. In the face of Omega, you cannot conceal your true desires.'*

Jack listened closely.

'*Move forward or die . . .*' he said. 'That's what we just experienced. Sphinx got here about a day ago and that first maze closed off. It remained open for one rotation of the Earth.'

His eyes scanned the mummified tattooed scalp.

'*Once you pass the shining stair, there is no going back,*' he repeated. 'That's the entry tunnel. Once that Vandal and I tumbled onto and over the metal step in the tunnel, that big sliding stone dropped behind us and we couldn't go back. We *had* to move forward and jump across from the entry tunnel to the half-bridge.'

Jack said to Lily, 'We were in too much of a hurry earlier to realise just how specific these notes are. They're instructions for surviving each maze of this Labyrinth.'

Lily said, 'We have to assume Sphinx has them as well. Likewise, the Omega monks and Rastor—'

Jack was still peering at the ancient skull.

His eyes narrowed as he saw something.

'Wait a second . . .' he said slowly. 'These aren't just instructions written down between random symbols and drawings. This is a *map*, an actual map . . .'

'What do you mean?' Lily said.

But Jack was now muttering excitedly to himself as he peered more closely at the tattoos.

'These are the five entry tunnels *here* in the centre, with all five converging on a point . . . which means we're *here*. Oh my God, it's a spiral . . .'

Lily said, 'What are you talking about?'

'Okay, look.' Jack indicated the centre of the tattooed scalp:

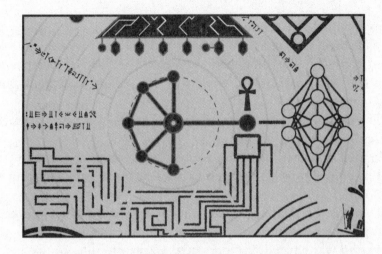

'This is a map that starts in the centre and radiates *out and around* in a clockwise spiral. See, we just came through this middle section, the one with five lines converging to a point. We're now to the right of it, under that image of the ankh.

'But, look closely, you can see that we have no choice now but to turn *downward*, toward this box-shaped chamber with six lines branching off it: four in front of us and two at the sides.'

As he examined the map, he noted that prominently featured on both of its sides, at nine o'clock and three o'clock, were two famous ancient tree symbols: on the left side, the Kabbalistic–Sephirot Tree of Life, and on the right, the Norse Tree of Death.

He recalled that his mother, Mae, had seen an image of these two sacred trees side by side inside the Vatican's most secret vault:

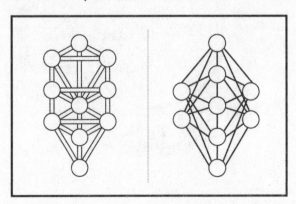

Jack thought about the two ancient images.

With their similar arrays of lines and circles, it was easy to get them confused. But they were different. The Tree of Death used *thin* lines and *nine* circles, while the Tree of Life used *thick* lines and *ten* circles.

Similar though they were, they also came from very different places in the world.

In the Kabbalistic doctrine, born in the Palestine region, the Tree of Life guided mortals through various stages of enlightenment to 'Heaven'.

The Tree of Death, on the other hand, hailed from northern Europe where it was known as *Yggdrasil*, the tree from which the god Odin was hanged. It represented a grim afterlife, or 'Hell'.

Jack also remembered someone at the Great Games mentioning in the same breath the four legendary kingdoms, the three secret cities and the 'two sacred trees'. They were important.

'This is all coming together . . .' he breathed. 'Here. Now. In this place.'

He traced his finger around the skull in a clockwise direction, starting in the centre and spiralling around it:

Now that he was looking at it more closely, he even noticed thin jagged lines connecting some of the images around the edge of the skull, reinforcing his theory.

'You start in the middle and if you keep going around the circle, through the various mazes, passing through the Tree of Life at nine o'clock, you eventually reach the final image, the Tree of Death, over on the right side at three o'clock, where presumably the Throne resides.'

He and Lily swapped looks.

'A maze of mazes,' she said. 'And that closed-off tunnel before was the Emperor's Route: a short and direct path to the Tree of Death and the throne there. But as you said, it's been closed off so now everyone has to go the long way round.'

'Right,' Jack said. 'So we're here, at this box with the six lines branching off it.'

They gazed out at the abyss before them, with the hand-rungs leading across its ceiling to the six doorways and their ledges.

'These lines on the scalp look like tunnels to me, long ones, complicated ones, endless ones,' Jack said. 'But only one reaches the Tree of Life at nine o'clock. So we have to pick the correct one.'

Lily said, 'Then let's start using the instructions. The next one is: *To find the endless tunnel, take the doorway below the image of Ningizzida.* Okay, who or what is Ningizzida?'

Jack said, 'Ningizzida was a very old Assyrian serpent god, traditionally represented as two snakes slithering up a pole, like a caduceus. He was also known as the God of the Tree of Life. Like they did with a lot of other ancient deities, Christianity basically stole him and inserted him into the Garden of Eden as the snake who tempted Eve to eat the apple from the sacred tree. You were pretty young at the time, but we encountered a pit inside the Hanging Gardens of Babylon named after Ningizzida. Had a lot of snakes in it.'

'The God of the Tree of Life,' Lily said, looking across at the images above the six tunnel mouths. 'All six of those images look like the Tree of Life, plus a snake. But look closely and you can see they're all a tiny bit different. You need serious historical knowledge to get through this place, but it's also designed to confuse you. Get you to hurry and make a mistake in your haste.'

'You're right.' Jack nodded, seeing it.

'See, three of them aren't the Tree of Life at all,' Lily said. 'Rather, they're the Tree of *Death*.'

'It's that one,' Jack said, pointing at the image second from the right. 'It's the Tree of Life—thick lines, ten circles—and it's got two serpents wrapping themselves up it. Ningizzida.'

Lily gave him a meaningful look. 'If you're wrong, and this tunnel—or rather, these tunnels—really are endless, we're going to go some distance before we realise we've gone the wrong way.'

'Like you said, this is all about knowledge. These traps and choices exist so that only the right people—the worthy—make it to the end of the Labyrinth,' Jack said. 'This choice here is the ultimate test of knowledge: are you willing to bet your life, and the lives of your companions, on what you know? I can and I will.'

He pointed again at the door second from the right. 'It's that one.'

'All right, stay here, I'll go first,' Lily said.

'Now, wait a—'

'No,' Lily said firmly. 'You always go first. You gotta let me take the lead sometimes and now is one of those times, since you're still a little emotional.'

'All right,' Jack said.

And so Lily reached up, grabbed the handholds embedded in the ceiling and crossed the dark abyss.

Jack watched tensely as she moved hand-over-hand along the line of ancient rungs.

After a minute of climbing in this manner, Lily came to the other side of the shaft and hung for a moment above the ledge in front of the tunnel mouth Jack had chosen.

For Lily, it was really quite frightening.

Hanging high above the abyss messed with her sense of distance and before she let go she wanted to make absolutely sure she was wholly above the ledge and not in any way short of it.

She let go of the hand-rung . . .

. . . and dropped.

Watching from the other side, Jack caught his breath.

But Lily landed safely on the balcony—turning to smile and give him the thumbs up.

Jack exhaled.

'I'll go next,' Jack said to Easton. 'Then you, then Smil—'
He was cut off by a sudden loud noise.
A gunshot.
Followed by several more.
And then panicked shouts coming from one of the other five tunnels.

'Move, move, move! Fuck! They're right behind us!'

'*My eyes! I can't see!*' another voice cried.

Alone on her balcony ledge, Lily whirled as she heard them, too.

The voices had come from the tunnel right next to hers, the one with the broken-open statue shells.

Lily stared at the tunnel's mouth in tense anticipation.

She shot a worried look over at Jack and Easton across the shaft.

'They took the wrong tunnel,' she whispered.

Whoever it was, they'd chosen that tunnel and evidently followed it until they realised it was the wrong one. But by the time they doubled back, the two silvermen 'statues' guarding the doorway had broken out of their shells and gone in to kill them.

Then a man burst out of the adjoining tunnel, staggering and stumbling, and fell flat onto his face on the balcony ledge.

He wore the jet-black battle fatigues of a Knight of the Golden Eight, but he was young. He was a Squire.

The young mercenary grunted in pain as he landed on his chest.

Trying to stand, he reached for the doorframe—feeling for it as if he were blind—and as he did so, Lily recoiled.

It looked like a length of pale string trailed from his hand, only it wasn't string.

It was his skin.

His own melted skin.

Lily stared, stunned, at the whimpering young man.

His black battle helmet was oddly deformed. It looked like it had lost its shape under some kind of intense heat and had melted against his scalp to become one with his head.

And then Lily saw his face.

In addition to the many heat blisters on it, there was also something that was truly grotesque about it.

The young Squire had streaks of *white fluid* below each of his eyes. It ran down his cheeks, as if he were crying milk.

'What the hell—?'

Then Lily realised what the liquid was.

The whites of his eyeballs had melted.

'Jesus God in Heaven . . .' she breathed. '*Look not in their faces, or thine eyes will not see again,*' she quoted from the skull.

The blinded Squire managed to pull himself up using the door-frame, leaving smears of his semi-liquid skin on it.

He whimpered rapidly in his terror: 'Oh, Momma, Mommy, please help me . . .'

This hardened killer was calling for his fucking mother.

'Momma, please . . . ahhhh!'

With shocking suddenness, a metallic gold claw reached out from the darkness of the Squire's tunnel and yanked him violently back into the darkness.

A crunching sound followed and a moment later, the Squire's severed head came rolling out of the tunnel and dropped into the abyss.

Lily gulped.

From the other side of the shaft, ninety feet away, Jack also stared in shock at the scene. He'd seen the whole thing.

And then both he and Lily heard a voice from the other tunnel.

A voice shouting, 'Move it! Get out of my way!'

A voice that they both knew.

The voice of Dion DeSaxe.

In the nanoseconds of time in which the mind operates, as Jack saw Lily standing there, alone, on the other side of the shaft beside the tunnel with all the chaos emerging from it, he realised what had happened here.

This test really was all about knowledge.

A day ago, Sphinx had entered the Labyrinth, followed by Ezekiel and his Omega monks: both of those groups had studied the lore of the Supreme Labyrinth, so they knew about things like the Emperor's Route, the Trees of Life and Death, and Ningizzida.

Dion had arrived at the Labyrinth some time after them. Jack recalled the radio intercept he'd heard from Sphinx to Dion, calling Dion to the Labyrinth and ordering him to bring some Squires of the Golden Eight with him.

So Dion had obeyed and done just that.

But he didn't have the requisite knowledge.

The spoiled son of royalty, ever confident in the belief that he would rule simply by virtue of his lineage and his wealth, he had not paid enough attention to his history lessons. He didn't know about Ningizzida.

And so he'd taken the wrong tunnel.

He must have ventured down it for a time—many hours at least—until he'd come to a dead end.

Then he'd turned back, and walked for the same number of hours the other way . . .

. . . only to discover that the stone statues flanking the entrance to his tunnel had come alive and—given the *gold* claw that had

reached out and grabbed the blinded Squire—maybe something else had, too.

On her ledge, Lily was arriving at the exact same conclusion, when suddenly a second Squire stumbled out of the adjoining tunnel mouth.

Like the first Squire, his armour and skin were gruesomely melted. But this man's helmet was missing.

Lily could see that his hair had been burnt off and his facial skin was melted through to the bone. He gripped a length of climbing rope in one hand and looked fearfully in every direction.

He was in a total panic, searching for an escape.

He squinted hard.

His eyes were not as damaged as the first guy's had been. While they had discharged some white fluid, he could evidently still see, but it clearly took effort.

The length of rope in his hands had a grappling hook at its end.

An instant later, Dion DeSaxe himself burst out of the tunnel and shoved his way past the Squire.

Lily saw the young king's distinguishing feature instantly: the translucent plastic mask he wore over his disfigured lower jaw, covering the hideous wound he had received at the conclusion of the Great Games when Alby had shot him through the face.

His eyes, she saw, were also partially melted. But his body was unharmed.

Whatever superhot substance had splashed over his men had not touched him. Typical Dion. He'd been hiding behind them.

It was lucky Dion came out when he did, for at that exact moment, the metallic gold claw lunged out from the shadows of the tunnel again, clutched the Squire beside Dion by the throat and yanked him back into the darkness.

As he was sucked from view, the Squire screamed and dropped the rope and hook.

Dion scooped it up.

Then, without any hesitation, he dived off his balcony, leaping toward the next ledge over—Lily's—holding the grappling hook in his outstretched right hand as he did so.

The hook caught Lily's ledge.

Lily was momentarily taken aback.

Here was this man—this vile young man who had told her once that after he married her, he would violate her every night with his brother, Zaitan—now dangling at her feet above the abyss.

Lily's first thought was to kick the hook and dislodge it, but could she do such a thing?

Hell, yes.

She lunged forward and raised her boot to kick the grappling hook.

'Not so fast,' Dion said, his hideous semi-melted eyes looking up into hers. 'Or else you go with me.'

He must have had it clipped to his belt.

As he gripped the grappling hook with his right hand, he revealed his left hand, holding a grenade.

Jack watched helplessly as, ninety feet away from him, Dion climbed up onto Lily's ledge.

It was literally Jack's worst nightmare: this royal asshole holding his daughter at his mercy.

Jack drew his pistol. Maybe he could—

'If you shoot me, this grenade goes off and she dies with me, Captain!' Dion called across the shaft.

Jack swore.

Dion stepped up fully onto the ledge.

Lily faced him. He was a foot taller than she was.

Her disgust must have shown.

Dion smirked. 'Come now, darling. Do I look so hideous?'

With his translucent facemask and the milky white fluid trickling from his eyes, the answer was a resounding yes.

'Couldn't happen to a bigger douchebag, Dion. You were always so wrapped up in appearances.'

He winced, the agony he was in clearly visible. 'But I've *changed*. I've learned to live with pain. First, my face, now my eyes. My men looked at the goldman in there, so their eyes liquefied completely, but I only caught a glimpse of him, so mine just ache like a motherfucker. We managed to get back here, only to encounter two silvermen.'

He looked at the ledge on which they stood and the doorway leading away from it.

'You, however, seem to know exactly where you're going. Thank you for showing me the way.' He smirked again. 'You always were a smart little bitch, Lily. I hated that about you. Let's see if you're smart enough to dodge this.'

Then he drew a pistol, aimed it right at Lily's forehead and before Lily—or Jack, watching from the other side of the shaft—could do anything about it, he fired.

Somehow, Dion's shot missed.

He couldn't have been more stunned.

He was only five feet away from Lily. No-one could miss from that range.

But Lily was ready for it and she took advantage of his shock and moved at lightning speed.

She leapt forward, clutching one hand around Dion's grenade hand—keeping the grenade's spoon depressed—while with her other fist, she hit him right in the nose.

Dion's nose broke, exploding with blood, and he grunted as he staggered back a step.

As he did, Lily wrenched the grenade from his grasp—still keeping the spoon depressed—and punched him again, once, twice, each time in his already broken nose.

'You can handle pain, huh?' she said furiously. 'Well, I want you to feel every one of these.'

In each ensuing punch there was a well of anger, retribution, payback.

She hit him four more times in his busted nose, turning it into a pulpy bloody mess.

Dion reeled under her blows.

Then his heels touched the edge of the ledge and the newly minted King of the Underworld—once a handsome and wealthy prince with women and money and not a care in the world—looked at Lily with his deformed jaw, his broken nose and his semi-melted eyes.

'Come, now, Lily, surely we can—'

'You wanted to keep me as a sex slave, to share with your brother, you prick. Guess what: you picked the wrong girl. See if *you* can dodge this.'

And with those words, she jammed the grenade into the front of his pants and shoved him off the ledge.

Dion screamed as he dropped off the ledge.

He had fallen about ten feet when the grenade detonated, blowing his mid-section apart, and he fell into the abyss in two ragged pieces.

Then he was gone, vanishing into the darkness, and the shaft was silent.

Dionysius DeSaxe—the wicked son of Hades, the loyal protégé of Sphinx, the cruel prince who, with his brother Zaitan, had tortured women and hunted minotaurs—was finally dead.

Using the hand-rungs in the ceiling, Jack, Easton and Smiley crossed the shaft and joined Lily on her ledge.

When Jack landed beside her, Lily rushed into his arms and wept. 'Oh, Dad, he—'

Every fear, every ache, every raw emotion she felt toward Dion came rushing out in great wrenching sobs.

'—he was a monster.'

'He sure was, kiddo,' Jack said, holding her tightly. 'But he's not any more. You got him good. That bastard's not gonna hurt anybody any more.'

He held Lily away from him. 'Having said that, young lady, isn't it strange how his shot missed you from point-blank range? I was wondering where that old Warbler had got to. I actually searched for it at the farm a while back but couldn't find it. *You* took it.'

Lily pulled a disc-shaped device from her chest pocket. It was one of Wizard's old inventions, called a Warbler, a device that disrupted the flight of subsonic projectiles, like bullets.

Lily said, 'I found it one day last year in the work shed at the farm. It reminded me of Wizard, so I kept it on me. I didn't know if it even still worked, but I'm sure glad it did.'

Jack shook his head. 'I think Wizard would be very pleased to know he just saved your life. After all this time, he's still with us.'

'Yeah.'

'Oh, and Lily,' Jack added, 'you're never going first ever again.'

★ ★ ★

They examined the doorway to their tunnel.

The two stone statues standing to attention on either side of it were unmoving, still. If there were silvermen or anything else inside them, they weren't emerging yet.

Cracking a new glowstick, Jack peered into the tunnel.

It was maybe ten feet wide and a faint breeze blew out from it. Beyond that, it was especially dark and eerie.

As he did this, Easton brought Smiley over to Lily, pointed at her and said, 'Bronzeman. I order you to protect her, too.'

Lily nodded. 'Thanks, Easton.'

Jack was still looking down the dark tunnel.

'The Endless Tunnel,' he said. 'Something tells me we're in for a long walk, folks.'

The four of them entered the tunnel.

THE ENDLESS TUNNEL

While perhaps not literally endless, the tunnel turned out to be very, very long.

It was square in shape, maybe eight feet to a side, so Jack could walk upright.

It had walls made of huge stone blocks positioned together so perfectly that Jack and the others could barely spot the seams.

There was one other thing about this tunnel that was particularly noteworthy: it was not entirely dark.

Embedded in its ceiling every fifteen metres or so were small glowing spherical orbs, each the size of a golf ball.

They pulsed an ominous shade of red, blood red, bathing the tunnel in a creepy crimson glow. It wasn't a strong light, but after their eyes adjusted to it, it was enough to see by.

Jack was glad for that because Lily only had a regular flashlight and Easton had his barrel-mounted one. And all Jack had was his helmet-mounted penlight. He wanted to preserve their batteries. Anytime they could make do with another light source, they would.

It was just as well, because they walked for hours.

During that time, they passed sixteen pairs of sentinel statues. Each time they came to them, they skirted them warily and in silence, but no silvermen emerged from the stone statues.

They pressed on through the red darkness.

★ ★ ★

They walked in single file.

Smiley led the way, followed by Jack and Lily, then Easton.

At first they talked as they walked, but as the hours ticked by, they began to walk in silence.

After a time, moving along behind Jack, Lily began to notice something more in his silence.

His head was bowed, his steps more of a trudge than the usual springing stride. He had withdrawn into his mind, into himself.

Zoe, Lily thought.

She skipped up beside him. 'Hey there, champ. How you doing?'

He blinked out of his reverie, caught.

'To be honest, not so good, kiddo,' he said. 'My mind's a mess. Got all kinds of thoughts running through it. How I can't believe she's gone, how she was taken so suddenly, why I didn't hang back with her, how much I loved her, how much I already miss her, how I can't really comprehend going on without her, and why I should bother saving a world that will never know or even care about her sacrifice—'

'All right, stop right there, mister!' Lily snapped with surprising sternness.

As she said it, she jumped in front of him, halting him in mid-stride.

Jack stared blankly at her.

Easton paused a few steps behind them, not daring to intervene.

Lily pointed right at Jack. 'Okay, listen up and listen good, because I'm only gonna say this once and I only *want* to say it once. Put those thoughts away for now. Put them in a box in the back of your mind, somewhere out of the way. You can wallow in them later, but right now, you and I have a universe to save. Zoe was on the same mission, and if you give it all away now you give up what she was fighting for, too.'

Tears welled in Jack's eyes.

Lily saw them. She wanted to cry, too—cry her eyes out—but she couldn't yet.

She had to hammer this home.

'I'm not going to stand here and say that what happened doesn't suck. It does. But you're *Jack West fucking Jr.* You found the Seven Ancient Wonders and the Six Sacred Stones. You're the fifth greatest warrior, the guy who won the Great Games and *you didn't come this fucking far just to come this fucking far!* You never give up, even when you're hanging by your fingernails with all the odds in the world stacked against you!'

And then Lily's voice cracked and she couldn't hold back her own tears.

'You'll see her again, Dad. You will. But right now *you're still here*. And we got some really bad dudes to stop. Grieve later, but not now. All my life I've watched you and wondered what it is that makes you a hero. And I figured it out: it's *trying* when nobody else thinks it's even worth trying, when the odds really are stacked against you or when your friends and family are taken away from you. You've done this all your life. And maybe this is the hardest example of that—going on without Zoe—but this is *who you are*. This is *what you do*. We still have a job to do and I need you fully focused to do it!'

She stopped speaking.

Jack's eyes were still downcast.

Then, slowly, he began to nod.

When he looked up at her, there was fire in his eyes.

'I understand, kiddo,' he said in a low voice.

Lily hugged him tightly.

'Oh, Dad, I'm so sorry,' she said as she gripped him.

Jack just held her.

Then they separated and, together, began walking down the endless tunnel again.

'Nice speech, by the way,' he said.

'Don't ask me to do it again. It all just kinda came blurting out. Stream of honesty, I guess.'

'Tell me what you *really* think next time.'

'That's what family is for,' she said as she took his hand and they walked onward into the darkness.

Most of the time, the tunnel either sloped steadily downward in curving arcs or stretched away in long flat straight sections.

On a few occasions it bent upward, via sets of broad steps that spanned the width of the tunnel.

Eager to catch up to their rivals, Jack, Lily, Easton and Smiley the bronzeman jogged in the descending and flat stretches. They walked when the tunnel ascended.

During one of those long trudges up a set of wide stairs, Easton said, 'Minotaurs in the Underworld tell story about this Labyrinth. Old story, famous story. About prince named Theseus and minotaur named Asterion.'

Jack nodded as he walked. 'Sure. That's a very famous legend outside the Underworld, too.'

Easton's eyes lit up. 'Really? The story of the evil prince Theseus and the hero minotaur he left to die in the Labyrinth? Wow.'

Walking beside Easton, Lily raised her eyebrows. 'I'm actually a bit hazy on the whole Theseus-and-the-minotaur story, Easton. Since we've got nothing else to do while we walk, why don't you tell it to us as you know it.'

Easton nodded enthusiastically. 'Of course, Miss Lily. Is great legend.'

And so he began.

'When famed warrior Hercules won Great Games at Underworld for King Zeus, Zeus go to Supreme Labyrinth.

'At that time, Zeus's brother—Poseidon—was King of Sea. As homage to his all-powerful brother, Poseidon send his son, the prince Theseus, to accompany Zeus into the Labyrinth. Theseus bad man, cruel prince. He bring three other minor princes with him as royal escorts for Zeus.

'Zeus's other brother was Hades, King of the Underworld. Hades give Zeus a gift of nine minotaurs to act as porters in Labyrinth, to carry his supplies and equipment. The leader of this team of minotaurs was Asterion.

'Asterion smart minotaur. Honest and hard-working. He very proud to do this task.

'After Zeus use Emperor's Route to reach throne and prevent Omega, he go to leave. But Prince Theseus tell Zeus that he wish to linger behind, to take final look at amazing Labyrinth. So Zeus leaves.

'Theseus stays with his three prince friends and suddenly they begin killing minotaur porters.'

'Wait! He starts *killing* them?' Lily exclaimed. 'Why?'

'For sport. Many royals think minotaurs dumb animals. Good for nothing except simple labour and killing. Theseus one of those.'

'What happened then?' Jack asked quietly.

Easton said, 'Theseus and the other princes proceed to slaughter minotaurs. Laugh and chortle as they hunt them in passageways of Labyrinth using arrows and swords. It awful scene. Minotaurs scream and wail as they butchered by the young princes.

'But one minotaur, Asterion, he escape. Not only escape, but he actually disarm and kill one of Theseus's friends. Wounds two others and even manages to cut Theseus himself in single combat.

'With Theseus knocked down and wounded, Asterion hurry outside and as he emerge from Labyrinth, he see Zeus in the distance, arriving back at his camp of tents. Asterion flee in other direction, over mountains and away into desert.

'When Theseus emerge from the Labyrinth, he tell Zeus false tale: that *minotaurs* revolted and started attacking princes, so he had to kill them and only just escaped with his life. Theseus not tell Zeus that he himself murdered his two wounded companions—finished them off—so that they not be able to reveal the truth of what happened.

'From that day on, Theseus considered great hero: the man who slayed the murderous minotaurs who probably would have killed Zeus, too. Also from that day, minotaurs considered deceitful, untrustworthy, and treated badly, lower than dogs.'

'Because the victors write history,' Jack said.

Easton nodded sadly. 'Yes.'

Lily said, 'And over the years, through countless retellings, Theseus's version becomes the story that we all know: his dead friends become sacrificial youths, Asterion becomes a monster in the Labyrinth, and he becomes the brave hero who entered the Labyrinth to slay it. What a jerk.'

Easton said, 'But that not the end. After escaping Labyrinth, Asterion go on great journey. After travelling for long time, he find his way back to Underworld and he tell minotaurs of his tale. Minotaurs very proud of Asterion. Keep him hidden from King Hades. Asterion live in honour—but also in hiding—in minotaur city in Underworld. When he die, he given honourable burial under shrine in most sacred temple inside minotaur city. That is the true tale of Asterion and the great villain Theseus.'

Jack shook his head as he continued down the tunnel, taking this in. Lily did the same.

History, they both knew from hard experience, was a strange thing. It morphed over time with every retelling.

When one word changed, whole stories changed. Like with King Canute: a very wise king who said he could *not* hold back the tide. He became known to history as a proud king who thought he could hold back the tide.

Even *recent* historical events, like the deaths of JFK and Princess Diana, became so shrouded in untruths and innuendo that no-one knew what had really happened.

Myths were worse.

If you couldn't know what really happened to Princess Diana

as recently as 1997, how could one *ever* know what happened to Theseus and a minotaur sometime around 1200 B.C.E.?

Jack turned to Easton as he walked. 'Thanks for telling us that story, Easton. It's good to know Asterion's side of it.'

They came to the top of the stairs they had been climbing to see another long section of flat tunnel stretching away from them.

The dim crimson orbs in the ceiling receded into the distance, getting smaller and smaller.

Jack sighed. 'Okay, folks. Start jogging again.'

THE UNDER-TUNNELS

They had gone a few kilometres down this new flat section of the tunnel when they came to a feature they had not encountered before.

They stopped, cautious.

It was like a kink in the tunnel, a downward one.

Eight stone steps spanned the width of the tunnel, going down. They opened onto a short flat section maybe twenty metres long before a second set of stone stairs led the way back up again.

Jack edged down the stairs and paused on the second-to-last step.

The little sub-tunnel was partially flooded.

A shallow layer of water covered its floor, about a foot deep.

In the middle of the tunnel, ringed by the water, was a waist-high stone pedestal with a five-fingered handprint sunken into its top.

Jack knew what that was.

The handprint matched the mark on his palm, the one that he—and Lily and Zoe—had acquired when they'd performed the Fall.

'What's this?' Lily asked as she and Easton stopped beside Jack on the step just above the water's surface.

Jack said, 'The Labyrinth is making sure that only someone with the mark can proceed.'

His eyes darted upward, scanning the ceiling.

'Wait a second,' he said. 'I've seen a trap like this. In that chamber in Santorini—*there*.'

He pointed up at them.

Arrayed in a pattern around a single crimson orb in the ceiling were a dozen small greystone pellets. They jutted out a centimetre or two from the otherwise flush surface of the ceiling.

'Greystone pellets?' Lily whispered.

'Exactly,' Jack said. 'This is just like what I saw in Santorini. Something in here triggers an inflow of water. So this lower section of tunnel—let's call it an under-tunnel—fills with water. When the rising water reaches the ceiling, it touches the greystone pellets and turns the whole flooded under-tunnel to solid stone.'

'Sealing it off completely,' Lily said. 'Plugging it.'

'That's right.'

'So what triggers the inflow of water?'

Jack jerked his chin at the floorstones under the water. 'I'm guessing one of those floorstones is a trigger stone. Looks to me like at least one set of our rivals came through here. They triggered the water, but placed their palm on that pedestal and stopped it. If we want to pass through, I figure we have to do the same. Stay here, I'm going first this time.'

Jack stepped cautiously into the shin-deep water.

No sooner had his boot hit the first submerged floorstone than five gushing streams of water blasted out of circular holes in the walls of the under-tunnel.

The water level rose fast.

Jack sloshed forward through it and slammed his palm down on the handprint on the pedestal.

The inflow of water stopped.

Jack smiled at Lily and Easton. 'Come on.'

They hurried through the under-tunnel, followed by Smiley, but when they rose up the steps at its far end, they stopped dead in their tracks, for a shadowy figure stood in the darkness before them, blocking the way.

Jack whipped out his gun, gunslinger-style.

The man in the tunnel didn't move.

He just stood in the dead centre of the passageway, on a podium of some kind, bathed in the dim glow of the crimson orbs lining the ceiling.

He was broad-shouldered and tall. His head almost touched the eight-foot-high ceiling.

But the figure still didn't move.

Jack exhaled with relief.

It wasn't a person.

It was a statue. On a pedestal.

Jack edged toward it.

There were some objects on the floor on the other side of it, low mounds in the darkness.

As he came closer, Jack saw what they were.

A body and . . . something else.

The body wore tan combat gear and lay face-down on the floor-stones, dead.

The 'something else' had, well, once been a pair of bronzemen.

Only these bronzemen's limbs had melted into formless lumps that had since re-solidified. The only evidence that remained of their former humanoid shapes were their heads sticking up at odd angles from the lumps of re-hardened molten metal.

Jack arrived at the statue.

Tall and man-shaped, it stood with its back to him.

It was similar in design to the bronzemen and silvermen, only taller and made of gold.

A goldman, Jack thought with a jolt of fear, recalling the golden claw that had seized Dion's men earlier.

He was about to step past the goldman when something else occurred to him: two lines from Imhotep's skull.

Speak not in the presence of the gold ones: only in silence may you pass.

And:

Look not in their faces, or thine eyes will not see again.

As he looked at the human body and the melted bronzemen on the floor, he also recalled the injuries Dion and his Squires had acquired: melted eyes and skin.

Jack turned to Lily and used sign language:

Don't speak. Signing only.

Tell Easton no talking.

Wait there. Dead body ahead. Going to investigate.

Don't look at the statue's face.

Lily nodded back at him, signing, *Okay*.

This was, Jack reflected, another bonus of knowing Alby. It was because of Alby that Jack, Lily and Zoe had learned sign language many years ago. Some people—people like Dion—might have considered being deaf a weakness, but here it was a strength.

Jack gazed up at the back of the goldman statue.

It towered over him, facing the other way.

Its pedestal was about a foot high, so the goldman, almost touching the ceiling with the top of its head, must have been close to seven feet tall. Its metallic golden body shone dully in the blood-red glow of the ceiling orbs. Its arms ended at fierce-looking claws. It had definitely been a goldman that had been pursuing Dion's group.

How am I going to do this? Jack thought.

Just keep my eyes down, I guess. And don't look back at its face.

Jack peered into the darkness beyond the goldman.

About fifteen metres past the body and lumps on the floor, he saw another under-tunnel.

He signed to Lily, *Tunnel ahead. Going to check it out.*

Lily nodded in reply.

Jack swallowed and, keeping his eyes determinedly downcast, slowly and carefully stepped around the goldman.

The statue didn't move.

Didn't come alive. Didn't lunge at Jack or tear him to pieces.

It didn't do anything.

It just stood there, ominously still.

Moving with his eyes down, not daring to even peek at the statue, Jack found himself thinking of the biblical story of Lot's wife: the woman who, as she and her husband fled the city of Sodom, had been commanded by God's angels not to look back. But Lot's wife had disobeyed, stealing a glance back at the city, and for her sin, she was turned into a pillar of salt.

And suddenly the *direction* that the statue was facing made sense to Jack.

It was designed to ensnare anyone fleeing *back out* of the endless tunnel.

Dion's tunnel must have had a similar goldman statue in it.

Maybe, in their ignorance, Dion and his men had spoken in its presence and awakened it. Or they had got past it, only to hit a dead end in their tunnel and when they'd turned back, one of them had looked at its face.

Either way, it took all of Jack's self-control not to look back at the thing.

Every fibre of his curiosity wanted to turn and examine it, but he kept his eyes aimed determinedly down and forward, away from the big gold automaton.

In the dim red glow of the orbs in the ceiling, he came to the body slumped on the floor of the tunnel.

It was an Omega monk.

Jack could tell from the greystone hourglass hanging from a chain around his neck. It was intact.

Jack pocketed the hourglass. Greystone had come in handy once before, in the English Tunnel under Mont Saint-Michel. It might come in handy again.

The monk was also not wearing traditional Omega robes. Instead, he wore tan combat gear and a gunbelt.

It didn't matter. Nothing he could have worn would have protected him from what had happened.

As had been the case with Dion's Squires earlier, assailed by some superintense source of heat, his clothes, boots and helmet had become one with his skin.

His body was an unholy mix of cloth, leather, skin and bone.

The monk had been gripping a gun. That had also melted and become part of his fingers. His other hand had deformed completely and was now just a puddle of disgusting goo at the end of his arm.

What happened here? Jack thought.

He leaned in close to examine the face of the monk.

It was revolting. The skin of his face had sloughed off, revealing his jawbone and teeth—

The monk gagged.

Jack sprang back.

This horribly melted man *was still alive*.

The monk hacked out a hideous choking cough, upchucking a gout of blood as he did so.

Jack recoiled.

In a hoarse whisper, the monk started mumbling: 'If we can't get to Keter, Malkuth will lead us to the other realm. If we can't get to Keter, Malkuth will lead us to the other realm . . .'

Jack frowned.

Keter? Malkuth?

He knew those terms.

They were from the Kabbalah.

The Kabbalah was a collection of ancient mystical teachings that were said to predate all the world's major modern religions. It had acquired a certain mystique over the millennia since its secrets were known only by a certain few 'initiates'. It was mainly concerned with, on the one hand, the eternal and divine realm of existence, and on the other, the mortal, tangible world that we live in—which it famously depicted in diagrammatic form in the Tree of Life image that Jack and the others had seen earlier.

In Kabbalistic lore—and indeed on the Tree of Life—*Keter* was the uppermost celestial plane, or, for want of a better word, Heaven. *Malkuth* was the opposite, the lowest level of the Kabbalah and the entryway to the darker underworld.

In his near-death state and unbearable pain, the monk was rambling, repeating some kind of mantra from his studies about the afterlife.

'. . . If we can't get to Keter, Malkuth will lead us . . .'

As the dying monk kept muttering, Jack scanned the tunnel around him, careful not to look back at the goldman.

The stone walls on both sides of the fallen man, he noticed, were pockmarked with many large slashing indentations that radiated outward, as if someone had detonated something in here and the blast had seared *into* the walls in a kind of spray pattern.

His gaze fell on the two re-solidified bronzemen and suddenly he saw a mark on the floor next to them.

Shaped like a small black star, it was a scorch mark of some kind, as if a grenade had indeed gone off here and left this charring on the ground.

Jack looked up at the ceiling directly above the mark.

And he saw it.

Or, rather, he *didn't* see it.

A crimson orb should have been directly above the scorch mark, but instead of an orb, there was just an empty socket.

An orb had dropped out of that socket and hit the floor.

The orbs don't just provide light . . . Jack realised.

If they fall out of the ceiling and hit the floor, they explode, releasing some sort of heat blast . . .

He looked again at the deformed Omega monk and the melted

lumps that had once been bronzemen. He also thought about Dion and his Squires.

Something extremely hot had assailed them all, something so incredibly hot that it had melted their equipment to their skin and turned bronzemen to liquid. Although, notably, it hadn't affected the goldman at all.

That was when he remembered another of Imhotep's warnings:

Beware the liquid fire.

Jack looked from the scorch mark on the floor to the empty socket in the ceiling . . . to *all the other red orbs* running down the ceiling in a line.

Jesus. There were hundreds of them in here, and just one had done this.

Jack had been in deadly places before, but nothing with this level of lethality.

Keeping his head downturned, he signed to Lily:

Come over now.

Keep flashlight off. Stay silent.

And do not—do not—look at the statue's face.

Our lives depend on it.

Moments later, Lily, Easton and Smiley joined Jack and, with the goldman in the tunnel still not moving, they scurried away into the next under-tunnel.

They left the dying Omega monk to his fate. He just kept whispering hoarsely through his melted lips: '. . . If we can't get to Keter, Malkuth will lead us to the other realm . . .'

They hurried into the under-tunnel, setting off its water trap, but Jack quickly pressed his palm to the pedestal there and the water stopped and they raced up its far stairs.

The goldman did not follow.

They stepped up from that second under-tunnel into another long flat section of the main tunnel and Jack's relief at passing the goldman instantly vanished.

Something was wrong here.

It took him a moment to realise what it was: this section of the tunnel was darker.

Totally dark.

It had no red orbs in its ceiling, just a line of maybe ten empty sockets where they should have been.

Jack tensed. *Possible trap?*

Not yet willing to use his helmet flashlight, he reached into his pack, grabbed his night-vision goggles and put them on.

With his head bent, he saw the floorstones at his feet in the green glow of night vision.

Then he swung his head back up to look at the tunnel and in that haunting glow he saw a figure with sharpened teeth rushing at him in a screaming rage.

The figure slammed into Jack, hurling him back onto the floor and knocking the night-vision goggles off his head.

Darkness. Blackness.

He was totally blind.

And then his attacker was on top of him, punching and scratching at his face.

Jack fended off the flurry of blows. As he did, he heard Lily scream plus scuffling noises.

A twee voice squealed: 'Can you fight while blind! Can you, can you!'

In the split second before his goggles had been dislodged, Jack had caught a glimpse of his attacker:

A Vandal: nimble and wiry, it had been wearing a pair of its own night-vision goggles.

It could see and Jack couldn't.

And there was at least one other Vandal in here, attacking Lily—

Boom.

Amid all the movement, Jack heard a dull echoing thud from somewhere behind them.

Was it the goldman?

Had it awakened?

Uh-oh.

He still couldn't see a thing. Just infinite black.

The Vandal on top of Jack was still attacking him—hissing, punching and biting—so Jack raised his titanium left forearm to protect his face, and not knowing that it was made of metal, the

Vandal bit viciously into it and squealed in surprise and pain.

'Ow!'

Jack took the chance and lashed out at the darkness with his titanium fist, hoping to land a punch.

It landed.

He heard the Vandal's nose break and the little man howled and in the pitch darkness, Jack's metal hand found its throat and grabbed it.

With his other hand, Jack levelled his pistol at where he thought the Vandal's head was and pulled the trigger.

Bang!

In the tight confines of the tunnel, the shot echoed loudly. Jack's ears rang.

There was the sound of a splatter and the Vandal in his grip went limp. From point-blank range, he'd blown its head off.

Boom. Boom.

More dull thuds. Heavy footsteps.

Tossing away the body of his dead attacker, Jack turned, his eyes adjusting to the darkness, and by the very dim light of the red orb in the previous under-tunnel, he could just make out the shadowy figures of Lily and Easton engaged in a struggle with the second Vandal.

He was too far away to help, but then he saw Smiley step up from the under-tunnel, snatch the Vandal off Lily and hurl it down the stairs, back into the under-tunnel.

The Vandal tumbled down the eight steps and splashed into the watery floor of the under-tunnel.

In the dim red light down there, Jack saw it scramble to its feet and look back the other way—

—when it froze.

And screamed, in both terror and pain.

Boom. Boom.

'*Argh!* No! My eyes!' The Vandal clutched its eyes, fell to its knees and began to wail in agony.

Boom. Boom. Boom.

And suddenly Jack saw a pair of gold legs arrive in front of the stricken Vandal and stop above him.

Because of the angle of the ceiling, Jack couldn't see the gold-man's face—which might have saved his life—but he saw the big thing's golden claws reach down and lift the Vandal from the floor and calmly rip the little man in two.

The Vandal shrieked.

Blood gushed.

'Lily, Easton, run!' Jack whispered as he pulled them the other way and they raced down their tunnel toward the next under-tunnel fifty metres away.

Boom. Boom. Boom.

The goldman was coming.

Jack saw its shadow rising from the steps, silhouetted by the low crimson light. He spun, not daring to set eyes on the thing's face.

They reached the next under-tunnel . . .

. . . and paused.

It was different from the others and in a significant way: this under-tunnel had been completely clogged with greystone.

A perfectly flat layer of greystone lay flush against its upper rim, like freshly poured concrete.

Jack could see what had happened instantly: this under-tunnel had filled with water and that water—after it had touched the grey-stone pellets in the under-tunnel's ceiling—had then been turned to greystone.

Only, thankfully, someone had dug *through* it.

A crude round hole—created by a jackhammer of some kind and just big enough for a person to crawl through—bored *through* the greystone like a jagged stone pipe, down and into the under-tunnel.

Jack figured that Sphinx, coming through here first, had deliber-ately allowed this under-tunnel to fill with water and plug entirely with greystone.

But then one of the other groups in here—probably the Omega monks, given the dying man Jack had seen—had come prepared with a device to dig through the concrete-like greystone.

'Lily, go go go,' he urged. 'Easton, you, too.'

Into the tight space they went, bellycrawling on their chests, hurrying as fast as they could.

Jack went third and Smiley brought up the rear.

After about a minute of wriggling, they emerged in a new, long section of the main tunnel—lit by red orbs again—and they ran headlong down it.

After a minute or so, the booming of the goldman's footfalls faded into the distance and they figured it hadn't been able, or willing, to crawl through the greystone hole.

It was only once they had run for about ten full minutes that Jack dared to stop and let them all catch their breath.

'Goddamn,' he said, 'this is one vicious labyrinth.'

They pressed onward, down the tunnel.

They encountered a dozen more under-tunnels—two of which were clogged with greystone yet also jackhammered with crawl-holes—and three more goldmen, which they skirted in silence, always careful not to look at their faces.

But in the main, the tunnel just continued in long sweeping stretches, maintaining its gentle downward grade.

They walked for almost a whole day, covering miles in the crimson gloom.

'I hope we chose the right tunnel,' Lily said. 'You wouldn't want to come all this way and hit a dead end.'

Jack nodded. 'I think that's what Dion did. Took the wrong tunnel, wandered for hours and then had to turn around.'

At one point in their travels, Jack paused to examine one of the red orbs in the ceiling.

Climbing onto Smiley's shoulders, he gently extracted one from the ceiling and peered closely at it.

The little orb pulsed with red light, throbbing.

Very carefully, Jack pressed it with his titanium left index finger.

The orb's outer skin flexed under the gentle pressure.

'Looks like it's a liquid inside a thin membrane. Doesn't seem like it would take much of an impact to crack the membrane, either. "Beware the liquid fire."'

'You think this is what melted all those other guys' skin and clothing?' Lily asked. 'And those bronzemen, too?'

'Yep,' Jack said.

They kept walking, onward and downward.

After a time, they reached a point where Jack knew they had to risk getting some sleep.

And so Smiley stood guard while they slept for a few hours.

Jack slept fitfully, his dreams shot through with nightmares.

When he woke, he found Lily sitting over him, stroking his shoulder saying, 'Easy now. It's okay, Dad.'

'Thanks, kiddo.'

When they rose, they continued down the endless tunnel. After two more hours, they encountered something in the tunnel that they had not seen previously.

An intersection.

Their tunnel split in two.

'Which way do we go?' Lily asked. 'Left or right?'

Jack looked at her, perplexed. 'I don't know.'

THE SECRET ROYAL WORLD II

TROY, THE ROYAL REDOUBT AND THE RED HORIZON STAR

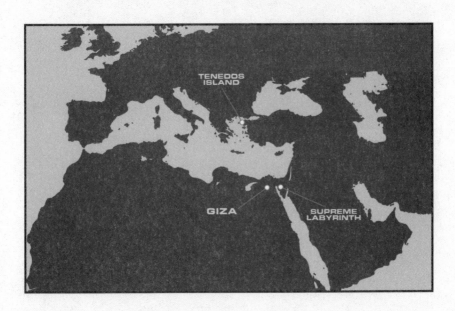

Do not trust the horse, Trojans! Whatever it is, I fear the Greeks, even when they bear gifts.

VIRGIL, *THE AENEID*

TENEDOS ISLAND
AEGEAN SEA NEAR THE TURKISH COAST
27 DECEMBER, 0900 HOURS

The seaplane touched down beside Tenedos Island, a particularly nondescript island not far from the mouth of the Dardanelles Strait.

As the crow flies, Tenedos Island is about twelve miles from Hisarlik on the Turkish mainland, the commonly accepted location of the famed city of Troy.

But no tourist buses or boats come to Tenedos. It is a quiet place, strictly for locals only.

Inside the seaplane sat Nobody Black, Iolanthe and Bertie. They had sped here overnight, pausing only to sleep.

On the way, they had checked in with Pooh Bear and Stretch and learned about their daring kidnapping of the royal banker, Sir John Marren, at Salzburg Airport in Austria.

Iolanthe frowned. 'That was a bold move, gentlemen. Definitely something that no-one in the royal world would have seen coming. But be careful. Marren is a ruthless man. Watch him closely.'

Pooh Bear and Stretch also informed them of the worldwide scattering of the royal families and how those families were fleeing in great haste to three secure locations: Xian in China, Hohensalzburg Fortress in Austria and, the most important one, Raven Rock in America.

'This is how the rich and powerful prepare for the new world order,' Nobody said bitterly. 'They scurry to their fortresses to sit out the storm and wait with bated breath to welcome their new emperor.'

'Sadly, yes, that's exactly what it is,' Iolanthe agreed.

Now, in the light of day, as their seaplane bobbed on the water, Nobody, Iolanthe and Bertie looked up at Tenedos Island.

There wasn't much to it.

Mid-sized and plain, vineyards lay over much of its sloping terrain. The dry climate was apparently good for grape growing, but it didn't exactly make the island easy on the eye. It was brown and dry, drab.

A few large white-walled mansions dotted the island's eastern coast, looking back at Turkey from commanding positions on the hills and bluffs.

The building of these massive estates, Iolanthe said, was a relatively recent phenomenon: wealthy families would purchase a vineyard—a classic trophy purchase—and then build a vacation mansion on the land above it. Many of the grand houses sat empty for eleven months of the year, occupied only by housekeepers and support staff.

The island's population was less than three thousand.

As he looked up at it, Nobody pursed his lips doubtfully. 'You're saying *this* is the site of the lost city of Troy? It doesn't really look like the site of a great empire and a famous war.'

'This is it,' Iolanthe said. 'But as I said back in Italy, the Trojan War wasn't fought at a *city*. It was fought at a vault. The vault of the royal banker.'

'What about all those stories about the search for Troy by Schliemann?' Nobody said.

'Pleasant fairytales,' Iolanthe said. 'And fairytales that Heinrich Schliemann told repeatedly in order to make a lot of money. His story captured the public's attention because of its compelling narrative—that Schliemann had used the descriptions of the landscapes in Homer's *Iliad* and *Odyssey* and Virgil's *Aeneid* to find the location of Troy. But it was all entirely fanciful. He found something, sure. Some old buried walls over in Turkey.'

Nobody cocked his head. 'So what do *your* royal history books say?'

Iolanthe grinned. 'That Schliemann didn't find Troy at all.'

Nobody said, 'And I bet all you folks in the royal world were perfectly happy to let him and the world's media think he was successful.'

'We sure were.'

'So what's the truth?'

Iolanthe pointed at Tenedos Island, indicating one particularly large estate that ran from some low ocean-level cliffs back up a high grassy hill.

A white marble mansion lorded over an enormous vineyard and the broad lawn that stretched down to the cliffs. In the otherwise dry and brown island, the lawn was a burst of vibrant emerald green.

The whole estate was, Nobody thought, very sleek and new, more American in its styling than Turkish or Greek. It looked like something from the Hamptons.

This was exemplified by what lay at the bottom of the estate's sloping lawn: an enormous gabled white boathouse embedded in the cliff face.

'The truth,' Iolanthe said, 'is that this estate sits atop the ancient vault of Troy, an all but impregnable vault that was managed by Priam, the then Master of Coin to the four legendary kingdoms. The royal banker.

'In his two great works, *The Iliad* and *The Odyssey*, Homer said that the King of Troy was an honourable man named Priam. Priam was indeed honourable because he was guarding the most important vault in the world, one containing innumerable treasures of the four kings.

'The Trojan War was actually a colossal Greek mission *to rob* the vault of Troy—and it did ultimately end with a stratagem involving a gigantic horse. Only not as you probably think.

'As part of his duties as the Master of Coin, even today the royal banker watches over the treasures of the four kingdoms, many of them priceless. These treasures, naturally, are now kept in more modern vaults.

'They are no longer thick-walled treasuries carved into the ground underneath temples or castles. Rather, they are titanium behemoths located inside modern buildings with state-of-the-art laser scanners and biometric defences.'

Iolanthe paused.

'But just as the technology underpinning these vaults has changed over the centuries, so too have their locations. As the locus of global power shifted, the sites of the vaults did, too. Two thousand years ago, the primary vault was located in the safest place of the time, central Rome. During the Dark Ages, it lay in a crypt buried deep beneath a mountaintop monastery in France. These days, as the fulcrum of global power has shifted to the West, there are two main vaults, one in Switzerland, the other in the United States.'

Iolanthe held up a finger.

'But the four kingdoms do venerate history and this is a weakness of theirs that we can now exploit. For, over the millennia, out of a deep sense of respect for past glories, the kingdoms have kept intact some of the older, no-longer-used vaults. Indeed, to have an old vault on one's property is seen as a mark of prestige in the royal world.

'One such vault—the primary vault of its time, the tumultuous era around 1200 B.C.E.—does indeed still stand and it holds the copy of the crown that we seek. The vault of Troy.'

She pointed at the huge estate on the coast of the island of Tenedos.

'And the vault of Troy lies underneath *that* mansion.'

'How do you know this?' Nobody asked.

'Because I've seen it. I've been inside it.'

'You've been inside it? Were you on a research trip or something?'

'No.' Iolanthe smiled. 'I was attending a wedding. A very big society wedding.'

★ ★ ★

She explained.

'The island of Tenedos—the whole island—has been owned for a thousand years by the Zampieri family, one of the richest families in history and one of the most influential in the royal world. The Zampieris made their fortune during the rise of Venice as a seagoing empire and during that time, they acquired many islands in the eastern Mediterranean.

'And when the only daughter of the family patriarch, Giovanni Zampieri, decided to get married, her wedding was held here, on Tenedos.

'It was an astonishingly lavish affair while still remaining stylishly understated, as is the royal way. The ceremony was held on the lawn you can see, looking out over the sea. But the reception was held *inside* the vault underneath the property, the vault of Troy. Now, I've seen a lot of remarkable things in the royal world, but that vault was something else. It didn't have any recent treasures inside it. As I said, those had long been taken to more modern facilities. But it did still have on its walls and in its alcoves some statues and items from the Trojan period which were simply too big to move from the vault and which were nothing short of breathtaking.'

'Like the copy of the Crown of Priam?' Nobody asked.

'Yes, it's particularly striking,' Iolanthe said. 'We can't waste any time. Chloe might have realised her error by now and be on her way here. We have to get in and out before she arrives with her muscle.'

It turned out that, apart from a few custodial staff, the Zampieri estate on Tenedos Island was empty.

According to some grizzled fishermen at the town's wharf where Nobody brought their seaplane in to dock, the Zampieri family had departed from their hilltop mansion the previous evening rather suddenly.

That in itself wasn't particularly unusual. They had left instructions for the maids and gardeners to keep the estate in good order and to expect them back in a few months.

'After the world has changed forever,' Nobody said as he, Iolanthe and Bertie drove from the main town in a rented car, heading in the direction of the Zampieri estate.

Iolanthe nodded. 'They left for the safety of their royal rendezvous point.'

They got the lie of the land quickly.

A couple of fat security guards manned the entry gate to the estate.

A few more roamed the perimeter fences listlessly. They were lazy local rent-a-guards, used to an easy gig in a quiet place. One was asleep at his post.

Nobody and Iolanthe quickly took care of the guards idly manning the estate's massive boathouse under the cliff and, with Bertie joining them, hurried inside it.

Inside the giant boathouse, tied up to the dock there, was an enormous megayacht. It was a huge shining thing, four storeys tall and two hundred feet long. And fitting entirely inside the warehouse-sized boathouse.

Iolanthe ran right past it.

'This way,' she said.

She guided them to an old rusty iron door set into the rough stone wall at the rear of the boathouse. The wall was clearly part of the cliff face that the boathouse backed up against.

Iolanthe used a drill on its lock and hurled the door open. Its rusty hinges squealed with disuse.

They hurried through it and down a long stone-walled canal with paths cut along its sides. The canal was about as wide as a train tunnel and clearly carved by the hands of men.

After running for about a hundred metres, guided by the beams of their flashlights, the three of them emerged in a wider space.

Nobody froze.

They'd arrived at a stone jetty—essentially an underground dock for ancient boats—and the ceiling above them shot skyward into darkness.

But even then he could see some features in the gloom.

Towering statues—each fifty feet tall and cloaked in shadow—lined the high walls on either side of him.

And right in front of him, in pride of place in the centre of the space like some kind of prized museum exhibit, mounted on a steel cradle, was an old Greek-style trireme boat.

It had a tall oak mast and ports for the oars that were once rowed by slaves in ancient naval battles.

'It's a ramming ship,' Nobody breathed in wonder. 'An old Greek ramming ship.'

Iolanthe shared a knowing look with Bertie.

'Professor Black,' Bertie said, 'this is the most famous ramming ship in history. Look at its bow.'

Nobody did . . .

. . . and he gasped.

The bow of the ancient vessel was made of shining bronze and it had been formed by some brilliant metalworker of old into the shape of a huge horse's head.

The bronze horse head was gigantic, easily twenty feet high, and it was reared back, its mouth open in a fearsome snarl. Nobody saw that its jaws were bared so wide that a full-grown man could easily stand in them.

And suddenly he got it.

This underground holdfast.

The Greek ramming ship.

With a huge horse's head on its bow.

'Oh, no way . . .' he said.

'Yes,' Bertie said.

'Yes,' Iolanthe confirmed. 'This vault, the impregnable vault of Troy, was the focus of the Trojan War. And this vessel is the battering-ram ship that finally penetrated the vault and disgorged the Greek raiders hidden within its belly through its mouth.'

'The Trojan Horse . . .' Nobody said.

Iolanthe nodded. 'It's really all kinds of cool, but it's not what we're here for. We're here to examine *him*.'

She pointed at one of the towering statues embedded in the right-hand wall: a beautifully preserved, fifty-foot-tall statue of a man with handsome features and dressed in ornate robes. The statue was astonishing in its detail. The rings on the man's hands were perfectly realised in stone, as were his piercing eyes, strong nose and curly hair.

And nestled on that curly hair, also carved from stone, was a crown.

'This statue,' Iolanthe said, 'is of Priam, the King of Troy. And *that* on his head is a copy of his ancient crown.'

Nobody risked a smile.

'This is great,' he said. 'And, all things considered, it wasn't all that hard—'

Right then, chillingly, a voice came from the darkness.

Chloe's voice.

'*Hello, Iolanthe. Took you long enough to get here.*'

The voice was distorted. It was coming from an unseen speaker or cell phone of some kind.

'*You know, I once read about a terrible fire at the King of Land's hunting estate in Wales sometime in the 1800s—one that destroyed many treasures—but I wasn't sure if the Crown of Priam was one of those treasures, so I had to check. It didn't take me long. I knew exactly where to send my people to look in the Royal Hall of Records. I spent a lot of time in that place reading and exploring when you were gallivanting around the world attending all those glittering royal parties.*

'*Unfortunately for you, my people have already come and gone through this vault and found the information we needed. The answer is London, by the way. It's time your mission ended, you spoilt little rich girl. It's time for you to die. Ta-ta.*'

A shrill beep rang out.

And sixty seconds later a colossal explosion ripped through the massive space, filling it completely with a blast wave of flames and smoke that destroyed *everything* in the historic vault: the supertall statues, the stone dock and even the famed boat with the horse-shaped bow.

It was a blast of such ferocity that no-one could have survived it.

It happened so fast that there was no time for Nobody, Iolanthe and Bertie to escape back out through the entry canal.

When the smoke and dust finally cleared, in the light of Bertie's dropped flashlight, the ancient vault of Troy lay broken and destroyed.

Its statues had fallen from their alcoves—including the one of Priam—and they now lay in shattered pieces on the floor. The famed Greek ramming ship, the source of one of humanity's most enduring stories, had been turned to splinters, its bronze horse head now lying askew on its side.

And no-one—not Iolanthe or Nobody or Bertie—remained alive in there.

A7 MOTORWAY BETWEEN LYON AND MARSEILLE, FRANCE
28 DECEMBER

'Begging and screaming,' the man in the twenty-thousand-dollar suit said evenly.

He made for an incongruous sight: seated in a small cell in the back of a speeding police van with his hands flex-cuffed, and yet dressed in a perfectly tailored Brioni suit. His fingernails, Stretch saw, were manicured.

He was Sir John Marren, the royal banker to the four legendary kingdoms.

And right now, he was sitting inside the back of the van as it sped down the eerily empty A7 motorway toward Marseille, in the custody of Jack's people, having been duped by them on the tarmac in Salzburg, Austria.

In the police van with him were Stretch, Pooh Bear, Sister Lynda and Dr Tracy Smith, who was up front driving.

'That's how you're all going to die,' Marren said. 'Begging for your lives and screaming in agony.'

Marren was maybe sixty years old, with a sharp nose and a high forehead. He wore his hair slicked back, making his forehead seem longer. He was fit and healthy-looking in the way that rich people with private yoga instructors are, with polished pink skin that matched his manicured fingernails.

Pooh Bear said, 'Oh, that's charming.'

Marren snorted. 'I've watched stronger men than you cry like babies on the torture slab and plead to die. This will not end well for any of you.'

Having learned that—in anticipation of Sphinx succeeding inside the Supreme Labyrinth—the members of the secret royal world were rushing to three secure rendezvous points in Europe, China and America, Stretch and Pooh Bear had decided to head for the most important rendezvous point, the one in America: Raven Rock, outside Washington, D.C.

But if they were going to do that and stop Sphinx's plan, they needed to do it in another ride.

The Egyptian president's plane was both way too visible and way too trackable. Figuring it was only a matter of time until Marren's people came after them, they'd dumped the plane in Lyon—the city and its airport silent thanks to a Siren bell—parking it inside a hangar at the airport there.

Then they'd stolen an abandoned police van from the airport and begun the journey for Marseille where they planned to acquire another, less conspicuous plane and start their journey across the Atlantic, heading for the eastern seaboard of the United States. It was a circuitous route, but they had no other choice; they needed to stay out of sight for a while.

They also needed to know more about what Sphinx's plan actually was, which was why they had kidnapped the royal banker so brazenly.

Stretch said to Marren, 'On some of the phone intercepts we heard, your royal friends mentioned something called "the transition". What is that?'

Marren smirked. 'What the fuck do you think it is? The transition to a new ordering of this world. An entirely new system of rule, one without governments or dictators or puny little kings. A system with one man at its head, Sphinx, and a ruling class of royals working as his governors, and all the populations of the world brought to heel.'

Pooh Bear said, 'That's why he needed the Siren bells. He puts entire populations to sleep and only wakes those he wants.'

Marren shrugged. 'The bells are the ultimate tool for enforcing obedience. Problems in the Middle East? Put everyone there to sleep and never wake them again. Need a new slave class of workers? Put an entire workforce to sleep, transport them to some new country—I don't know, say, the Philippines—and wake them up chained inside a factory.'

Sister Lynda shook her head. 'You're monsters.'

'We're *rulers*,' Marren shot back. 'The world's become a shithole. Too many people, taking up too much space. It's time to fix it, to restart things. We begin that by culling the weak: put a couple of billion souls to sleep and let them fucking die. Everybody else serves us, the ruling elite.'

'"You will wake as slaves,"' Tracy Smith quoted from the driver's seat. 'You honestly believe that.'

'Our world will be better for it,' Marren said. 'Human beings are sheep, easily led. They like more than anything *to know their place*. They will know it precisely when they wake up after the Omega Event.'

Pooh Bear said, 'Why were *you* going to Washington, D.C.? Why not stay in Europe, in Salzburg?'

'When we perform the transition, we will do it from the White House,' Marren said. 'It is the closest thing to the seat of world power. When Sphinx emerges from the Labyrinth, he will make his announcement of this new world order from the White House, surrounded by the bells and his new royal governors.'

Pooh swapped a look with Stretch as they both digested the full extent of Sphinx's plan: a wholesale takeover and reordering of the world.

Stretch jerked his chin at Marren's suitcase. 'The master lists of all the royal families and military people loyal to the royal world: they're in that?'

'Yes.'

'We'd like to see those lists, please. When we defeat you, we're going to need to know the names of everyone who was part of your giant take-over-the-world plan.'

Marren nodded sagely. 'Go fuck yourselves.'

'We have people who can crack the security codes protecting that case. We'll get those lists, one way or another.'

'You haven't been listening to me,' Sir John Marren said. '*You cannot win this.* Look at you, a ragtag bunch of misfits, led by an idealistic fool who is probably already dead inside that maze. *You are fighting against a royal organisation that has been preparing for this time for centuries.* Things are in motion and they cannot stop now. Bells are ringing, whole populations are falling asleep, the heavens are shifting, the very universe itself is about to realign. No. You won't get anything from me. The only thing that will happen, as I said, is that you will all die begging for your lives and screaming in agony.'

They drove on and he would say no more.

RED SEA COAST, EGYPT
26–28 DECEMBER

It had taken the two big-bearded pilots, Sky Monster and Rufus, a whole day and a half to ride their motorcycle-and-sidecar across the mountainous landscape of the Sinai to the edge of the Red Sea.

They stopped twice to grab some sleep under the star-filled sky.

This was all rather new to the two airmen.

For one thing, they were not used to staging rescue missions without their more outwardly heroic partners, Jack West and Aloysius Knight.

For another, they just weren't used to doing it on the ground. Both men felt like fish out of water or sailors trying to adjust to their land legs after many months at sea.

Deep into the second night of their travels, they crested a rocky hill on their motorbike and beheld the Red Sea.

Sky Monster hit the brakes.

'Goddamn . . .' Rufus breathed.

The Red Sea stretched away to the starry horizon, glittering and vast, reflecting the light of the full moon.

But it was what lay on it that caused Rufus to say what he said.

By the brilliant light of the moon, they saw a flotilla of nine naval vessels anchored off the coast.

Occupying pride of place in the centre of the mini-fleet, towering above all the others, was an aircraft carrier. It was simply gigantic, built to a different scale than all the others. Destroyers, frigates and a cluster of support ships flanked it like parasites.

'An aircraft carrier?' Sky Monster said, confused. 'Who would have a carrier near here—?'

'That's a Russian carrier,' Rufus said flatly. 'You can tell by the bow angle of the launch deck. That's the *Admiral Kuznetsov*. Big bastard. Look at what's beyond it.'

Sky Monster did and he saw it.

An enormous multi-levelled oil rig.

Perched atop six colossal pillars that were themselves mounted on two huge floating hulls, the rig stood almost as high above the waterline as the aircraft carrier's control tower did.

It had four levels packed with pipes and office structures, plus a helipad that jutted out from its forward end. At its tallest point, a cluster of antennas stabbed upward at the sky.

The huge rig was positioned about a mile out from the shore. It was a mobile vessel that floated on the surface, tethered by a cable to a concrete plug on the seafloor.

Rufus nodded at the rig. 'That's the Red Horizon Star-4. And it looks like it's got some serious naval protection.'

It was hard to tell in the darkness, but there seemed to be something in the water *in between* the rig and the carrier, something large that did not reflect the moonlight.

Helicopters flitted like insects between the Russian naval ships and the rig . . . and a makeshift airfield that had been set up on the desert shore. A cluster of white demountable buildings flanked a runway of hardpacked sand, all of it lit by floodlights.

Sky Monster gazed hard at the scene: the airfield, the rig, the carrier.

It was an awesome display of military power.

'Whatever the surface point of the Labyrinth is, these guys have known about it for some time,' he said. 'I bet that rig is really owned by some secret royal assholes. Probably been sitting here for years, on top of some kind of weird deposit, making sure no-one else finds it.'

'Look! There!' Rufus said, pointing at the dusty airfield by the shore.

Sky Monster peered that way and saw them: Alby and Aloysius, lying asleep inside a pair of outdoor cages, guarded by Squires of the Golden Eight and some bronzemen.

'We gotta bust them out, but how?' Rufus said.

Sky Monster bit his lip in thought. 'I don't know yet, but we have to figure out something.'

A MAN NAMED JACK

PART II

THE SCHOOLYARD FIGHT

If you can keep your head when all about you
Are losing theirs and blaming it on you,
If you can trust yourself when all men doubt you,
But make allowance for their doubting too

. . .

If you can meet with Triumph and Disaster
And treat those two imposters just the same

. . .

Yours is the Earth and everything that's in it;
And—which is more—you'll be a Man, my son!

'IF—'
RUDYARD KIPLING

It is a recurring dream of Jack's, a memory from his childhood.

He is thirteen.

In the principal's office.

His nose is bloody. He has a black eye and a cut lip. The left sleeve of his shirt is torn off. He is covered in dirt.

He's just had the shit kicked out of him.

The principal shakes his head. 'Jack, what in heaven's name were you thinking, getting into a fight like that?'

'I don't know, sir.'

'Don't give me that. You're a smart kid. You *do* know. Those boys are *three years older* than you. Tenth graders. Practically men. You're lucky the teachers came by when they did.'

Jack says nothing, stares at the floor.

'I've called your parents. They're on their way here right now. Take you home. Or maybe to the hospital.'

My parents, Jack thinks. He already knows what his father's reaction will be.

Jack's parents collect him from school.

During the car ride home, he sits in the back seat, silent.

His mother turns around. 'Come on, Cub, talk to us. What happened?'

'Those older boys were going to beat up my friend.'

'Which friend?' his mother says.

'Sumil. Sumil Gupta.'

'The skinny little nerd from India?' his father snorts. 'The one with the gigantic glasses?'

'Yes. Sumil.'

'Fucking little weirdo. Why can't you have normal friends like your sister—'

'And you defended him?' his mother interrupts.

'Sumil's really smart,' Jack says. 'I mean *really* smart. Much smarter than me. But he's small and not strong at all. I've seen those tenth graders. They're cruel and mean. They would have hurt Sumil bad. Like, put-him-in-hospital bad.'

'So you thought you'd step in and take on a group of sixteen-year-old thugs?' his father says incredulously. 'And take the beating for him?'

'Yes.'

Jack says it tonelessly, expressionlessly.

'Say that again, son?' his father says.

'I said yes. That's exactly what I did. I took the beating for him. I knew I couldn't win. But I also knew I could take their hits while Sumil couldn't. I just had to keep fighting long enough until he got away or a teacher came by.'

'Fuck me,' his father says. 'I can't believe you're my son.' He resumes driving, shaking his head.

But Jack's mother turns around in her seat again, smiling, her eyes shining with admiration.

'I'm so proud of you, Cubby. Want to get some ice cream?'

A year after that incident, Sumil Gupta was accelerated a couple of years and left Jack's regular high school to attend a selective school.

He would go on to study complex mathematics and computer science at Stanford University and ultimately found a software company. He was a billionaire many times over.

As an adult, Jack kept in touch with him and Sumil—the busy billionaire in his office on Sand Hill Road—always took his calls.

Always.

Whenever they caught up in person, Sumil would thank Jack for defending him that day in the schoolyard.

Jack would just smile and say, 'I knew even then, Sumil, that you had something to give the world. What I could do then was take a punch. So by taking those punches, I figured I was helping the world.'

THIRD TEST OF WORTH

THE CITY-MAZE

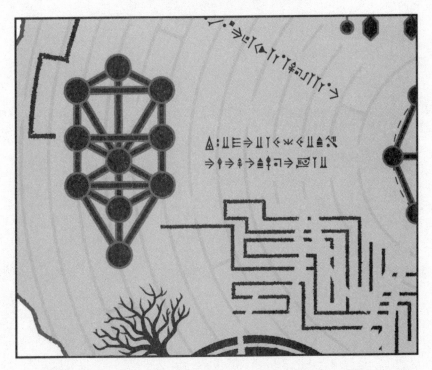

Moses held out his hand over the Red Sea, and the Lord
drove the sea back with a strong wind . . . The water was
divided, and the Israelites went through the sea on dry
ground, with walls of water on both sides.

EXODUS, 14:21

THE ENDLESS TUNNEL
27 DECEMBER, 0606 HOURS (LOCAL TIME)
TWO DAYS TILL OMEGA

Jack and Lily still stood at the junction in the Endless Tunnel, with Easton and Smiley behind them.

Jack frowned. 'Two choices.'

'Yeah, but the consequences of making the wrong choice are severe,' Lily said. 'It could set us back hours, days even, and we don't have that time.'

Jack scanned the floor of both passageways, searching for evidence of which way their competitors—Sphinx, Ezekiel and Rastor—had taken.

But he saw nothing: no bootprints or disturbed dust.

'Wait.' He looked up. 'Imhotep's skull guided us into this tunnel when it talked about those images of Ningizzida. Didn't it also say something about—'

He hurriedly pulled out the mummified skull of the ancient Egyptian genius.

'Can you read the inscriptions that referred to the Endless Tunnel again?'

'Sure.' Lily scanned the skull. 'Okay. The first one says: *To find the endless tunnel, take the doorway below the image of Ningizzida.* Then it says: *In the tunnel, always to take the sinister fork.*'

Jack turned back to face the intersection. 'The *sinister* fork. It could work. Some mazes work that way . . .' he said aloud.

Easton said, 'Excuse me, but what does Captain Jack mean?'

Jack nodded at the intersection. 'We take the left fork. The sinister fork is the left-hand one.'

'Oh, of course,' Lily said, realising.

Jack saw her get it. 'You may have a natural-born gift for languages, but your old man still knows a thing or two.'

Lily turned to Easton to explain. 'In languages all over the world, from German and Vietnamese to Chinese and Polish, the word for *right* or *right-handed* also means correct, better or lawful, while the word for *left* or *left-handed* means evil, sinful or unlawful. Our modern word *sinister*, which we associate with wickedness, actually derives from a much older word, *sinistra*, which means *left*.'

Jack said, 'This reference from Imhotep isn't a riddle. It's a simple instruction. We just take the left fork. Indeed, to get safely through this maze of tunnels, at *every* junction we must always take the left fork.'

And so they stepped down the left-hand fork, venturing further into the darkness.

They walked for another six hours.

The tunnel maintained its steady downward slope.

They encountered three more forks and at each of those they turned left.

'How do we know for sure that taking the left fork is the correct option?' Lily asked at one point in their long walk.

'We can't know,' Jack said. 'We'll only know it was the correct choice when we arrive at some grand new maze or we turn a corner and hit a dead end.'

As the hours ticked by, they passed through three more under-tunnels and crept by two more statue-like goldmen until—after almost twenty-three hours of steady trudging—Jack turned a stone-walled corner and suddenly the tunnel in front of him plunged dramatically downward in a dead-straight and very steep decline.

'This is new,' Lily said.

'We must be close to the next maze,' Jack said.

They increased their pace, hurrying down the superlong, super-steep descent.

At the bottom, they passed through an arch and abruptly the walls of the tunnel around them changed.

No longer were they made of uneven carved stone.

Now they were smooth and made of concrete-like greystone.

Jack touched one of the walls. 'Someone *built* this. We've entered a structure of some kind.'

A few metres later, their tunnel ended at a blank grey wall—a dead end—and Jack's heart fell at the thought that he'd made a terrible mistake, that they had come all this way for almost a whole day only to—

'Look!' Easton pointed up at the ceiling above the end of the tunnel.

In the flat stone ceiling above the dead end, a narrow shaft shot upward into darkness. Hand- and footholds lined it.

Jack exhaled with relief.

'I think we just reached the end of the Endless Tunnel,' he said.

And so up they went, straight up.

They climbed close together, with Jack in the lead followed by Lily, Easton, then Smiley.

Looking ahead of him, Jack became aware that the shaft narrowed gradually as they rose, as if they were climbing up the inside of a giant telescope. He could also see a dim glow at the very top of the shaft, one that looked like reflected daylight.

After about ten minutes of climbing, they came to a horizontal passageway that, to Jack's great surprise, led to a square stone doorway at the end of which was, indeed, sunlight.

Jack froze.

Something lay beyond the doorway.

Three somethings: three slumped human figures, out in the sunlight, flanked by two obelisks.

It looked like they were lying on a stone rooftop of some sort and beyond that rooftop, Jack saw a wider sunlit space with *lots* of other stone roofs.

Jack edged closer to the door, gun up, with Lily, Easton and Smiley behind him.

As he came nearer to them, Jack saw that the slumped figures were more dead bodies: two of Rastor's grey-clad Serbian troopers and, a little farther out, a smaller body with a red face, a Vandal.

Intrigued, Easton stepped past Jack, out through the doorway to examine the dead Serbian soldiers—

'Easton, wait, no!' Jack lunged after him.

Too late.

Fizzzzzzz – whap!

A bullet fired from somewhere beyond the doorway sizzled through the air and slammed into Easton's right shoulder, spinning him backwards.

Jack caught him and yanked him back into the safety of the tunnel.

'You okay?' Jack whispered.

Easton grimaced in pain but nodded. Jack applied pressure to the wound as Lily arrived beside them and pulled a bandage from her pack.

As if in response to that first shot, a flurry of many more gunshots rang out from outside.

Blam!-Blam!

Boom!-Boom!

Bang-bang-bang!

Jack's trained ear could tell immediately that they came from several different guns: Steyr AUG assault rifles, pistols and at least one sniper rifle.

Jack guessed that the shooter who had hit Easton was a sniper left behind by Sphinx: probably the same one who had killed Rastor's Serbians in this very doorway.

But in firing that shot, the sniper had drawn the fire of the other parties already here.

Jack was processing all this—half crouched in the doorway holding Easton while Lily bandaged the wound—when movement caught his eye.

'What the goddamn hell . . .' he breathed in horror.

The Vandal that had been slumped on the floor *was getting up*.

It wasn't dead . . .

Like a ghoul rising from a grave, it stood slowly, at first facing away from Jack, and he saw that it had something duct-taped to its back, near the shoulderblades, something small and round.

Then the Vandal turned and levelled its red-rimmed eyes at Jack.

'Hello, Captain! I've been waiting for *you*!'

As it spoke, Jack saw that this Vandal was actually handcuffed and that the cuffs were attached to a longer rope looped around one of the nearby obelisks.

It wasn't here of its own accord. And the thing taped to its back . . .

Jack frowned, mystified and concerned.

What was this about—

Then the Vandal took a step toward him. 'My master Sphinx left me behind to kill General Rastor. But Rastor captured me and taped the little red thing to my body. Then he tied me to this obelisk and told me to wait for *you* to arrive. He said when you did, I was to say I am his farewell gift for you.'

The Vandal took another step forward. Ten feet away.

The little red thing . . .

And suddenly Jack realised what the object taped to the Vandal's back was and his blood went cold.

A red orb, taken from the ceiling of the Endless Tunnel.

And then Jack's horror was complete as he looked into the Vandal's eyes and realised—too late—what a fucked-up and deadly trap Rastor had set for them.

'Rastor's turned this Vandal into a walking bomb,' he said. 'He must've left a sniper of his own to—'

As soon as Jack said it, another shot rang out, the report of a sniper rifle fired by a grey-clad Serbian sniper on one of the other nearby rooftops.

The sizzling round hit the orb taped to the Vandal's back . . .

. . . and the Vandal exploded.

The little red man just disappeared, blasting out into a thousand pieces in a *ferocious* blast.

And Jack, Lily and Easton, huddled in the doorway so close to the explosion, had no way and no time to avoid it.

Just as Rastor had planned.

Jack had seen the hideous effects of an orb explosion earlier in the Endless Tunnel: it melted human skin and reduced bronzemen to lumpy puddles.

Now, he got to *see* a blast, at least for a split second.

It was a truly terrible thing.

Struck by the sniper round, the crimson orb on the Vandal's back blew out with shocking force.

A starburst of roaring liquid fire sprayed out from the exploding Vandal, razing-incinerating-splattering everything within a thirty-metre radius. Anything that the fireball so much as *touched* immediately sizzled and hissed, as if struck by searing acid.

There was nothing Jack could do.

Rastor had outsmarted him.

Only then, to his complete surprise, at the exact moment that the Vandal blew apart, a figure stepped calmly and silently *in front of* Jack, Lily and Easton, positioning itself between them and the blast, turning its back to the explosion.

Smiley.

The superheated fire blasted into the bronzeman's back—sizzling and flaming—but thanks to the automaton's quick move, Jack and the others were shielded from the heat blast and spared from being hit.

A few whizzing droplets got past Smiley and sliced through the sleeve of Jack's jacket but thankfully missed his skin.

Other droplets nicked Lily's hair, cutting some strands clean off and leaving the edges smoking.

And then it was over.

The Vandal was gone. The blast dissipated. Spot fires burned.

Jack sprang out from behind Smiley, spied the Serbian sniper on the nearby tower, shot him right between the eyes, and then ducked back into the tunnel.

It was only then that Jack realised that Smiley hadn't moved since his heroic intervention.

Still bent protectively over Lily and Easton, Smiley's entire bronze back was bubbling, melting. Crude gobs of his metal body oozed downward before falling in dark drops to the ground.

Smiley fell to his knees with a *whump* and Jack, Lily and Easton pulled him deeper into the tunnel.

'He saved our lives,' Lily gasped.

'Smiley is good bronzeman,' Easton said, patting the automaton on its chest. 'Smiley obey order.'

'He sure did. But I think Smiley's fight is over,' Jack said, laying the sizzling automaton against the stone wall. 'We can come back for him, but right now we still have a job to do.'

Outside, the firefight between their enemies was still raging. Jack edged toward the light.

Staying in the shadows, he peered around the ancient doorway . . .

. . . and this time he actually got to see the larger area that lay beyond the door and his breath caught in his throat.

'Okay, now that's big,' he said.

**THE CITY-MAZE
IN THE RED SEA
(WHEN JACK ARRIVES)**

THE CITY-MAZE

Jack found himself standing at the rear of a flat stone roof of a soaring stone tower overlooking a *vast* circular stone city.

The city was ringed by a curving eight-hundred-foot-high wall of smooth greystone.

The sheer size of the wall made it seem like this city sat at the base of the largest dam in the world, only this dam went *all the way around the city* in a huge perfect circle.

And it was all open to the sky.

Indeed, the sky blazed bright and blue high above the scene.

The city was a dazzlingly complex mix of towers and domes, bridges and staircases, avenues and trenches, pyramids and obelisks, and in its exact centre, rising above the metropolis around it, was a spectacular multi-spired white-and-silver castle.

At the top of this castle was a superhigh gold-and-silver pinnacle that shot several hundred feet *further* into the sky, until at its peak one beheld a large golden throne that glittered in the light of the sun.

Jack gazed in wonder at the sight.

'A throne?' he said, perplexed. 'Here?'

It didn't make sense. By his reckoning, they were only halfway through the Labyrinth.

Lily crept up beside him. 'Did you say *throne*?'

He pointed at it and she said, 'Oh. Whoa.'

As the two of them scanned the white-and-silver castle, the low maze of buildings and the massive grey wall, Jack couldn't help feeling that, beyond the sheer magnitude of it all, he'd seen something like this before.

It hit him.

The Underworld.

Hades's old kingdom, in a remote corner of India.

The *style* of this place was the same, the whole look and feel of it.

The mix of rough-edged natural stone and smooth greystone; the complex city nestled around the central castle; and, of course, the utterly extraterrestrial nature of it all.

This was a place that had not been made by human hands.

It was older than anything humanity had ever constructed, bigger in concept, and built in service to a mission far beyond the knowledge of modern humans, let alone societies like that of ancient Egypt.

A flash of light from the castle—from its summit, at the base of the pinnacle—caught Jack's eye a split second before he heard the report of a gunshot, since light travelled faster than sound.

Three figures were at the top of the castle.

Jack recognised Sphinx and Mendoza.

The third man was a Knight of the Golden Eight and he was furiously firing a gun down at their rivals.

Before Jack could process this, heavy return fire from one of the lower buildings slammed into the castle's battlements around the shooter and hit him, and the Knight fell with a scream off the castle, plummeting for hundreds of feet before he disappeared into one of the alleyways in the labyrinthine city.

'We just walked into a hornet's nest with a throne in the middle of it and at least three groups of hornets already fighting,' Jack said.

Lily's eyes were on the throne at the top of the pinnacle, the throne that Sphinx was so tantalisingly close to reaching.

'It's the presence of that throne that bothers me,' she said.

'I know, we must have missed something,' Jack said. 'We can figure that out later. All that matters right now is that Sphinx is minutes away from sitting on it. But all our enemies are here, too, and they're his enemies as well, and they're pinning him down.'

And then suddenly, from their left, a streak of smoke extended from a buildingtop toward the central castle.

It was the telltale smoke trail of a shoulder-launched missile and it whooshed in a dead-straight line right toward Sphinx and Mendoza on the castle . . .

. . . only to whiz harmlessly past them, missing.

Even from this distance, Jack heard Sphinx laugh: 'Nice try, Garthon! But I have electromagnetic protection from such weapons!'

Jack spun to see General Rastor off to his left, standing on top of a tower to the south of the castle with his RPG launcher on his shoulder and his grey-clad soldiers at his side.

The general laughed.

'Is that so?' Rastor called back to Sphinx. 'Oh, Hardin, you never understood me and the lengths to which I will go to achieve my goal!'

THE CITY-MAZE
(WHEN SPHINX ARRIVED)

THE CITY-MAZE
SIXTEEN HOURS PREVIOUSLY

Sixteen hours before Jack arrived at the city-maze, a stupendous and historic thing occurred.

Sphinx and his entourage—Cardinal Mendoza, three Knights of the Golden Eight and two remaining Vandals—had steadily made their way here.

Racing to stay ahead of Brother Ezekiel and his Omega monks, but also being careful not to make a deadly mistake, they had picked the correct tunnel mouth out of the six choices, and then cautiously made their way through the Endless Tunnel with its under-tunnels, goldmen and junctions.

They had even stopped to sleep. Sphinx and Mendoza had long planned for this moment, done their research and even trained for it physically, and they were bearing up well.

And then, like Jack, they had come to this city-maze surrounding the castle.

Only when they came to it, it had been *underground*, the entire spectacular cityscape shrouded in vast echoing darkness.

Emerging from the Endless Tunnel, Sphinx found himself standing on a rooftop—the same rooftop Jack would arrive at later—jutting out from the colossal circular wall ringing the city and the castle.

As his men's flashlights illuminated the buildings nearest to them—towers surmounted with obelisks and exotic-looking temples—Sphinx inhaled sharply.

'We made it,' he said.

Mendoza was similarly awestruck. 'Good Lord, we did it.'

Sphinx aimed their most powerful light across the space, illuminating the incredible structure in its middle: a spectacular white-and-silver castle with many spires extending out from it like branches on a tree.

In the dark shadows, he saw the pinnacle reaching upward from the summit of the castle.

'The Life Throne . . .' he said softly.

Aiming their flashlights further upward, they saw that the entire city-maze—a space that must have been at least a mile across—was covered by an immense hemispherical dome. All by itself, this dome would have been an architectural wonder, but next to the city and the castle that it covered, it seemed merely functional.

Sphinx stepped forward . . .

. . . landing on a trigger stone in the floor . . .

. . . and setting off an ancient alien mechanism that literally made the earth shake.

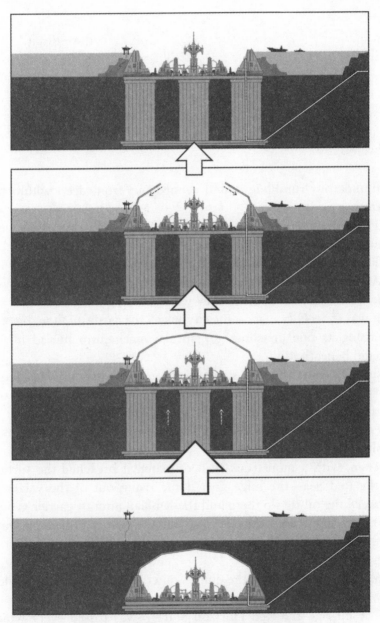

**THE RISING OF THE LIFE THRONE
AND THE CITY-MAZE**

A thunderous rumbling sound echoed out from deep within the Earth.

The ground shuddered so hard that Sphinx and Mendoza were almost thrown off their feet.

They looked all around themselves, unsure but also excited.

And then they felt the ground on which they stood *begin to rise*.

It wasn't just the rooftop they were standing on.

It was *the whole space*—the city-maze, the castle *and* the dome— all rising as one on some gargantuan mechanism buried in the ground beneath it all.

Indeed, under the vast space, three gigantic pistons built aeons ago by a long-lost civilisation, pushed the whole thing upward, out of the seabed and up through the waters of the Red Sea.

First the great dome created a giant bulge in the seafloor as it pushed up mud and dirt.

Then, with a monstrous rush of water, it breached the surface of the Red Sea—the huge grey dome rising out of the waves *in between* the oil rig up there and the Russian aircraft carrier group.

It was night-time outside and massive waves rolled outward from the emerging dome, making even the mighty aircraft carrier rock on the surface.

Seawater cascaded off the dome's outer flanks, running in rivulets down its surface, glistening in the moonlight.

The oil rig—the Red Horizon Star-4—was tossed every which way.

It swayed wildly. Some men on its helipad and lower levels were thrown clear off it into the sea, so rough was the rocking.

Its anchor cable, long attached to a concrete plug in the seabed, was torn free and the rig rocked on the mighty waves created by the emergence of the colossal structure.

And then, just as suddenly as it had begun, the rising of the immense ancient thing stopped, and it now just stood there in the night, this great grey dome, on the surface of the Red Sea, within view of the Sinai coast, looking like some megasized enclosed sports stadium.

Anyone still standing on the oil rig or on the decks of the naval vessels stared at it in speechless awe.

It dwarfed the carrier.

It dwarfed the oil rig.

Bigger than a dozen Great Pyramids, it dwarfed everything.

It was then that a final mechanism was triggered.

There came a great groaning sound and suddenly eight seams appeared in the giant grey dome and, like petals on a flower, eight segments of the huge roof all began to retract in perfect unison, withdrawing down into the outer wall ringing the city, allowing moonlight and fresh air to touch the city-maze and the castle for the first time in thousands of years.

Now the entire thing really did look like a supergigantic sports stadium: a breathtakingly huge hollow concrete ring, fully open to the sky, with its mighty eighty-storey-tall greystone ring-wall holding back the waves of the Red Sea, while in its middle—hundreds of feet below sea level—lay the city-like labyrinth, with its buildings of all shapes and sizes, and, poking up from the exact centre of the space, the high castle with the pinnacle and the throne mounted on it.

It was of another time, another civilisation.

This was momentous.

Stunning.

Historic.

Sphinx was not a man who was easily awed, but at that moment he was well and truly blown away.

He'd seen many strange and wondrous things in his capacity as a watchman of a secret city, but nothing like this, not on this scale.

He gazed out over the now open-air city, bathed in glorious moonlight, and at the towering grey wall ringing it.

To Sphinx's right, peeking over the rim of the outer wall, he could see the bow of the aircraft carrier, while off to his left, he could see the uppermost deck of the still-rocking oil rig: floodlights from both played over the massive space.

The Russian carrier was, of course, under his command.

As was the oil rig.

It had long been owned by loyal royals, their job: to stand guard over this site, like the watchmen at the Three Secret Cities did. The crew on the rig could not know what lay below the seabed, but their ground-penetrating radars had long shown that there was something large down there connected to the ancient places of the world.

Sphinx eyed the throne at the centre of the maze.

'The Life Throne,' he said. 'It's going to take us time to traverse this city-maze and reach the castle.'

Mendoza added, 'And to sit on the throne, you must scale the castle and pass through its holy doors in the correct order.'

'You have the decoded writings from the Kabbalah about ascending the Tree of Life?' Sphinx asked.

'I do, sire.'

'That's all we ne—' Sphinx cut himself off, hearing something.

An echo from somewhere back in the Endless Tunnel.

He gazed at the narrow ladder-shaft they had climbed to get here. It had, during the spectacular rise of the megastadium, extended its tight walls to become an even longer ladder-shaft.

Sphinx froze, listening.

'We mustn't linger. We left some Vandals to slow our rivals and plugged up a few of those low tunnels with greystone, but they will eventually get here.'

He turned to his three Knights: 'Gentlemen, it is time to earn your places in the world to come. Jaeger Sechs, you will come with the cardinal and me. We must penetrate this city-maze and get to the castle and the Life Throne atop it as quickly as we can.'

He nodded at the other two: 'Jaegers Sieben and Acht'—Hunters Seven and Eight—'you will do whatever is necessary to keep our competitors from reaching that castle. Whatever. Is. Necessary. Understand?'

The three Knights of the Golden Eight nodded curtly.

'Aye, sir.'

'Yes, sir.'

'Yes, sir.'

Sphinx said, 'Let's move. Destiny awaits.'

And so, by the light of the moon and the seaborne floodlights, Sphinx, Mendoza and Jaeger Sechs—Hunter Six—set out into the maze, crossing a few superhigh bridges that connected the outer rim to some towers.

They then descended some steep rail-less stone staircases that took them into the inner part of the maze, before ascending others that were even steeper.

At the start and finish of each bridge or staircase, they always passed through an ornate stone archway.

It was a long and circuitous route: left then right, up then down, stairs and ramps, trenches and bridges.

Their progress was slow.

They marched through the night.

'Can we not call in a helicopter to fly us directly over to the castle?' Jaeger Sechs asked early in their journey.

'No,' Mendoza said. 'Absolutely not. Like many of these labyrinths, this maze and the castle are connected by unseen mechanisms. Unless one passes through all the archways of this maze, one cannot ascend this throne. There are no shortcuts when the fate of the universe is at stake.'

They had been traversing the city-maze for about two hours when the first gunshot smashed off a stone wall above their heads.

The monks of the Order of Omega had arrived . . .

. . . and the battle of the city-maze began.

It would rage for the next twelve hours: a running battle between Sphinx's Knights and the Omega monks.

Both forces tried to make their way to the centre of the open-air city-maze, exchanging volleys of gunfire—at first under the night-time sky and then in daylight as the sun rose.

Commanded by Brother Ezekiel, the Omega monks had come prepared and they took to the battle with zeal.

Their biggest hold-up was the two Knights of the Golden Eight that Sphinx had left behind.

The two Knights put up a good fight, but the monks overcame and shot them and soon the monks were racing at full speed into the inner sections of the maze—exchanging fire with the running figures of Sphinx, Mendoza and Jaeger Sechs up ahead.

Sphinx charged across the maze, head bent, under the constant gunfire of the monks.

But his lead had been good and it held.

After fourteen hours of nonstop movement and near-constant

sniper fire, he and his team had almost reached the centre of the vast circle and the base of the castle.

Firing their guns at their pursuers, Sphinx, Mendoza and Jaeger Sechs came to a final bridge—long, slender and rail-less—that led across a sheer greystone ravine to the magnificent castle itself.

They had passed through all the archways of the city-maze and now the castle loomed above them, white and silver, glorious and mysterious, at the far end of the long high bridge.

Sphinx risked a grin.

'We made it—'

Which was precisely when a rocket-propelled grenade fired by Brother Ezekiel slammed into the bridge and blew it apart.

Sphinx watched in horror as the slender stone bridge in front of him exploded in its middle and its crumbling pieces fell away into the ravine.

'Fuck!' he swore.

He couldn't get across.

His fast-moving eyes saw another bridge giving access to the castle but—given the backtracking and the extra alleyways and bridges he'd need to traverse to get to it—he figured it would take him at least an hour, maybe two, to reach it.

But he had no choice, so he sucked it up and hurried on.

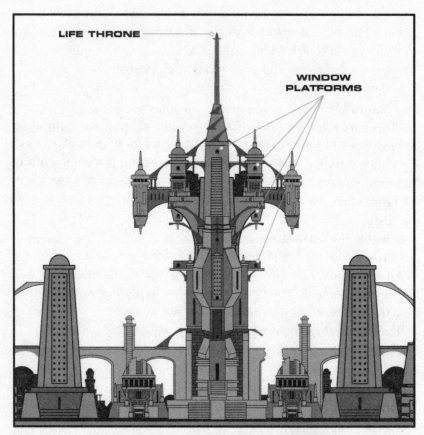

LIFE THRONE

WINDOW
PLATFORMS

THE CASTLE AND THE LIFE THRONE

Day had fully arrived as Sphinx ran around the castle.

The delay with the broken bridge had cost him two hours but he finally came to the castle and raced inside it as bullets from the Omega monks strafed the walls all around him, Mendoza and Jaeger Sechs.

'Talk to me,' Sphinx said urgently, looking up at the interior of the castle above him.

It was a high hollow space, with many soaring stone stairways crisscrossing it.

All the stairways, he saw, in some way touched ten window-platforms arrayed around the castle and each of these platforms was accessed via ancient archways on landings.

'How do we solve this final maze?' Sphinx said.

Cardinal Mendoza was riffling through the notes that he carried with him.

'We call this the Life Throne, but its full name is actually the Throne *of the Tree of Life*,' Mendoza said. 'Indeed, this whole section of the Supreme Labyrinth is depicted on my tattoo as the Tree of Life.'

He pointed to a copy of the tattoo on his head:

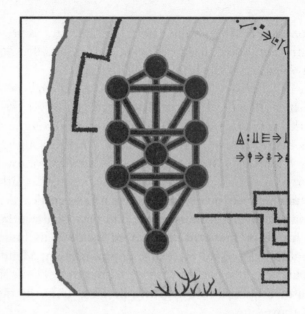

'In order to reach the throne at its summit, we must ascend it in the sacred *order* of the holy tree, which, fortunately for us, was laid out in the Kabbalah.'

Mendoza pulled out a diagram of the castle and also a drawing of the Kabbalistic Tree of Life with a set of arrows drawn on it.

Mendoza said, 'The Kabbalistic Tree of Life represents the sacred path from humanity/Earth at the bottom—called *Malkuth*—to divinity/Heaven at the top—known as *Keter*.

'As the lowest rung of the Tree of Life, *Malkuth* is all things physical. It is also the barrier between the realm of life and the underworld, the realm of the Tree of Death. *Keter* is the opposite. It literally means *crown*. It is where a man becomes a god.

'To get from the bottom to the top, you must follow the path in the correct order. Some believe this is a spiritual path, one of enlightenment. But it isn't. It's all about scaling *this* castle, here, in the Supreme Labyrinth, to get to the Throne of the Tree of Life. Look at this diagram of the castle now . . . and see how the path fits the layout of its window-platforms perfectly.'

The cardinal quickly scribbled the arrows from the picture of the Tree of Life onto the drawing of the castle:

Sphinx's eyes lit up as he saw the connection.

'A transformation from humanity to divinity.' He smiled. 'From man to emperor. Let's move!'

The first archway stood before them. Three sets of upward-leading stair-bridges sprang away from its roof in three different directions.

The archway was a large dark cube-shaped structure decorated with black horn-like protrusions and fearsome-looking statuary. Short stairways led to its roof and it had a broad well in its floor.

Obeying the arrows on the diagram and invigorated at being so close to success, Sphinx and his team dashed up the right-hand set of stairs leading up from that first archway to the next one high above it.

And so Sphinx ascended the interior of the castle swiftly, finding order in its otherwise baffling maze of crisscrossing internal stairways.

He was three-quarters of the way up when Ezekiel and his Omega monks arrived at the bottom of the castle.

The Omega monks fanned out to positions both inside and outside the castle, firing pistols and sniper rifles up at Sphinx, Mendoza and Jaeger Sechs, but it was to no avail. The stairways and landings blocked their shots and Sphinx was simply too far ahead.

Then, at last, Sphinx ascended the final stairway and he burst out into sunlight, arriving at the summit of the castle, high above the circular city-maze.

The view took his breath away.

He actually now stood even higher than the rim of the colossal ring-wall holding back the sea, and he could see, off to the east, the Russian aircraft carrier and the Sinai coast. To the west, he could see the oil rig, the Red Horizon Star-4.

A cheer went up from some Russian officers on the carrier's flight deck. They pumped their fists in triumph.

While he was at the top of the castle, Sphinx still stood at the bottom of the pinnacle that led up to the Life Throne, a dizzyingly high needle of silver and gold that was shot through with carved handholds.

It was essentially a supertall cylinder, about one hundred and fifty feet tall and twenty feet wide, with decorative images of huge snakes winding around it and small ledges protruding from it.

Abruptly, gunfire slammed into the stone all around him, from a new source.

Jaeger Sechs spun and returned fire to two Omega snipers perched on a tower to the east. He killed one of them, only for the second sniper to nail him in the chest and Sechs went sailing off the castle, falling for thousands of feet to his death.

Sphinx didn't care.

He was so close to his goal. He turned to face the pinnacle and looked up at it.

He scanned the bending paths of hand- and footholds running up the needle and eventually reaching the throne at its top.

Sphinx reached for the first hand—

Whoosh!

A missile whizzed by his head, missing him by mere feet.

Sphinx whirled—

—to see General Rastor standing on top of one of the towers to the south of the castle, with a missile launcher on his shoulder.

Sphinx laughed: 'Nice try, Garthon! But I have electromagnetic protection from such weapons!'

'Is that so?' Rastor called back. 'Oh, Hardin, you never understood me and the lengths to which I will go to achieve my goal!'

This was, of course, the moment when Jack arrived on the scene, emerging from the Endless Tunnel.

Jack saw Jaeger Sechs exchange shots with the Omega snipers, get shot and fall; saw the RPG missile whoosh past Sphinx on the castle's summit, and heard Sphinx's exchange with Rastor.

'We might be too late,' Jack said.

'There has to be a way,' Lily said.

And then, to their horror, Rastor did something completely unexpected and the scene descended into a whole new level of anarchy.

It was Sphinx's comment about having electromagnetic protection that must've made Rastor do it, Jack figured.

Sphinx, Jack deduced, must have himself been wearing some kind of Warbler, an electromagnetic shield that deflected subsonic projectiles like bullets and shoulder-launched missiles.

True to his reputation for wild tactics and strategies, Rastor simply chose a different way to counter Sphinx.

He hefted his RPG launcher onto his shoulder and fired it again . . .

. . . only this time, he didn't aim it at Sphinx on the castle.

No, this time he fired it *at the wall* ringing the entire site.

In a split second, Jack realised what was about to happen.

'Oh, Jesus God in Heaven,' he breathed. 'This is going to be so bad.'

Rastor's missile streaked across the space and *slammed* into the top section of the massive grey wall over on the western side of the city-maze.

The rim of the wall exploded, blowing out in gigantic chunks of greystone, the blast creating a V-shaped opening in the structure.

And then—catastrophically—through that newly formed opening, came the inrushing sea.

It poured into the city-maze—an instant waterfall, mighty and powerful—a flooding, cascading, devastating body of seawater that gushed en masse through the shattered section of the wall.

Jack's jaw dropped.

The water tumbled and bounced down into the buildings of the city-maze, smashing some of them to smithereens, before hitting the bottom in a churning mass of whitewater.

As the water hit that lowest level, it immediately fanned out, rushing in deadly twenty-foot-high tsunamis down the alleyways on the western side of the stadium-like space.

Jack was entranced by the sight.

But then a scream of rending metal made him look up and he saw the inflowing waterfall at the top of the wall heave an enormous man-made object into view.

'Oh, come on . . .' he gasped as he saw it.

It was the oil rig. The one that had been located to the west of the immense stadium.

The mighty upward rise of the city-maze must have broken the rig's anchor cable; probably snapped it like a thread.

This meant that when Rastor's missile broke open the wall, the inward flood of water carried the oil rig into the city-maze!

The rig must have been twenty storeys tall but against the colossal scale of the megastadium, it looked puny.

Carried on top of the inward-rushing body of seawater, it snagged on the lip of the outer wall and came to a lurching, jerking halt, one of its huge pontoons catching on the jagged edge of the exploded-open gap.

Seawater gushed past it on both sides, shoving it, pushing it, causing its pontoons and pillars to bend and squeal . . .

. . . and Jack saw men on it, clutching onto its helipad—even diving *into* a helicopter that was tied down on the helipad—or hanging on for dear life on other decks, screaming for help, until . . .

. . . with an ear-splitting metal shriek . . .

. . . one of the rig's pontoons snapped and the oil rig jerked again, coming free of its snag, and, riding the crest of the incoming waterfall, it dropped away from the rim of the outer wall and fell, fell, fell, down the face of the mighty grey wall—the tiny figures of men sailing down through the air beside it—until part of its torn anchor cable, flailing after it, caught on the jagged upper rim of the broken wall and the whole rig jerked to a halt again, *suspended* from the lip of the wall by the now-taut cable.

It hung there precariously from the supertaut length of cable, its decks now turned vertical, high above the buildings on the western side of the city-maze, with seawater pouring past it on both sides.

'This Rastor guy is totally insane,' Jack said.

The sudden creation of the colossal waterfall caused the whole city-maze to shake and, up on the castle's peak, Sphinx had to hang on tight to stop himself from falling off as the castle beneath him shuddered.

But Rastor wasn't done.

He re-aimed his missile launcher—this time at the eastern rim of the wall—and fired it again.

The missile streaked across the city-maze . . .

. . . and hit the rim again, only now on the other side.

Another showering explosion.

More flying boulders of greystone.

And another waterfall was instantly created.

And within moments another man-made vessel carried on the ensuing wave of inflowing water came thundering over the rim of the wall.

The Russian aircraft carrier.

Jack West had seen many astonishing things in his life, but few could match this one.

He gaped in awe at the sight, instinctively stepping back.

The carrier appeared *above* him and just off to the side, impossibly huge, its gargantuan underbelly exposed as it roared over the wall on the inrushing waterfall.

This was an entirely different experience from the fall of the oil rig.

The rig's fall had taken place over on the opposite side of the city-maze, perhaps a mile away. The rig had also been much smaller. It had squealed as its spindly legs had been dragged awkwardly over the broken wall.

The aircraft carrier, on the other hand, was much larger and much heavier *and this was happening right next to Jack's position on the eastern flank of the wall*, barely twenty metres away from him, Lily, Easton and Smiley.

The carrier's bow came over the wall first, cresting on the gushing wave of seawater, bursting through the gap Rastor's missile had created.

Its sharp prow, with the leading edge of the flight deck surmounting it, nosed high into the sky, peaking for a split second . . .

. . . before it tipped and fell.

THE FALL OF THE RUSSIAN CARRIER

Jack watched in amazement as sixty thousand tons of Russian aircraft carrier plummeted nose-first down the side of the ancient grey wall.

The carrier looked like a falling skyscraper as it rushed past Jack's rooftop in a blur of grey metal.

It was over three hundred metres long and it created a deafening grinding sound as it thundered past Jack and the others, smashing *right through* the towers and temples of the ancient city.

The immense weight of the carrier made its descent a thing of awesome destruction: a rampaging fall that obliterated everything in its path, turning ancient structures to dust in an instant.

As the carrier fell, it was literally raining tiny aircraft off it.

Fighter jets, recon planes and helicopters went tumbling off its almost-vertical flight deck, falling off in clusters.

They cartwheeled through the air by the dozen—looking like toys flung by some invisible giant—smashing through the bridges of the city-maze or blasting into obelisks and temples. Many burst out in fiery explosions as they struck the solid stone structures and their fuel tanks ruptured.

The carrier's control tower rushed past Jack and he actually saw the tiny figures of its command crew inside getting thrown around—

—before it was gone, flashing by in an instant, replaced by the stern of the ship as—

—suddenly a big Russian Kamov Ka-27 search-and-rescue

helicopter was flung off the flight deck and came whirling through the air right at Jack's little group!

The big chopper spun laterally as it sailed through the air.

'Look out!' Lily yelled.

She shoved Jack out of the way, just as the giant helicopter slammed into the rooftop right where Jack had been standing.

The chopper cleaved a chunk out of the rooftop as it banged down against it, hitting Lily with a glancing blow, hurling her ten feet backwards into the wall at the rear of the towertop.

Lily hit the wall and slumped, her eyes snapping closed, knocked out.

Jack then watched in horror from the ground as one of the chopper's rotor blades came swinging round, superfast, right at her immobile body.

The swinging blade was going to cut her in two when all of a sudden Smiley was there—lunging forward, even though his back was horrifically melted, moving again!—stepping in front of her, shielding Lily with his body, and the bronze automaton took the full force of the blow in his metal chest as the rotor blade slammed into him.

The impact knocked Smiley to the ground but it also stopped the rotor, and it just hung there, vibrating and ringing.

'Damn, I love that robot,' Jack said to himself.

While all this was happening, the enormous Russian aircraft carrier was *still* freefalling into the city-maze, when—

CRUUUUUUUNCH!

Its mighty fall stopped.

Catastrophically.

Its bow *smashed* into a squat, trapezoidal building at the base of the maze, a structure that was sturdy enough to withstand the carrier's immense descending momentum.

The carrier's bow caved in, crumpling like an accordion, and the great fall was halted.

But while its fall had stopped, the carrier's humiliation wasn't yet complete: for it was then that *more* seawater—still flowing over the wall into the megastadium above and behind the Russian carrier—now began flowing down the length of its flight deck in the form of a tumbling wave.

Jack staggered to his feet.

Spray from the nearby waterfall doused him.

He wiped it from his eyes and tried to take in his new situation.

He was suddenly on his own, on the northern side of a new and large gash in his towertop, separated from Lily, Smiley and Easton.

Easton—with his now-bandaged shoulder—was crouched in front of Lily, who lay against the rear wall, unmoving. Smiley sat on the floor near them, still.

'Is she okay!' Jack called anxiously from across the gap.

Easton touched Lily's throat. 'She has pulse. Just unconscious.'

Jack exhaled.

But his predicament was now clear: Easton was wounded and Lily was out cold. And Smiley had taken such a beating, it looked like he'd shut down.

Jack was on his own.

He looked around himself.

From where he stood on his half of the shattered towertop, he was almost perfectly level with the stern of the down-tilted carrier. Its massive propeller hung in the air near him, still rotating slowly and dripping with water.

'How the hell did you get here, Jack?' he whispered to himself.

Over on the castle, Sphinx had also been shocked by the arrival of the Russian aircraft carrier.

As the carrier slammed to a halt against the base of the city-maze, the castle rocked even more violently than it had before and Sphinx was thrown off his feet.

He and Cardinal Mendoza were both hurled back down the last

flight of stairs they had ascended and were lucky not to be thrown completely off the towering castle structure.

'Fucking Rastor!' Sphinx yelled as he tried to get back to his feet.

The megastadium looked like a disaster site.

It was flooding from the two gaping voids high up in its ring-wall.

An oil rig hung from the western flank.

An aircraft carrier lay nose-down, ass-up, like a beached whale on the smashed buildings on its eastern side.

Russian sailors and flight-deck crew—hurled clear of the carrier as it had fallen in here—bobbed in the water, screaming and wailing for help.

And on the top of all that, the maze of buildings and alleyways was filling with fast-rising seawater.

But Rastor still wasn't done.

He withdrew a fist-sized cube of greystone from his pack and tossed it into the seawater filling the maze.

As everyone in that megastadium knew, just a pinch of greystone could turn a sizeable body of water to stone. A cube this big would easily do the job here.

The response was instantaneous.

The water filling the megastadium turned grey . . . then darker . . . almost black . . .

. . . and then it hardened into deep grey-coloured stone, essentially creating a new floor for the enormous space.

The hapless Russian sailors who had been bobbing in the water were suddenly trapped in the solid greystone—encased in it—and their wails either became more pained or they stopped crying out completely as the greystone solidified *over* them.

Rastor bounded out from his position, running across this new layer of solid ground, racing for the central castle before the still-incoming water flooded this new layer.

Near him, Ezekiel and his monks did the same.

From his position on the rooftop, Jack saw all of this.

And suddenly his mind clicked into overdrive.

He'd finally caught up with his rivals and he still had a job to do: stop Sphinx or Brother Ezekiel from sitting on that Throne; stop Rastor from destroying it; or even sit on it himself.

And in his desperation he saw it.

Saw the way to catch up fully, to make up over a dozen hours in a few minutes.

He glanced across at Lily, still unconscious. He couldn't wait for her. He had to do this now.

And with those thoughts in his mind, he bolted off the rooftop.

THE RIG AND THE CARRIER FALL IN

THE RIG AND THE CARRIER COME TO REST

Jack bounded down the nearest series of rooftops, looking like a parkour free-runner.

He raced across two roofs, passing through a pair of obelisks, before he leapt as far as he could off the edge . . .

. . . and landed *on the deck of the adjacent aircraft carrier.*

The carrier's long flight deck sloped away to his left, stretching down to the base of the city-maze.

This was his shortcut to the castle.

At the bottom end of the flight deck—indeed, the bow of the carrier was now embedded in it—was the new greystone 'floor' of the whole vast space.

Ankle-deep water flowed down the length of the flight deck and Jack's feet splashed in it as he dashed down the steep slope.

But then, from behind him, there came a terrible sound: the roar of metal scraping against stone.

Jack spun as he ran—

—as suddenly *another* vessel came riding in on the eastern waterfall, crested the rim, and landed with an almighty crash *on top of* the aircraft carrier's flight deck!

It was a Russian destroyer.

'Fuck me . . .' Jack gasped.

The ship was huge.

Like the carrier, it had been too close to the megastadium when Rastor had blown open the eastern section of the wall and it had been sucked in behind the carrier.

But then, as if the sight wasn't already totally crazy enough, it became completely terrifying as the destroyer's bare hull *began to slide down the carrier's flight deck* toward him!

'You have got to be kidding me.'

The giant destroyer rushed at him, creating an ear-piercing shriek of metal on metal as it skidded down the steeply-sloping flight deck.

Jack could hardly believe what he was seeing.

He'd outrun sliding stones, spiked iron balls, even flaming boulders before.

But he'd never had to flee from a beached warship.

He sprang into action, racing to the port-side edge of the deck and swung himself off it, gripping it by his fingers as the steel grey hull of the massive destroyer screamed by inches away from his fingertips, kicking up sparks that sprayed all over Jack's helmet.

And then, with a metallic shriek, the Russian destroyer ground to a halt *on the carrier's back*, rolling a little to one side as it did so.

Jack hauled himself back onto the flight deck: he had a slim metre of room to stand on as he stood there in the shadow of the warship beached on the deck.

It towered over him. Confused shouts in Russian echoed from its decks.

'This is nuts,' Jack said.

He continued down the sloping flight deck, staying close to the hull of the destroyer, on its port side.

As he came to the bow of the beached destroyer, down near the low end of the carrier's flight deck, he suddenly heard voices—speaking in English—and he froze, staying back out of sight.

Two Omega monks had evidently had the same idea and had been moving down the starboard side of the carrier's flight deck, on the other side of the destroyer.

'Move, move, move!' the first one yelled to the second. 'Ezekiel is going to bring down this whole castle with RDX—destroy it—topple the throne *and* Sphinx! Then he will venture into the deadlier half of the Labyrinth that leads to the second throne, the Throne of the Tree of Death! The passageways to it are reached through the arch of Malkuth! Come, we must hurry before Ezekiel blows the explosives!'

Jack remained hidden behind the beached destroyer's bow.

Another throne?

At the Tree of Death . . .

He didn't have time to fully process that comment now.

For right then, he saw the tiny figure of Ezekiel appear at the base of the central castle . . .

. . . laying explosives.

Ezekiel planted them on the southern side of the magnificent castle: a cluster of superpowerful RDX charges.

The plan was simple.

When they went off, they would cause the castle to topple southward—bringing down this Throne and Sphinx while allowing Ezekiel to pass through the arch of Malkuth at the bottom of the castle and enter the second half of the Supreme Labyrinth.

Ezekiel was just about to set the timer on the array of explosive charges—

—when a sniper round sizzled through the air and slammed into the armour plating on his left shoulder, hurling him off his feet.

As the ground around him was strafed with bullet-fire, Ezekiel scrambled for cover, snapped to look up and saw a sniper on a nearby temple.

Damn it. Sphinx still had one last protective sniper.

The sniper—mortally wounded but not yet dead—unleashed more withering gunfire at Ezekiel, pinning him down.

'Fuck! I can't blow the charges!' Ezekiel yelled in frustration. 'I can't stop Sphinx getting to the Throne!'

From his position on the carrier's flight deck, Jack saw all of this: saw Ezekiel down at the base of the castle, taking cover as Sphinx's rearguard sniper kept him pinned.

Then he looked up to see Sphinx and Mendoza appear again at the summit of the castle, at the base of the pinnacle leading up to the Throne.

Sphinx gripped the first handhold.

He was going to make a climb for it.

Rastor's men fired at him, but their bullets whizzed harmlessly past Sphinx, protected as he was by his Warbler.

And suddenly Jack knew.

There was nothing to stop Sphinx.

He was going to get to the Throne, sit on it, and rule the world.

'No . . .' he gasped. 'There has to be a way to stop him.'

He bit his lip, thinking hard, his mind racing.

And then, as he looked out at the magnificent castle in the centre of the gargantuan space, he noticed the pattern of its window-balconies.

'The *castle* is the Tree of Life,' he said aloud.

And then he whispered, '*Life is rule, death is life,*' reciting the line that appeared on both Imhotep's skull and on the metal wall they'd seen barring the Emperor's Route.

Now, the Labyrinth performs its role, the Thoth glyphs on that metal wall had said.

In it, as outside it, Life precedes Death.

Ascend the pinnacle of Life or sit in the embrace of Death, it matters not to Omega.

The realisation hit Jack like a bolt of lightning.

'There are *two* thrones in here. The Tree of Life is one throne. The Tree of Death is another . . .' he said softly. 'The Throne of the Tree of *Death* was the throne that the Emperor's Route would have taken Sphinx to. But you can also reach it by going the long way round, through the *whole* Labyrinth. Only when you do it that way, *Life precedes Death*: the Life Throne comes first and the Death Throne comes later. And you can sit on either one to avert the Omega Event, since Omega doesn't care.'

He recalled tracing a spiralling path around the tattooed map on Imhotep's skull earlier:

The path he'd traced had gone right through the symbol of the Tree of Life at nine o'clock: where this Throne lay.

Jack blinked in shock.

There was another Throne that he could get to.

He was still in this.

He could figure out the details later.

Right now, he had to stop Sphinx from sitting on this one.

He looked desperately around himself, searching for something, anything, he could use to—

And he saw it.

Oh, Jack. Are you that crazy?

No choice.

No time.

Do it.

Jack spun and ran *back up* the carrier's flight deck and started clambering up some netting on the side of the Russian destroyer mounted on the back of the aircraft carrier.

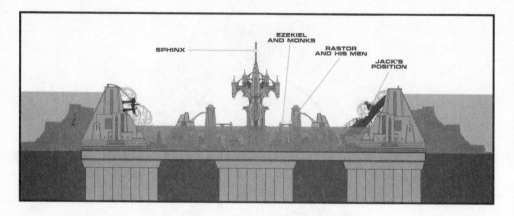

On the golden pinnacle, Sphinx climbed quickly.

On the side of the Russian destroyer, Jack clambered upward.

Sphinx gripped every hand- and foothold with grim determination, staring fixedly up at his goal.

Jack scrambled over the destroyer's handrail, dropped clumsily onto its deck.

Sphinx was only thirty metres below the Throne now and ascending fast, his confidence growing.

Jack ran forward along the deck then scurried up a metal ladder.

Sphinx panted as he climbed. Twenty metres from the Throne.

Jack slipped into the dark cabin of the Russian destroyer's main forward gun.

It was, to be frank, a big fucking piece of artillery: a whopping 130mm cannon capable of firing fearsomely large rounds at a cyclic rate of thirty rounds per minute.

Jack found a panicked young Russian sailor still in the gunner's chair. He hurled him out through the door, slammed it after him, and slid into the seat . . .

. . . and peered out through the sight-window to see . . .

. . . dead ahead, across the cityscape of temples, obelisks and towertops, the pinnacle with the Throne on it, with Sphinx barely twenty metres below it.

With the destroyer beached on the carrier's steeply down-tilted flight deck, its gun was aimed too low. Jack needed to raise its angle a few degrees, so he started turning dials and flicking switches, causing the long 130mm gun barrel to rise on its massive gears.

Sphinx was ten metres away now. So close. His eyes gleamed. His lips turned up in a satisfied smile.

Ezekiel was still under fire from Sphinx's rearguard sniper.

Rastor and his men were still racing across the new greystone floor of the city.

The waterfalls kept raining seawater into the megastadium.

And then the gun barrel stopped its rising as Jack brought the pinnacle into his sights.

'Rule this, Sphinx,' he said.

He slammed his fist down on the firing switch, unleashing the awesome firepower of the warship's cannon.

Boom-boom!-boom-boom!-boom-boom!

Six booming shots blasted out from the mighty cannon.

The roar of the shots reverberated across the megastadium.

Sphinx's Warbler might've been able to repel small subsonic bullets and shoulder-launched missiles, but it was no match for a fusillade of massive 130mm shells.

Jack's shells *slammed* into the golden pinnacle, one after the other, impacting against it with astonishing power, and immediately . . .

. . . the ancient pinnacle cracked at its peak, bare metres above Sphinx . . .

. . . and the golden and silver spire broke . . .

. . . and in almost eerie slow motion, the top of the pinnacle, with the all-powerful Throne of the Tree of Life at its tip, began to tilt and fall.

Now it was Jack who smiled.

'Bullseye, motherfucker.'

Still on the pinnacle—so close to his goal yet now so far away—Sphinx could only watch in dismay as the top of the pinnacle was blown apart by Jack's fire and dropped away into the flooding city-maze.

'No!' he cried. 'Noooo!'

He immediately slid back down the pinnacle to rejoin Cardinal Mendoza at its base.

The decapitation of the great spire made the sniper harassing Ezekiel look up, a move that got him killed.

Ezekiel and his monks immediately whipped up their own assault rifles and shot the sniper dead.

Ezekiel already knew what the next option was. 'Monks, to the tunnel entrance under Malkuth! Go, go, go!'

Rastor saw the spectacular fall of the gold-and-silver pinnacle from the floor of the maze and he smiled broadly.

'Oh, Captain West, that could only have been you!' he exclaimed with delight, looking over at the destroyer and its smoking forward cannon. 'Only you are bold enough to do such a thing!'

A second later, he saw Jack—tiny at this distance, but unmistakable in his fireman's helmet—emerge from the big gun's firing cabin.

Rastor said, 'What a gamble you have taken. But do you even realise what you have done? Do you know what the dark side of the maze entails? I can only thank you for it.'

To his troops, he called, 'Men! To Malkuth! Now! Before it floods! Move!'

As he looked down at the flooding city-maze—with an oil rig sus-pended on one side of it, hanging from some kind of cable, and the enormous down-turned carrier lying on the other side—and the now pinnacle-less castle in its middle, Jack realised that this race had entered a new, more desperate phase.

He saw Rastor and his troops fire zip-lines across their side of the city-maze and whiz down them on flying foxes, zeroing in on the base of the castle.

He saw Sphinx and Mendoza atop the decapitated castle: they disappeared into it, hurrying back down.

He saw Ezekiel and his monks on Jack's side of the city-maze, hurrying across the last few bridges.

They were all converging on the castle, heading for its base.

Gazing out at the castle and the unique pattern of window-balconies on it, Jack now analysed the finer details.

He again saw the *pattern* of the window-balconies clearly: saw how each one represented a node of the Tree of Life.

He recalled the dying monk he'd encountered in the Endless Tunnel repeating the phrase: 'If we can't get to Keter, Malkuth will lead us to the other realm. If we can't get to Keter, Malkuth will lead us to the other realm.'

It hadn't been some old holy mantra.

It had been his *orders*.

If the monks' plan to get to Keter failed, they were to move on to the second option, Malkuth.

This was confirmed by the comment about Malkuth that Jack

had overheard the other Omega monk say on the carrier's flight deck earlier.

Malkuth was the bottommost node of the Tree of Life. As such, it was also the entry point to the lower realm of existence—that of decay and wickedness, turpitude and pain—at the end of which was the fearsome Tree of Death.

In here, that meant the second Throne.

The line from Imhotep's skull and the metal wall echoed in his mind again:

Life is rule, death is life.

Jack guessed this might mean that the reward for whoever sat on this throne, the Life Throne, was the power to *rule* over everyone else. And if death was life, then maybe the reward for sitting on the Death Throne was the same thing. Then again, it might be something much simpler: the privilege to *keep living.*

Whatever it is, he thought, *now that this Throne has been destroyed, this is an entirely new race. We're still in the game and no longer that far behind.*

We . . . he thought, pausing.

He glanced back at the towertop where he had left Lily, Easton and Smiley.

Easton was still crouched over Lily. She was moving, rubbing her head. Smiley sat motionless next to her. The destroyed Russian search-and-rescue helicopter lay near them, beside the gash it had carved into the tower's roof.

It's not 'we' any more, Jack thought sadly. First Zoe had been killed in the entry maze. And now Easton and Lily had been struck down. Even Smiley was out of commission.

It was just him now.

And he couldn't stop. He had to go on, even if he had to do it on his own.

'Well, jackass,' he said grimly to himself. 'Are you gonna take your own advice? You didn't come this far just to come *this* far, did you?'

And with those words, he looked out at the base of the castle:

he had to get there and he had to get there before it got covered over with water.

He took a deep breath, girded himself, and then he started running down the flight deck as fast as he damn well could.

Jack raced down the length of the aircraft carrier's downwardly tilted deck.

As soon as he emerged from behind the bow of the beached destroyer, the two nearby Omega monks saw him, but Jack just turned as he ran and shot them both in the head. He didn't have time for that shit.

He holstered his gun as he came to the forward end of the flight deck and, without missing a step, he leapt off it onto the flat roof of a tower with a temple on it.

After that, he raced across a high bridge at full speed—all while the roiling seawater beneath him rose quickly.

Another bridge met him . . .

. . . only its middle had been blasted apart with explosives sometime earlier that day.

Jack never stopped running.

He just drew his Maghook from his backpack as he ran and fired it at a higher bridge, latched it on, and swung across the wide gap.

He landed on the other side, reeled in the Maghook and kept on going.

It was a hell of a run, and thus he made his way to the castle, until he was only one long slender bridge away from it and he could see Ezekiel and his last two remaining Omega monks at the other end of the bridge, about to mount a high hill of stairs that led to the castle's base.

He also saw, off to his left, Rastor and some men come swooping

in on a zip-line *and overtake Ezekiel*. They arrived at the castle's entrance, fired more shots that took down one of Ezekiel's monks and hurried inside it.

Rastor stepped inside the castle structure.

He gazed up at its soaring hollow interior, with its crisscrossing stairways and impossibly tall columns. It looked like the mightiest cathedral ever constructed.

The archway of Malkuth stood before him, in the exact centre of the bottom level.

It was an evil-looking thing, shot through with carvings of demons and devils, serpents and jackals. Every angle on it was sharp, giving it a menacing aspect.

It was also actually quite large—it was probably seventy feet tall—but against the scale of the space around it, it looked small.

Three soaring stairways leapt upward from its spiked roof, while inside it was a round rimless well that plunged into darkness.

'That's our path!' Rastor called to his men.

They hurried for the archway and climbed down into the wide well, the first team to enter the second half of the Labyrinth.

High above Rastor, Sphinx and Mendoza were bounding down the stairways of the castle's interior.

'Damn it, fuck!' Sphinx swore as he saw Rastor and his troops hurry into the archway of Malkuth.

Rastor had taken the lead in this race.

And Sphinx was well aware of what Rastor wanted: to destroy the other Throne and let the whole universe collapse.

'Hurry!' Sphinx urged Mendoza. 'We can catch him in the second half of the Labyrinth, but we can't let him get too far ahead!'

They hurried into the well shortly after.

★ ★ ★

Jack kept running, out across the last long bridge.

The spectacular white-and-silver castle rose up before him, mounted on its hill of stone steps.

The incoming seawater kept rising beneath him—now maybe fifty feet below his bridge and filling fast.

Jack never stopped running.

He couldn't stop.

The water was rising quickly below him and would overwhelm his bridge in seconds.

Jack continued up the hill of stairs just as the water behind him swallowed the bridge.

Half a minute later, he burst inside the castle and beheld its soaring nave.

He arrived just in time to see Ezekiel and his last remaining monk lower themselves into a well inside a large cube-shaped structure at the bottom of the vast hall.

Malkuth.

The entry to the underworld, to a second series of mazes that led to the Throne of the Tree of Death.

Jack hesitated, spun to look behind him.

Out through the main doorway, he saw the city-maze—complex, ornate and in any other circumstance, a site that would have been one of history's greatest archaeological discoveries. It was now half-flooded by the incoming seawater.

He saw the tiny figures of Easton, Lily and Smiley over on the eastern wall, now hopelessly separated from him by broken bridges and heaving seawater.

You have to go on, he thought.

Alone.

And so he turned and hurried for the archway of Malkuth.

Coming to the deep stone well, Jack peered tentatively over its rimless edge.

He was worried that Ezekiel might be down there waiting with a rifle pointed up at him.

But no gunfire came.

On second thought, Jack figured, Ezekiel was probably more worried about the seawater that was about to flood into the well and whatever maze of tunnels was down there and so had bolted away.

Jack clambered down the hand- and footholds cut into the stone wall of the well, descending into the darkness with only the flashlight on his fire helmet to guide him.

At the base of the well was a long flat tunnel.

Except for the dim light coming from the well, it was entirely dark. It had no crimson orbs in its ceiling. By the look of it, it stretched eastward, back toward the Sinai Desert.

Jack hurried down it until, after about a kilometre, it angled upward as a steep stepped tunnel.

Hundreds, maybe thousands, of stairs rose up into blackness—

A dull roar echoed from behind him.

It sounded like a powerful indoor waterfall.

'Oh, shit,' he gasped. 'The floodwaters just arrived in the castle.'

He charged up the stairs.

Ran as fast as his legs would carry him.

The roar from the tunnel behind him grew louder, the sound of rushing, crashing water.

★ ★ ★

Jack couldn't see it, but back in the megastadium, the rising waves of seawater had reached the castle . . .

. . . and slithered inside it . . .

. . . stretching across the castle's slick stone floor, reaching like a living creature for the archway of Malkuth in the middle.

When it reached the well, the incoming seawater just poured down it in shocking quantities, like bathwater swirling down a drain.

It was now filling Jack's tunnel underneath the megastadium, and until it reached the same level as the sea above, it would keep pouring in.

Jack pounded up the ascending tunnel.

He heard the first wave of seawater lash against the base of the stairs, heard it rising up through the darkness below him.

And then the water was nipping at his heels and he knew he wasn't going to be able to outrun it, but then suddenly he came to level ground and he dived full-length onto it and—amazingly—the body of rising water that had been about to catch him suddenly abated, stopped, pulled back, just below this section of level ground.

Jack gasped with both relief and exhaustion.

He'd reached sea level.

He let his head fall against the ground.

In the heavy silence that followed, he heard footsteps in the darkness ahead of him: the sounds of his rivals racing away into this second half of the Labyrinth, *but now in a new order.*

Rastor and his Serbian troops.

Then Sphinx and Mendoza.

And then Ezekiel and one remaining monk.

All still ahead of Jack, but no longer by very much.

He was back in the game.

Jack looked back at the lapping waves of seawater filling the tunnel behind him, blocking it off from any more contenders but

also from his teammates.

Sure, he was back in the game, but now he was in it totally and completely alone.

THE RED HORIZON STAR-4
THIRTY MINUTES EARLIER

Around the same time that Jack arrived at the megastadium and looked out over the city-maze within it, a Russian transport chopper was flying toward the oil rig known as the Red Horizon Star-4.

The chopper had taken off a few minutes earlier from the temporary airfield on the shore.

Inside it were Alby Calvin and Aloysius Knight, flex-cuffed and guarded, prisoners of the Knights of the Golden Eight.

Having been held in their cages at the airfield for two nights, they were now being taken to the oil rig.

The chopper flew low and fast across the short stretch of turquoise water between land and rig.

Even though it was a big helicopter, it looked positively tiny as it passed over the gargantuan megastadium that had risen up from the waves of the Red Sea during the night.

Both Alby and Aloysius peered in awe at the colossal grey ring-wall and the many buildings of the city-maze. The glittering gold Throne of Life poking up from its exact centre looked absolutely majestic.

Alby even glimpsed tiny armed figures racing across one of the bridges down there.

'Shit just got real,' he said softly.

'You can say that again,' Aloysius agreed.

Minutes later, the Russian chopper landed on the helipad of the Red Horizon Star-4 and Alby and Aloysius were shoved out of it by the two Squires guarding them.

As he was marched across the helipad, Alby looked back at the megastadium: from up here, he could see over the grey wall and down into the maze.

One of his guards jabbed him with the butt of his rifle, making Alby face forward again and he saw who was waiting for them.

Jaeger Eins, the leader of the Knights of the Golden Eight.

'Albert,' Jaeger Eins said, 'it's so nice to see you again.'

He nodded at Alby's new artificial left hand. 'I don't mean to be unkind, but I must say I preferred your original hand.'

Alby clenched his jaw.

Jaeger Eins smiled nastily. 'I also liked your friend, Mr Adamson, at least before I cut off *both* of his hands and drowned him in his cage.'

Alby's eyes blazed with rage.

He remembered very clearly how at the Golden Knights' fortified headquarters at Aragon Castle on Ischia Island, Jaeger Eins had tortured Julius Adamson: cutting off Julius's hands with a super-sharp ancient filament weapon before dropping poor Julius into the water to drown.

Eins had then given the filament weapon to Dion DeSaxe and he had calmly cut off Alby's hand with it.

'I liked Julius a lot, shithead,' Alby said.

'What's this rig?' Aloysius cut in. 'Some secret royal observation post?'

'It's more than that,' Jaeger Eins said. 'The company that owns this rig is a royal company that owns many drilling rigs, including all the ones in this part of the Red Sea. It has sat here for years, drilling small amounts of oil but in truth watching over a strange and enormous formation of greystone under the seabed that, according to ground-penetrating radars, was hemispherical in shape. And then, today, it rose up all by itself, this glorious city containing the Throne of the Tree of Life.'

Jaeger Eins indicated the gigantic ringed city.

'We are about to be witnesses to history. Lord Sphinx, the new emperor of the world, is about to ascend the Throne of Life. The universe will be spared and he will become the undisputed ruler of every person on this planet.'

'And you want us to see it?' Alby said.

'Oh, no. Not at all,' Eins said, calmly pulling a small velvet box from behind his back.

Alby froze at the sight of it.

He felt a visceral response at seeing it.

He knew that box: it held the small, hand-wielded, harp-shaped filament weapon that Eins and Dion had used on him and Julius.

Eins said, 'Albert, Albert. After all the excitement at the gates to the Labyrinth, I had a few things to do. But I was informed that you had been captured, along with Captain Knight. Now that I have some time, I ordered my men to bring you here, so I could have a little fun with you before I killed you. Albert, because you have been such a consistent bane to our plan. And Captain Knight, because of those times in the past where you captured targets that I would have been paid a lot of money to kill.

'This is how it will go: first, I will slice off a few key pieces of your bodies: your feet and hands, to immobilise you both, then your noses, ears and tongues. And then, when you are lying here on this helipad pleading with your *tongueless fucking mouths* for me to stop, then—only then—will I kill you out of mercy.'

Alby said nothing.

'You know,' Aloysius said, 'you're not a very nice man. I sense a lot of anger issues in you.'

Jaeger Eins stepped forward menacingly, holding up the filament weapon.

'You're right, Captain. I am not nice. Not in any way. I am going to enjoy this very, very much—'

An explosion boomed from nearby.

And suddenly *a whole section* of the rim of grey ring-wall

right next to the rig *blasted upward* in a billowing cloud of flames and dust, sending thousands of stone chunks spraying into the air.

And with that explosion, everything on the rig went to hell.

The explosion was, of course, the result of Rastor's first shoulder-launched missile striking the western side of the ring-wall.

The blast tore a hole in the rim of the massive wall and sea-water immediately began to funnel through it en masse, into the city-maze.

And the rig, so close to this new hole in the wall, rocked wildly and then . . .

. . . lurched sickeningly *toward* the maze, carried on the mighty rush of inflowing water.

With the floating oil rig's anchor free of the sea floor, suddenly the Red Horizon Star-4 was swept like a bath toy—its decks tilting wildly, almost through forty-five degrees—toward the broken wall surrounding the city-maze and the colossal waterfall of seawater gushing over it.

On the helipad, as the rig lurched, Jaeger Eins was hurled to the ground.

Alby and Aloysius fell, too.

So did their two guards.

Quick as a cat, Aloysius took the opportunity to side-kick one of their Squire-guards, sending him sliding down the length of the helipad and off its lower edge, into the raging waters below.

Alby saw his chance and, still handcuffed, he dived toward Jaeger Eins and unleashed a double-fisted punch that broke the nose of the leader of the Knights of the Golden Eight.

Having stunned Eins, Alby snatched the filament weapon from Eins's grasp and quickly used it to cut his flex cuffs.

The glistening fishing line–like wire sliced through the plastic flex cuffs easily, it was that sharp.

He dived over to Aloysius and cut his cuffs just as . . .

. . . borne on the seawater funnelling through the broken rim of the ring-wall, the rig came to the top of the wall . . .

. . . and was swept over it.

And suddenly Alby's world went vertical.

As the rig toppled over the wall and plummeted into the city-maze, Alby and Aloysius searched for any handhold they could find.

They both ended up diving *into* the Russian helicopter on the helipad, since it had been tied down to studs on the pad earlier and was still affixed to it.

Alby didn't see what happened to Jaeger Eins but everybody else on the helipad—or on *any* exposed deck of the oil rig—was thrown off the falling vessel.

And then, as the rig freefell into the city-maze, *WHACK!*, its fall halted instantly and shockingly.

From his position inside the chopper, Alby didn't know what had caused the sudden stop.

Then he looked up and saw that the oil rig's anchor cable was reaching back up to the top of the wall and was now stretched taut.

The anchor cable must have caught on the wall and now the rig—turned sideways, almost perfectly ninety degrees—hung off the colossal ancient wall with seawater gushing down on either side of it.

Something flashed in Alby's peripheral vision and he ducked as Jaeger Eins came rushing out of the rear cabin of the chopper, leading with a knife.

Alby dodged the blow and, on a reflex, swiped at Eins's face with the filament weapon.

It happened so fast that at first Alby didn't realise what he'd done.

The lower half of Jaeger Eins's face *slid gruesomely off the bottom of his head.*

All of it—jaw, teeth and nostrils—one second they were there, the next they were gone.

A whole chunk of his face below the nose had been instantly excised, leaving only exposed flesh and a clear view into his throat in its place. He'd been turned into a living Picasso painting.

Above the grotesque mess that was his lower face, Jaeger Eins's eyes bulged in pure disbelieving shock.

He howled a mouthless cry of pain that was inhuman in its agony.

Alby didn't give a fuck. He pressed his advantage.

Slash, slash.

The first slash cut off the grip of Eins's knife *plus* his whole knife hand, causing the knife to fall away.

The second slash cut off his other hand.

And suddenly Jaeger Eins, the cruel leader of a cruel gang of assassins who had never been accountable to anyone, was a broken and disfigured wretch.

Alby clenched his teeth as he leaned in close to Eins's ruined face.

'This is for my friend, Julius,' he said grimly.

He kicked Eins out of the chopper and the Golden Knight fell away into the roiling waters at the base of the mighty waterfall, doomed to drown in fear and agony as water rushed unimpeded into his exposed throat, and Jaeger Eins was never heard from again.

Alby and Aloysius now found themselves stranded on the oil rig hanging sideways from the western rim of the ring-wall, with all its decks turned vertical.

There was nowhere they could go and nothing they could do. They could only watch as Jack's battle with Sphinx and Rastor and Ezekiel played out.

They watched in awe as the Russian aircraft carrier came thundering over the far rim of the wall and slammed down onto the ancient buildings on that side. Then they saw the Russian destroyer come in behind it and get beached on the carrier's flight deck.

They stared helplessly as they saw the tiny figure of Sphinx scaling the gold-and-silver pinnacle leading to the Life Throne.

And then they reacted with stunned joy as, without warning, the beached destroyer's gun boomed and a couple of its shells hit the Life Throne's pinnacle and broke it, foiling Sphinx's climb.

At that, Aloysius said, 'That determined bastard is still alive. Only Jack West would do something that crazy.'

And sure enough it was Jack.

For, moments later, Alby and Aloysius—still watching from the transport chopper lashed to the helipad of the side-turned oil rig—cheered as they saw the tiny figure of Jack racing down the length of the aircraft carrier and leap-swing-and-bound his way across the city-maze to the central castle, never giving up.

And then Jack hurried inside the castle and was gone, and the city-maze was suddenly quiet except for the two waterfalls of sea-water filling it.

After a time, the deep *whump-whump-whump* of a helicopter caught their attention and a fearsome-looking Russian Werewolf attack helicopter lowered into view right in front of their vertical helipad.

It hovered menacingly in front of Alby and Aloysius, bristling with guns and missile pods, while they sat huddled inside their chopper still tied to the side-turned rig's landing pad.

'It was nice knowing you, kid,' Aloysius said. 'Rufus told me he really enjoyed working with you on your mission to Libya. Wish I could've got to know you better.'

'You, too,' Alby said.

'What a shitty fuckin' way to go,' Aloysius said.

A second later, the Werewolf's six-barrelled forward mini-gun whirred to life, a vicious tongue of flames flashing out from it, and a withering torrent of gunfire blazed at them.

A MAN NAMED JACK

PART III

AFTER THE SCHOOLYARD FIGHT

'Daddy? Do you have a family?' [Lily asked.]
Jack smiled. 'Yes. I do.'
'Brothers or sisters?'
'One sister.'
'Older or younger?'
'Older, by two years. Although . . .'
'Although what?'
'Although she's not older than me any more. Her name
was Lauren. She's no longer older than me because she
died when she was thirty.'
'Oh. How did she die?' Lily asked.
'She was killed in a plane crash.' Jack's eyes became
distant. 'An airliner accident.'

THE SIX SACRED STONES, P. 227
(MACMILLAN, SYDNEY, 2007)

Jack is lying in bed.

It is night-time, hours after the schoolyard fight.

His father stands in the doorway, silhouetted, disappointed.

'Why can't you have normal friends like your sister?' he says.

It was like that Jack's whole childhood.

Two years older than him, Jack's sister Lauren had always been their father's favourite. She could do no wrong.

The praise of the great soldier, Jack West Sr—Wolf—was something Jack always yearned for but, for some reason, could never attain.

Wolf lavished Lauren with praise and gifts, attention and warmth.

With Jack it was the opposite: criticism and coldness, and physical violence—usually after Jack stepped in when Wolf had been beating Mae.

More than anything, Jack later realised, it was psychological warfare, practised over years.

Wolf's brainwashing of Lauren drove a wedge between her and Jack. Where once Lauren had been the caring older sister, she became critical of Jack, too.

It also had another effect: it turned Lauren against their mother, Mae.

So much so that when their parents divorced, Jack was astonished when Lauren chose to live with their *father*, even after the beatings he had inflicted upon Mae and Jack.

It was only years later, in their mid-twenties, after Lauren

discovered who their father really was that she reconnected with Jack and they became friends again.

And then she died.

In a plane crash at the age of thirty.

She never saw Jack battle their father for the six Ramesean Stones. Never saw him fight Wolf to the death above a bottomless abyss inside Easter Island. Never saw Jack defeat him.

The upshot of it all was that, as a child, Jack spent a lot of his time at home alone and isolated within his own family.

Some folks would have said this was a bad thing, but Jack never saw it that way.

It made him realise that, in any trial, as long as he hung in there, he could emerge from the other side and prevail.

THE TUNNEL BEYOND THE LIFE THRONE
28 DECEMBER, 0006 HOURS
ONE DAY AND FIVE HOURS TILL OMEGA

Jack trudged through the long dark tunnel on the edge of exhaustion.

The ancient passage stretched for miles. It mostly went gently uphill, in broad stairways and ramps, turning in sweeping arcs and the occasional sharp corner.

After he had made it up the initial flooding stairway, the crimson orbs reappeared in the ceiling, and Jack pressed on in their dim red glow, keeping his helmet flashlight off to conserve its batteries.

He walked for hours.

He'd been awake for over twenty-four hours and his fatigue became almost painful.

He knew he'd have to sleep at some point, but he couldn't bring himself to do it: he'd always see another corner up ahead and tell himself that he'd take a break when he reached it, but when he did, he'd just keep going.

He'd never felt so alone.

Zoe was dead. Lily and Easton had been felled in the city-maze. Even the loyal bronzeman Smiley, having stepped in front of that blast earlier, was no longer with him.

It was, in truth, much worse than he knew.

Jack didn't know that Iolanthe, Nobody and Bertie—in their search for the Blue Bell that could wake entire populations—had last been seen entering the vault at Troy moments before a massive explosion had ripped it apart.

Or that Alby and Aloysius, huddled on their tied-down helicopter on the oil rig's vertical helipad, had last been seen getting brutally fired upon by a newly arrived Werewolf attack chopper.

His team was in disarray.

His mission was in tatters.

And he was all that remained.

Here, trudging onward through an underground tunnel with his last ounces of strength.

And then, after nine hours of walking up that long tunnel, he turned a final corner and suddenly the tunnel ended at an ornate greystone archway with Thoth markings etched into it.

Beyond the archway, the path became a ledge that overlooked a wide and very long rectangular cavern.

As he took in the view and the shockingly complex maze that lay in the cavern before him, Jack said, 'Oh, fuck me.'

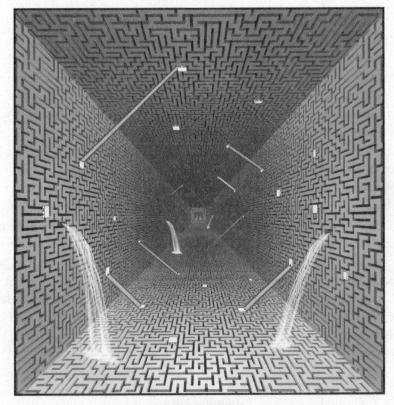

JACK'S VIEW

The cavern that spread out in front of Jack was exceedingly long—many kilometres at least—and the maze inside it was of a size, complexity and difficulty that he had not encountered before.

It was a *four*-sided maze.

And it was mind-bogglingly complex.

Its floor, walls and ceiling were all *covered* with countless slender trenches—hundreds of them, all zigzagging at right angles down the length of the superlong space, cutting across each other or stopping at dead ends.

Each trench was wide enough for a single person to walk through but also deep enough to stop that person from peering up over the walls.

Sphinx and Mendoza.

Then a third set—much closer to Jack, just two figures—Ezekiel and his last Omega monk.

An overwhelming fatigue gripped Jack.

The last twenty-four hours—without sleep—had drained him of almost all his energy.

If he was going to tackle this maze, he needed to do it with a clear head. He had to stop, if only for a moment, to rest.

He stepped back through the archway, gazing up at its Thoth markings, markings that no doubt explained this maze but which he couldn't read without Lily.

He retreated about ten yards into the tunnel and slumped onto his butt with his back pressed against the right-side wall.

He closed his eyes.

It would only be for a little while, he told himself.

He wouldn't go to sleep. He didn't have time for that. No, this would just be a short break.

Must keep going . . .

Can't stop . . .

Can't let the others get too far ahead . . .

Which was when, sitting there in that ancient tunnel with his back against the cold stone wall, he could no longer keep his eyes open and his head drooped against his chest and Jack West fell into a deep sleep.

Jack dreamed.

Images from his many adventures flashed across his mind.

Finding Lily inside the volcano in Uganda, a wailing newborn.

Raising her in Kenya, with Wizard and the original team.

Fighting Marshall Judah atop the Great Pyramid.

Seeing Wizard die in the tomb of Genghis Khan in Mongolia.

Battling his father, Wolf, above an abyss under Easter Island.

Surviving the Great Games in the Underworld.

Seeing his mother die at Rastor's hands underneath a Falling Temple in Jerusalem.

Waking inside his bedroom in his plane after the Great Games only to see Mephisto's red face and bared teeth right in front of his eyes—

—Jack jerked awake.

Damn it. He hated that nightmare.

He blinked, rubbed his eyes.

He didn't know how long he'd been asleep and thus how much time he'd lost to his rivals.

He began to heave himself off the ground—

'Hello there, Captain,' a voice said from his right.

Jack saw their boots first.

Then his eyes rose upward to find the familiar face of Brother Ezekiel, leader of the Omega monks, standing over him.

Beside Ezekiel was the other monk and he held a Glock pistol aimed right at Jack's face.

'What a pleasant surprise to find you here,' Ezekiel said. 'The maze ahead is long and difficult and we decided we needed to come back and regather our strength before we took it on. And look at what we find: you, on the floor, asleep and unguarded.'

Jack said nothing.

As he sat there on the ground, staring up into the barrel of the second monk's pistol, he sighed with a deep sadness.

So this was where it ended.

He was not just out of options and friends this time, he was out of *energy*.

The terrible fatigue came over him again, not so much from the physical exhaustion, but from the stark fact that he was going to die here, alone, in this dark subterranean place where no-one would ever find his body.

He would just *disappear*.

Ezekiel saw all of these thoughts on Jack's face.

'Oh, Captain,' he said mockingly. 'This is not your time to win the day and save the world. Once, it might have been, when that old prophecy about the five greatest warriors became real. But that time was but a precursor to this, the time of times, the end of all things and the beginning of a new age. An age that, sadly, will go on without you.'

Ezekiel turned to his brother monk. 'Kill him.'

The monk reasserted his aim at Jack's head and from a distance of four feet, pulled the trigger, and in the tight confines of the stone tunnel, the gun boomed loudly.

The bullet pinged with a spark off the stone wall beside Jack's right ear.

Somehow, amazingly, the shot had missed.

'What the hell?' Jack breathed.

'What the *fuck*?' the monk spat.

He fired three more rounds at Jack, but every bullet just veered away from Jack and ricocheted off the stone wall behind him as if he were protected by some kind of invisible force field.

The monk threw a confused look at Ezekiel—

—just as his head was knocked sideways with shocking violence by something that came shooting out of the dark tunnel to Jack's *left*, from the direction of the flooded city-maze.

The object slammed into the monk's head with terrific force and Jack heard a sickening crack as the monk's skull fractured in an instant and he collapsed to the ground, dead.

The object that had struck him clunked to the floor and Jack recognised it instantly: the bulbous silver magnetic head of a Maghook.

Ezekiel whirled to find the source of the Maghook.

Jack did, too . . .

. . . and he blinked in astonishment when he saw who stood there.

She stood in the middle of the tunnel gripping the Maghook's launcher like a gun, her feet planted in a perfect firing stance, wearing a sleek form-fitting black scuba suit and looking down the barrel of the launcher with deadly fucking eyes.

Zoe.

'Hey, honey,' she said. 'Hello, Ezekiel.'

Jack thought he saw more figures in the shadows behind her: Lily and—wait—Alby?

Christ, maybe I'm still dreaming . . .

'You . . .' Ezekiel growled at Zoe.

Zoe reeled in the Maghook and it whizzed across the floor, returning to the launcher.

'Now, boys,' she said, 'are we not playing nicely?'

Ezekiel reached for his gun.

But Zoe sprang forward quickly and kicked it out of his hand and it went skittering down the tunnel.

And as Jack sat there, dumbfounded, on the floor of the tunnel, Zoe and Ezekiel—the leader of an order of women-hating monks—fought.

Ezekiel seemed as shocked as Jack while Zoe was energised beyond belief.

However she had got here, she'd been storing up a wave of anger and now she was unloading it on Ezekiel.

Zoe attacked the monk furiously, punching him all over—in the face, throat and kidneys—forcing him back toward the ledge overlooking the four-sided maze.

'Don't like women, huh?'

Punch.

'Don't like the sound of our voices, huh?'

Punch.

'And this is for trying to kill my man.'

Punch. That final blow caused Ezekiel to stagger and Zoe took the opportunity to snatch the greystone hourglass that hung from his neck *and ram it into his mouth*.

The hourglass smashed inside his mouth and the grey powder puffed out in a little cloud as Ezekiel gagged—

—just as Zoe grabbed a water bottle from her belt and poured it into Ezekiel's mouth. Then she clamped her other hand over his lips, forcing him to swallow, causing the greystone to run down his gullet into his stomach.

The response came a few seconds later.

Ezekiel convulsed, his face turning purple.

The water inside his stomach was turning to stone and doing all sorts of internal damage.

He looked up in horror at Zoe, his eyes bulging red.

'Die knowing this,' Zoe said. '*You got beat by a girl.*'

And with those words, she side-kicked him off the ledge and the gagging-choking-dying monk went sailing down into the maze, falling a full hundred metres before he landed on one of the trench walls.

With the whiplashing impact, Ezekiel's head was snapped back at an obscene angle, his neck breaking instantly, and the leader of the Order of the Omega was no more.

Zoe raced over to Jack and wrapped her arms around him.

Jack wobbled in her embrace.

Over her shoulder he saw Lily and, yes, Alby hanging back, letting Zoe have her reunion with him.

But then Lily couldn't wait and she raced over and embraced Jack and Zoe as one.

'I really hope I'm not dreaming,' he said weakly.

Zoe held him away from her. 'You're not dreaming, handsome. I'm here.'

'But how did you—I mean—I thought you fell back in the—and then there was the Endless Tunnel to get through—and the flooded city-maze.'

'I know, I know,' Zoe said with her crooked Irish smile. 'I think you could say that I pulled a Jack West.'

Zoe explained.

As she'd fallen into the abyss with the massive inverted skyscraper and the pieces of the bridge falling all around her, she'd reached into her backpack and pulled from it the Maghook that she had brought into the Labyrinth and fired it at the wall. It found purchase and she'd swung over to the wall, slamming into it with such force that it took the wind out of her, but she managed to hang on.

It had then taken her a full two hours to scale the wall and reach the exit.

'What about the stone exit door?' Jack asked. 'It closed after we went through it.'

'I had two grenades on me so I gave them a shot. Planted them at the base of the door and blew them,' Zoe said. 'The door didn't budge—didn't get a scratch—but the stone floor *beneath* it cracked and a small hole was created, big enough that I was able to dig my way under the door. It wasn't exactly elegant, but screw elegance, it did the job.

'After that, Ningizzida showed me which of the six tunnels to take. Then I kept my eyes averted from the goldmen and took the left-hand fork—the sinister one—at every junction.'

Zoe smiled at Jack's reaction. 'You're not the only one who can solve ancient riddles, you know.'

'I've never doubted that. Not for one moment.' Jack shook his head. 'What about the city-maze around the Life Throne? It flooded shortly after I went down the well. I mean, the water chased me.'

Zoe nodded. 'That whole place is probably fully flooded by now. I arrived there shortly after the seawater rose up over the base of that castle in the middle. Found Lily, Easton and a very sorry-looking Smiley huddled beside a crashed Russian rescue chopper near the exit from the Endless Tunnel. Alby had just joined them, but I'll let him tell you his story in a moment.

'Lily and Easton told me everything that happened. Most importantly, Easton told me where he last saw *you*: running into the base of the castle just before it flooded over.

'So I grabbed some scuba gear for all of us from the crashed Russian rescue chopper and we went diving . . . swimming through the flooded city and down into the well at the bottom of the castle. Swam all the way up this tunnel until we reached dry ground. And we've been hiking up through it ever since. Got here just in time to see you sitting on your ass with those two monks standing over you.'

Lily leaned forward. 'I kinda helped there, too. I neglected to tell you I slipped my Warbler into one of your jacket pockets while you were sleeping earlier. Remember when you woke and I was sitting with you, rubbing your shoulder? That's when I did it. I don't know, I kinda just figured you might need it at some point.'

Jack reached into a zippered pocket of his canvas jacket and pulled from it the disc-shaped Warbler.

He shook his head. 'Thanks, kiddo.'

He smiled.

After feeling so alone, now, seeing these people he loved so much, he felt revitalised and recharged.

'God, I'm glad to see you all,' he said.

Alby then explained his presence.

He and Aloysius had been dead to rights on their vertical oil rig when the newly arrived Werewolf chopper had opened fire.

Only it hadn't been firing at *them*.

It had been firing at an armed Knight of the Golden Eight—the consistently nasty Jaeger Zwei—who had appeared above and behind them, climbing over the top edge of the vertical helipad with a gun in his hand.

The attack chopper's gunfire ripped Zwei apart, turning his entire body to mush.

When the roar of fire stopped, there came a squeal of feedback from the Werewolf's external loudspeaker, then a voice.

'Why, hey there, guys, sorry we couldn't get here a tad sooner,' the slow drawling voice said. 'Took Sky Monster and me a little while to steal this chopper. Want a ride off this rig?'

As he had peered at the Werewolf chopper, Alby recognised its two pilots and his face broke out in a wide grin.

It was Rufus and Sky Monster.

When he and Aloysius were safely aboard the Werewolf, Rufus had asked Alby where he wanted to go.

Alby had pointed across the vast city-maze at the towertop on which Lily and Easton sat with Smiley.

'There,' he'd said.

★ ★ ★

Minutes later, Rufus landed the Werewolf attack chopper on the towertop near Lily, Easton and Smiley with his melted back.

Lily and Alby hugged warmly as they were reunited, and the whole group—Rufus and Sky Monster, Alby and Aloysius—quickly swapped notes on what had happened to them all and how they might be able to help Jack.

And then Zoe had arrived and taken charge.

'We get some scuba gear and go in after him,' Zoe said.

'Absolutely,' Lily said.

Aloysius said, 'Mind if I stay out here with these two pilots? Got some things I'd like to do, some very destructive things.'

Zoe nodded. 'Do what you have to do, Captain.' She turned to Easton. 'Just take this brave minotaur and his bronzeman with you.'

Easton began to protest. 'But—'

'You've done your part, Easton. Smiley, too,' Zoe said kindly. 'And that bullet wound needs attention. Time for you to tag out. And I have a feeling that Alby wants to tag in.'

'Do I ever,' Alby said.

And so they separated.

Aloysius, Rufus and Sky Monster headed off in the Werewolf, taking the wounded Easton and the half-melted Smiley with them, while Zoe, Lily and Alby donned scuba gear and swam into the clear blue water covering the flooded city-maze, eventually arriving here to find Jack about to be killed by the two Omega monks.

When Zoe and Alby finished their tales, Jack smiled.

'I'm so glad you're all here, because we've got a hell of a maze to get through now.'

FOURTH TEST OF WORTH

THE FOUR-SIDED MAZE

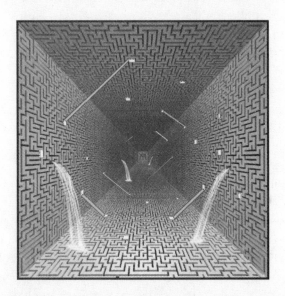

'There are many things in this world that cannot be explained, young one . . . Ask yourself, how did life itself arise on this remote planet? I am sure you are aware of the Cambrian Explosion, the sudden burst of complex life that occurred on Earth 500 million years ago. What caused it? How did life begin here?

'Humanity has been watched from afar for a long, long time . . .'

HADES TO LILY
THE FOUR LEGENDARY KINGDOMS PP. 141–2
(MACMILLAN, SYDNEY, 2016)

Lily gazed up at the Thoth text etched into the archway above the entrance to the four-sided maze.

'It reads:

> *And so the path to Death begins.*
> *Overcome the quadrilateral maze*
> *Board the golden cage*
> *And stand in judgement.*
> *Only then can you sit in the embrace of Death.*'

'Doesn't sound friendly,' Zoe said.

Jack said, 'I overheard some of the Omega monks talking about this second half of the Labyrinth. They said it was much nastier than the first half.'

Lily said, 'There's a final symbol carved at the end of the markings. It's also on Imhotep's skull. This one.'

She pulled out the skull and pointed at an image on it:

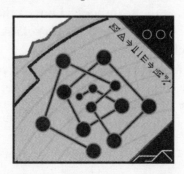

'What's it mean?' Alby asked.

'It's weird.' Lily frowned. 'It's a Thoth symbol that's been combined with an image, so it's hard to translate. It means something like "the turning sequence" or "the sequence of rotations".'

Jack looked from Lily to the four-sided maze.

He scanned the high grey-walled trenches in its floor, walls and ceiling; gazed at the white blockhouses that poked up from within them and at the waterfalls flowing from the spouts jutting out from the walls.

'That's the catch,' he said. 'Each maze in here has a unique feature to it. That "sequence of rotations" must be the catch for this one—'

He cut himself off as his searching eyes zeroed in on the trenches cut into the ceiling.

He'd noticed them before, noticed that something was *missing* from them.

'Hand-rungs . . .' he whispered.

'What?' Zoe said.

Jack was talking to himself now, thinking aloud. 'You don't swing from your hands across the ceiling. You *walk* on it . . . because the whole maze must . . .'

As he spoke, he kept staring upward, then he snapped to look out at the larger maze and the full realisation dawned on him.

'Dad? Hello? What is it?' Lily said.

Jack swallowed. 'Oh, man. We're in for a ride on this one.'

And, right then, it happened.

A deep grinding sound echoed from within the walls around them and abruptly, as the team looked out at the superlong maze, the whole immense square-shaped cavern *rotated*.

It was quite a sight.

The entire superlong maze—floor, walls and ceiling—*all rotated slowly to the left*, so that what, moments before, had been the left-hand wall was now the floor.

The effect was as shocking as it was sudden.

As the floor tilted quickly and passed through forty-five degrees, all the water that had poured into the floor's trenches from the waterfalls now sloshed wildly and, thanks to gravity, flooded downward, *as a wall of raging waves*, charging down through the trench-paths, bouncing off their many right-angled walls in an effort to settle on the new 'floor' of this cavern.

Then the giant unseen ancient gears that had caused the colossal rotation issued a deep muffled *clank* and the rotation ceased and the maze was still again.

'The only safe spots,' Jack said, 'appear to be the white block-houses. The rotation mechanism—the turning sequence—must be on a timer of some kind. You take refuge in a blockhouse and, from there, you figure out how you're going to get to the next blockhouse. But you only have a certain amount of time to navigate that section of the maze and get to the next blockhouse before the rotation mechanism kicks in again.'

Zoe said, 'And if you don't get to a blockhouse in time, you get washed down by the water. If you don't drown, you'll lose your bearings and become lost. If you get tipped out again by another rotation, you'll be hopelessly lost for good.'

Alby said, 'What about moving along the tops of the trenches?'

Lily shook her head. 'The builders of these kind of mazes tend not to like it when someone tries to cheat the system.'

Jack pointed at the nearest blockhouse, located a hundred metres into the maze, right in the centre.

'Okay, people. We don't have time to linger. Rastor and Sphinx are already moving through this maze. This is a test of memory and speed, under constant pressure. Look at the maze closely and find the correct route to that first blockhouse. We also need to time how often this thing rotates, because we'll have to get to each block-house before the next rotation occurs and hurls us off our feet.'

They observed the maze for the next thirty minutes.

Jack and Zoe used their stopwatches and, after three more colossal rotations—which brought the original 'floor' back to that position—they calculated that the massive elongated space rotated to the left approximately every ten minutes.

As they did this, Lily and Alby charted a course to the first blockhouse.

Once they were inside the trenches, they'd be working from memory, so they needed to know which way to turn at each intersection.

They came up with a system: at the first intersection in the trench-path, they deduced that they had to turn right, so they would call: 'One, right.' If at the second, they had to turn left, that would be 'Two, left.' And so on.

To get to the first blockhouse, for instance, there were sixteen turns to make, so Jack memorised the first four, Zoe the next four, Lily the next four and Alby the last four.

'All right, then,' Jack said. 'Time to make a run for it. Everybody ready? Good.'

And so they descended from the entry archway into the trench system and took on the four-sided maze.

★ ★ ★

TO THE FIRST BLOCKHOUSE

The trench system was tight and claustrophobic. Hard, grey and close.

The maze's massive side walls—over two hundred metres tall, the height of an office building—loomed high on both sides, shot through with snaking lines of trenches.

The floor on which they ran was covered in ankle-deep water that was slowly rising thanks to the waterfalls.

His boots splashing through the water, Jack raced through the trench-maze at speed.

The greystone walls blurred past him on either side.

He arrived at the first intersection.

Jack called, 'One: right!'

They all cut right.

At the next junction, he yelled, 'Two, left!' and they all jagged left.

As he ran, Jack realised that Zoe had been correct. Once you were inside it, the trench-maze was totally unnavigable. If you didn't have a plan to get through it, you'd get lost in no time. If you got thrown about by a sloshing wall of water during a rotation, you'd never get out.

And you'd die here.

After four intersections, Jack let Zoe take the lead and call the turns at the next four.

Lily took over next, then Alby for the last four.

After about nine minutes of running in this manner, they rounded a final corner and came to the first white blockhouse and dived into it . . .

. . . a bare second before the maze rotated.

It was a totally unbelievable feeling to be in the maze as it rolled.

It was both sickening and exhilarating at the same time.

The mighty grinding sound filled the air as unseen gears turned the vast space.

Safely inside the blockhouse, panting for breath, Jack and his team braced themselves against its walls as the whole structure around them rotated ninety degrees.

Out through the blockhouse's slit windows, they could see the maze rolling—could see the falling water of the waterfalls seem to change direction: now, instead of falling down the faces of the side walls, they fell vertically from the ceiling, slamming into the trenches that were now the floor.

Of course, gravity hadn't changed: it was the space that had rolled. The sides were now the ceiling and floor.

And then, with a resounding *clank*, the grinding and the movement stopped—and now Jack's blockhouse was mounted *sideways* on the right-side wall and they could see the next section of the maze ahead.

'Alby, Lily, did you figure out the way to the next blockhouse?' Jack asked.

'Sure did,' Lily said.

'Okay, while we're stuck here high up on the wall,' Jack said, 'see if you can map out the way to the blockhouses after that. When our wall becomes the floor again, we have to be ready to run again.'

★ ★ ★

As the group waited for the maze to rotate favourably again, how-ever, they saw something.

They saw two of Rastor's Serbian troops—evidently separated from their boss—poke their heads up out of the (current) floor of the trench-maze, trying to steal a peek at the route ahead.

In response, two red orbs immediately dropped from the ceil-ing above them, sailed down across the space, and landed in their trench right near them.

Two shocking blasts followed.

Twin fireballs filled their trench, lighting it up and obliterating the two Serbians.

Lily turned to Alby: 'That's why you don't go out of the trenches.'

They waited for the next rotation, but when it came, they didn't make a break for it.

That was because when the rotation occurred, their side wall turned *up* not down, and became the *roof* of the cavern, and every-one tumbled wildly inside the blockhouse and, with a scream, Lily fell toward the slit window and tumbled out through it . . .

. . . Alby dived full-length across the blockhouse and caught Lily's outstretched hand at the very last second while clutching the rim of the slit window with his artificial hand.

As the rotation completed itself, and their blockhouse went completely upside down, Lily screamed, dangling out the window two hundred metres above the floor of the maze.

Jack and Zoe hurried to help Alby and the three of them hauled Lily inside.

Now they were all sitting on the inverted ceiling of the blockhouse, with nowhere to go until the maze rotated again.

They used the time to confirm the routes for the next two runs: including to the next blockhouse, which had a diagonal footbridge stretching out from it to the next wall.

When the maze turned again, they bolted, making their way along the *wall* of the maze.

It was tough going. Zigging and zagging, climbing and crawling, they moved as well as they could along what was now the wall, wending their way through the trench-maze, arriving at the side-turned blockhouse with the diagonal bridge extending from it.

They arrived at it, diving through its door just as the maze turned again and they all huddled against the walls.

But as the rotation paused, they found themselves on the floor again, so Jack urged them not to stop and to keep going to the next blockhouse.

In short, it was hard work, and it required all of their attention, speed and energy. Sometimes they had to think quickly and move fast, at others they had to wait.

At one point when they stopped inside a blockhouse, Jack peered down the full length of the maze.

It stretched away into infinity, mind-bogglingly complex.

Every now and then, he glimpsed the moving flashlights of Rastor's and Sphinx's teams up ahead, moving steadily onward.

Jack checked the time.

It was 5:00 p.m. local time, 28 December.

'We've been going for over twelve hours now and it's going to take us many more to get through this thing. The Omega Event is going to occur at 3:06 a.m. GMT on 29 December. That's 5:06 a.m. local time.'

Zoe looked at her watch. 'So we have another twelve hours, that's all?'

'That's all,' Jack said. 'Twelve hours to get to the Death Throne. Sphinx wants to sit on it, while Rastor wins if he destroys it or if he *stops* anyone else sitting on it.'

He took a deep breath as he looked at the others.

'Keep going, everyone. We can't stop, no matter how tired we are. We can sleep after we've saved the universe.'

And so they progressed through the deadly rotating maze.

At times they made swift progress.

They even managed to get through a few rotations while standing *on* some of the diagonal bridges.

That was Zoe's idea, as a way to speed up their travel.

They would clamber along an *upward*-sloping diagonal bridge, and then, as the maze around them turned, its mighty gears grinding, they would stop, balancing carefully in the middle of the diagonal bridge.

Then the maze would rotate and the bridge would go from upwardly sloping to downwardly sloping. When the turning stopped, they would just keep running down it, onto the new 'floor'.

But more often, their progress was slow and they would only manage to make a short hop from one blockhouse to the next.

At other times, they made an error and had to hurry back to the previous blockhouse, so they didn't get stranded out in the open-topped trenches.

And then there were the occasions when they found themselves on a wall, where progress was extra difficult and slow, crawling and walking on the shelf-like walls of the trenches.

And, of course, there were those times when the rotation of the maze brought their blockhouse to the ceiling: at those times, they had no choice but to stay put inside the fully upside-down block-house till the next turn of the maze.

About five more hours in, they were working their way along a side wall when suddenly the maze not only turned sooner than anticipated, it turned *upward not downward*, and they were still twenty metres short of the next blockhouse.

As their side wall went up instead of down, it tilted their trench sickeningly, as if to tip them out of it, and Jack realised they were screwed.

They were all going to fall—almost two hundred metres—if not to their deaths, then scattered into the waterfilled maze.

He quickly yelled an order to Alby, then another to Zoe and Lily before—

—a second later, their previously vertical side wall went fully upside down.

If anyone had been there to see it, they would have stared in wonder.

Two hundred metres above the floor of the cavern, Jack and Alby hung from their upside-down trench—*one-handed*, by the fingertips of their titanium artificial left hands—with Zoe and Lily dangling from *their* waists.

At Jack's command, Jack and Alby had used their titanium fists to quickly punch shallow fingerholds into the stone wall of their trench, deep enough to get a grip.

And then Zoe had grabbed onto Jack's waist and Lily had clutched onto Alby's.

And so, as the trench came fully upside down, they hung there, dangling high above the maze, their feet swinging, waiting for the next rotation.

It was a feat no person with regular hands could do.

But Jack and Alby's titanium fingers weren't regular. In addition to being superhard, thanks to their mechanical servos, they were also superstrong, and they clamped onto their fingerholds with vice-like intensity until a few minutes later when, with a great groaning, the maze turned once more and their roof became a wall again and they all tumbled onto the side-wall of the trench, itself now a shelf once more.

They then hustled for the next blockhouse, dived into it, and, safe once again, gasped for air.

Alby turned to Jack, raising his titanium left hand. It was, after all, Jack's old one which he'd given to Alby after the incident with

Jaeger Eins and Dion and the filament weapon.

'This thing is awesome,' Alby said. 'Best second-hand hand in the world.'

'Better believe it,' Jack said. 'When Wizard built it for me twenty years ago, he promised it would be better than the hand I was born with. Turns out, it is.'

During that break, Lily figured out the rotation sequence.

'Oh, I see it now.' She gestured at the original symbol.

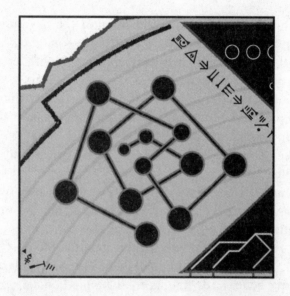

'This image represents the sequence of rotations, but it's tricky. The angles between the lines represent the *direction* of each rotation: see how some go to the left and some go right. But the *length* of each line shows the *duration* between each rotation: see how some are longer than others. That's how we got caught.'

Jack said, 'It looks like you got it figured out now. I'm so glad you guys caught up with me. There's literally no way I could have made it through this thing without you.'

Onward they went, through the long, rotating maze.

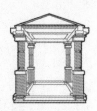

THE SECRET ROYAL WORLD III

THE NEW YORK OBELISK AND THE D.C. RENDEZVOUS

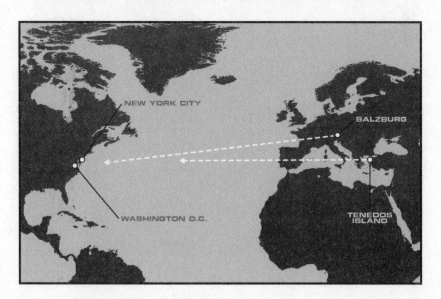

And he who was seated on the throne said,
Behold, I am making all things new.

BOOK OF REVELATION 21:5

TENEDOS ISLAND
AEGEAN SEA NEAR THE TURKISH COAST
27 DECEMBER, 0955 HOURS (LOCAL TIME)
36 HOURS EARLIER

Iolanthe, Nobody and Bertie stood in the darkness of the vault of Troy listening to Chloe's voice coming from a speaker in the darkness.

'. . . *Unfortunately for you, my people have already come and gone through this vault and found the information we needed. The answer is London, by the way. It's time your mission ended, you spoilt little rich girl. It's time for you to die. Ta-ta.*'

Then, a minute later, the colossal explosion ripped through the vault, destroying it and leaving no-one alive inside it.

In that minute, however, a lot happened.

A ring of red pilot lights blazed to life all around them: the pilot lights of twelve Semtex explosive packages wired together.

A shrill beep echoed out from the middle wad and Nobody leapt into action.

A former Navy man turned oceanographer and treasure hunter, he knew these kinds of explosives: they were sequential demolition charges, all connected by wires to a central control unit. He dived for the middle wad, jammed his finger down on the detonation switch and kept it depressed.

And nothing happened.

Iolanthe froze.

Bertie froze.

'What just happened? Or didn't?' Bertie asked.

Nobody gasped. 'I just stopped these bad boys from going off. Only there's a problem.'

'What?'

'I can't release this switch,' Nobody said. 'As soon as I lift my finger off it, all these Semtex wads will go off and they'll be mopping us off the walls and floor.'

Iolanthe gazed into his eyes. 'Oh, God.'

'Iolanthe,' Nobody added, 'it's more than likely Chloe left people to watch this place from somewhere outside, to make sure the explosives go off. They're probably on a boat offshore. If we go out, they'll kill us. If there's no explosion, someone is almost certainly going to come in here to make sure we're dead. You two have to get the information you need and get out. Then I'll release this switch and, well . . .'

Iolanthe swallowed. 'And die.'

'Yeah.'

A long silence followed.

It was Bertie who broke it. He had been looking up at the giant statue of Priam.

'Io, my sweet. I know how to overcome this situation.'

'How?'

'You two will leave—via Aeneas's door—and I will stay.'

'And die in the explosion?' Iolanthe said. 'Bertie, no . . .'

'I'm old, child,' Bertie said, gazing fondly at her. 'My life is all but over anyway. And you two make such a lovely couple. It'd be a shame to cut short your time together.'

'But—'

'No buts, girl!' Bertie snapped. Then, in one swift movement, he shoved Nobody away from the control unit, sliding his own finger onto the detonation switch as he did.

'Focus!' he barked. 'Look up there now. At Priam's Crown. At the inscription written on it in the Trojan tongue. That tells you the location of the Blue Bell. What does it say?'

Iolanthe blinked, trying to switch from emotional despair to academic focus. 'Er, well, it reads: "*The Blue Bell resides within the body of one of the two great Heliopolitan stone spires, the one that gives all life forever.*"'

Nobody said, 'What are the two great Heliopolitan stone spires?'

Iolanthe swapped a look with Bertie. 'Cleopatra's Needles. The two obelisks that once stood in Heliopolis but which now stand in London and New York.'

'Yes,' Bertie said.

Iolanthe added, 'They were both built by the pharaoh Thuthmoses III—a name, incidentally, that means Son of Thoth. The Blue Bell must be embedded inside one of them.'

'But which obelisk is the correct one? New York or London?' Nobody asked. 'Chloe said she went to London.'

Iolanthe nodded. 'She did . . . but that was a mistake.'

Iolanthe glanced at Bertie again, like a student addressing a teacher. 'The clue is in the final phrase: *the one that gives all life forever.*'

'It is,' Bertie nodded.

'It's the New York obelisk.'

'I think so, too.'

Iolanthe grinned. '*Chloe's going to the wrong obelisk.*'

'That she is,' Bertie said. 'Now, go. Run! You must flee from here immediately so our enemies think you're dead.'

'Oh, Bertie . . .'

'I have lived my life. Go and save the world, child, and live yours.'

Iolanthe gave the round-faced old monk a final embrace.

As they parted, Bertie pointed to a statue at the rear of the chamber: a tall statue of the goddess Athena.

'It's been a while since I read Virgil's *Aeneid*, but as I recall, the secret passage that Aeneas used to flee from Troy during the chaos at the end of the Trojan War lay behind a statue of Athena.'

Iolanthe hurried over to it and, sure enough, the huge statue was

a door and it swung open on an ancient hinge to reveal a rough-walled passageway behind it.

As Nobody joined her in the doorway, Iolanthe gave Bertie one last look.

'I love you, Bertie. I won't forget this.'

'I love you, too, my little moon of Jupiter,' Bertie said. 'Now go. In five seconds, I'll lift my finger from this detonation switch.'

Nobody and Iolanthe raced down the exit tunnel, running for all they were worth.

Five seconds later, a massive explosion rocked the passageway around them.

Bertie and the vault of Troy and all its incredible, priceless contents, were no more.

On a hilltop a mile away from the Zampieri estate, a lone spotter left behind by Chloe saw the explosion shake the landscape and blow out the doors of the boathouse.

The spotter rang Chloe's secure sat-phone number and reported this.

Chloe Carnarvon said, '*About fucking time. I've been delayed here in Salzburg. There's been an issue with the royal banker. But with Iolanthe dead, there's no hurry with the Blue Bell now. We don't need to have it before the Omega Event, just after, so I'll go to London tomorrow.*'

'Yes, ma'am.' The spotter hung up and departed.

He never saw Iolanthe and Nobody emerge from within the estate's main mansion thirty minutes later and flee in one of the servants' cars.

It took them a whole day of travel, but Iolanthe and Nobody eventually found their way to the Turkish mainland.

Their goal was to find a plane of some sort, any plane that could get them to New York City fast.

Ironically, they found one at a small provincial airport near Hisarlik, the town that tourists from around the world visit believing it to be the site of the fabled city of Troy.

They stole a private jet from that airport—a sleek Gulfstream IV—and took off immediately for New York City.

As night fell, Nobody put the plane on autopilot and joined Iolanthe in the main cabin.

She sat with her eyes closed, clearly still thinking about Bertie and coming to terms with his sacrifice.

When she looked up at Nobody, her cheeks were wet with tears.

Nobody handed her a tissue and as she wiped her eyes, he said, 'You gotta bring me up to speed here. You said Chloe was going to the wrong obelisk. Care to tell me why?'

'We caught a break,' Iolanthe said. 'Not a big one, it might only amount to an hour or so, but a break nonetheless. Chloe is going to smash open the obelisk in London, but it's the wrong one.'

'How so?'

'The crucial clue to finding the Blue Bell was in that final line of the inscription on Priam's crown: the Blue Bell is embedded inside the obelisk *that gives all life forever*.

'The two obelisks in London and New York were built by the Egyptian pharaoh Thuthmoses III and they are identical. Thuthmoses inscribed both of them with a dizzying array of hieroglyphs that are exactly the same. Except for one tiny detail that only a handful of people in the world know. Both inscriptions conclude with the description of the pharaoh as "Son of the Sun, Thuthmoses III", only the New York obelisk has one extra line. It finishes with: "Son of the Sun, Thuthmoses III, *who giveth all life forever.*"'

Iolanthe gave Nobody a hard look.

'When she finds nothing inside the London obelisk, Chloe's going to realise that she went to the wrong one. We need to fly directly to New York as fast as we can and go to the correct obelisk, the one in Central Park, and extract the Blue Bell from it before she realises her error.'

And so they flew across the Atlantic Ocean in the sleek private jet.

They took turns sleeping, to regather their energy.

Hours passed.

When they were a few hours out of New York, Nobody checked the flight patterns around the eastern seaboard of the United States.

What he saw disturbed him.

He walked back into the main cabin to wake Iolanthe but he found her already awake, staring out the window at the night sky.

'There's no air traffic at all over any of the major cities on the east coast: New York, Boston, Philly, D.C.,' he said. 'Zero chatter on the airwaves, too. Even the air-traffic controllers have gone silent.'

'What, oh . . .' Iolanthe said, distracted.

'Hey. You okay?' Nobody asked gently.

Iolanthe turned to face him. 'I was just thinking about what Chloe said to me, about what I've become.'

'What do you mean?' Nobody sat down across from her.

'For as long as I can remember, my whole life has been about looks and appearances, money and power. I really have been a spoilt bitch for a long time.'

Nobody nodded.

He looked at Iolanthe's shaven head and wounded nose.

'People can change, you know,' he said. 'And it looks to me like you've changed quite a bit. I mean, I've only ever known this version of you and, well, I mean, I like it.'

He shifted uncomfortably. 'I mean, hey, if we somehow survive this and the universe doesn't end, maybe, I don't know, I could take you out for dinner or coffee or something?'

Iolanthe raised her eyebrows. 'Are you asking me out on a date?'

'Well, yeah.'

Iolanthe shook her head. 'I don't deserve a guy like you. You're smart, you're nice, you're well above average in the looks department. Christ, you're wealthy, too. This is what I'm saying. All I've ever known are rich dukes and princes—'

Nobody smiled. 'Yes, but I don't live through my money. It just helps me do what I like to do. I still go to the supermarket and buy groceries; hell, I even buy Pepsi instead of Coke when it's on special. I doubt your royal rich boys ever set foot in a supermarket.'

'That's true.'

Nobody leaned forward, looked her squarely in the eyes. 'I won't lie. It's hard to change. But the first step is to acknowledge who you *used to be* and then decide to be different. Looks like you've been doing exactly that.'

Iolanthe rubbed her shaved head. 'But look at me . . .'

'I told you once, I like this look. It's got a cool punk-rocker vibe to it. More than that, it's *you*: you reduced to your pure self. No make-up, no manicures, no groomed eyebrows, not even any hair. This is as authentic as someone can get and I'm okay with that.'

Iolanthe shook her head again. 'Like I said, I really don't deserve a guy like you. But if we get out of this alive, I'll go on that date.'

Nobody smiled.

An hour or so later, with only a few hours till the Omega Event, they began their descent into New York.

NEW YORK CITY, U.S.A.
28 DECEMBER, 1900 HOURS (LOCAL TIME)
[29 DECEMBER, 0300 HOURS IN THE
LABYRINTH]
TWO HOURS AND SIX MINUTES TILL OMEGA

John F. Kennedy Airport, usually one of the busiest airports in the world, lay eerily deserted as Nobody's and Iolanthe's jet touched down on one of its runways.

Night had fallen, but the city that never sleeps was dark and silent.

Nobody and Iolanthe sprinted out of the plane and helped themselves to a nearby charter helicopter—a nice fast Bell Jet Ranger—which Nobody immediately flew toward the famous skyline of New York City.

They boomed over Queens, sweeping low over the freeways and flyovers that led to Manhattan.

Normally at this time of day, those thoroughfares would be clogged with slow-moving traffic.

Today, they were jammed—with countless cars, cabs, trucks and vans—but there was nothing normal about it.

There was no movement.

All the vehicles on the roads were still.

They lay askew or pushed up against each other, banked on the kerbs, or just sitting where they had been when the Siren bell had been rung here.

As their helicopter shot over the steel towers of the Williamsburg Bridge, Iolanthe and Nobody saw hundreds of cars frozen at all angles on the bridge, more victims of the bell.

And then their chopper was rushing through the canyons of New York City—with buildings on either side of it and empty streets below—before it burst out into open space above the wide green expanse of Central Park.

Nobody banked the chopper around, bringing it to the middle part of the park over by Fifth Avenue, and the giant flat building that was the Metropolitan Museum of Art.

Behind the Met, they saw it.

It rose above the trees, a great stone thing, grey and pitted, slender and tall; an ancient object truly out of time and place in this most modern of cities.

The New York Obelisk.

Cleopatra's Needle.

How the towering granite obelisk came to New York City in 1881 was a story in itself.

Just getting it from the docks on the Hudson River over to Central Park had been a herculean effort requiring specially made railway tracks, bridges and custom-designed lifting cranes.

A gift to the United States from the Khedive of Egypt, the obelisk had suffered in the modern polluted air of New York City. Even though it was cleaned often, soot and exhaust fumes had caked it in a layer of urban grime.

Nobody hovered their chopper beside the seventy-foot-tall obelisk. 'Okay,' he said, 'what do we do now?'

Iolanthe shrugged. 'The inscription on Priam's crown said the Blue Bell was inside the obelisk. I suppose we knock it over, even if history would frown on us for doing so.'

'That thing must weigh two hundred tons,' Nobody said. 'Okay, I got this.'

He edged the chopper toward the peak of the obelisk and, slowly and gradually, pressed forward on the throttle, causing the chopper's landing struts to push against the upper section of the stone spire . . .

. . . and the obelisk tilted . . .

. . . and fell.

It toppled like a tree before slamming down against the paved viewing area around its podium with a colossal *whump!* It was so heavy, it cracked the pavement as it struck it.

Nobody then landed the chopper beside the now horizontal obelisk and Iolanthe raced over to it, to discover that the heavy landing had also cracked the obelisk in a couple of weak spots.

Near its base, a crevice had appeared and Iolanthe grabbed a wrench from the chopper and used it to smash away at the crevice's edges, to reveal a hollow section inside the obelisk . . .

. . . where she found something wrapped in ancient bandages.

Something spherical.

The size of a basketball.

As Nobody watched, Iolanthe unwrapped the bandaging, revealing a stunningly beautiful thing.

A sphere made of brilliant blue metal.

The metal was perfectly crafted, with not a blemish or imperfection on it. It shone with a dull sheen that was clearly beyond the knowledge of humankind.

And it bore a small round hole in its base.

It was a bell, an ancient bell.

The Blue Bell.

Nobody grinned. 'We're back in this game—'

The roar of helicopters bursting out from behind some nearby skyscrapers cut him off.

Two military attack choppers.

A speaker on one of them squawked and Chloe Carnarvon's voice bellowed from it.

'Iolanthe! My, you are resilient. I see you've found the Blue Bell. But now there is nowhere else for you to run! I'll take that bell from you, thank you very much!'

Nobody and Iolanthe ran for their chopper, with Iolanthe clutching the Blue Bell in her arms.

While Nobody and Iolanthe had been zooming toward New York, Pooh Bear and Stretch's team had also been heading toward America, in a new plane they had acquired when they'd finally reached Marseille: an Air France 737.

They, however, were heading for Washington, D.C., to the main royal rendezvous point.

It was early evening and most of the lights in the plane were off.

With Pooh and Stretch were Dr Tracy Smith—expert on the Siren bells and the ear specialist who had devised the serum that reversed the sleep they caused—and Sister Lynda Fadel from the Order of Serene Maidens, the modern name for the Vestal sisterhood.

Plus, of course, their captive, the royal banker, Sir John Marren, who sat in a seat in the first class cabin, his wrists and ankles flex-cuffed.

The wealthy and powerful royal banker had spent the earlier part of the flight threatening and glowering at the team, but now he was asleep.

Pooh Bear sat alone in the cockpit of the darkened plane, keeping watch on the autopilot while the others remained in the first class section, taking turns sleeping and covering Marren.

Pooh Bear didn't mind. He'd always found it hard to sleep in the dry air of planes anyway.

As he sat alone in the cockpit, he pulled out a paperback

novel—Isaac Asimov's classic science fiction tale, *Foundation*—and by the glow of an overhead light started reading it.

It was an old copy. Pooh had read and enjoyed it many times.

He'd been reading for about thirty minutes when a voice from behind him said, 'You like Asimov, huh?'

It was Tracy Smith, standing in the doorway.

'I can't sleep,' she added. 'Never could on planes. It's something to do with the dry air. Mind if I join you?'

'Please. By all means,' Pooh said.

She slid into the copilot's seat beside him and gazed out at the gorgeous star-filled sky.

'You like sci-fi?' she asked.

'Why, I love all science fiction, but Asimov the most. He's simply marvellous. So imaginative. But this one, *Foundation*, is my favourite. I read it every few years, plus all the sequels. Have you read any of his books?'

'Sure. All of 'em. Including that one. Why is it your favourite?'

Pooh thought about that. 'I suppose because it's about the triumph of knowledge over force, wisdom over brute strength. I came from a family where strength was favoured over knowledge—my older brother was a terrible bully who beat me often, especially for studying. But when I retreated to my room and read this book as a boy, it nourished me, gave me hope. Which is your favourite?'

Tracy looked at him for a moment. It was an odd, almost penetrating stare.

Then she said, 'My favourite book in the *Foundation* series is the second one, the one where the Mule appears.'

'Ah, the Mule! What is it you like about him?' Pooh asked, interested.

Tracy said, 'I like that he's a mathematical anomaly. A true outlier who comes along and foils—at least for a time—Hari Seldon's mathematical plan. Life is full of random people and events like that and I thought Asimov wrote about that brilliantly.'

'You're so right,' Pooh said. 'The Mule is a wonderful creation.

A truly complex villain. Totally unique in fiction, one of Asimov's finest inventions. What did you think of the way Asimov . . .'

And so, by the dim glow of that reading light, the two of them chatted for the next few hours about books, reading and science fiction novels.

As they did, they didn't realise that they were being watched . . .

. . . not by any enemy, but by their friends, Stretch and Sister Lynda, back in the first class cabin.

Lynda was, quite simply, thunderstruck.

'They've been talking *for three hours*!' she whispered excitedly to Stretch. 'In all the time I've known her, I never saw Tracy talk to a man for more than three minutes. I mean, look at her, she's beautiful—slim and gorgeous—so all her life guys have approached her to chat her up. But she always had a rule: if they didn't ask her a question about herself or her opinion on something within the first minute, she would end the conversation then and there.'

'How did that go?' Stretch asked.

'Let's be honest, Benjamin, most guys talk about themselves. Not many of her conversations lasted long.'

Stretch laughed softly. He nodded at Pooh Bear. 'Well, she's in for a new experience, because my buddy up there is the last true gentleman on Earth. There's no human male on this planet who is more polite, courteous and conversationally generous than he is.'

'Is he single?'

Stretch laughed. 'To his mother's eternal anguish, yes, he is. He just never found the right girl.'

They continued to watch Tracy and Pooh Bear converse animatedly.

Lynda sighed. 'Who knows, maybe he *has* found the right one now. Be a shame if the world ended.'

At that moment, very suddenly, the plane's engines roared, thrusting unexpectedly, and the whole airliner banked wildly to the right.

Alarms sounded.

Anything not tied down went tumbling to the floor.

Then the engines roared again and the Air France 737 tilted the other way.

Staggering to keep his balance, Stretch raced up to the cockpit.

'What's going on?' he asked.

Pooh was leaning back in his seat, his eyes wide.

In front of him, the plane's steering yoke was moving *all by itself*.

Then the plane levelled off and began flying in a more settled way again.

Pooh scanned the dashboard, checking all the dials and indicators, his hands still held high, off the steering yoke.

'We've been hacked,' he said ominously. 'They found us. They finally found us. This plane is now being flown remotely by someone else. Somehow our friend Mr Marren must have alerted his people to his situation and whereabouts.'

He swallowed deeply, gave Stretch a long hard look.

'We're now being taken to wherever they want to take us.'

**RAVEN ROCK MOUNTAIN COMPLEX (SITE R)
BLUE RIDGE SUMMIT, PENNSYLVANIA
28 DECEMBER, 1900 HOURS (LOCAL TIME)
[29 DECEMBER, 0300 HOURS IN THE
LABYRINTH]**

An hour later, its landing lights blazing in the night, the Air France 737 landed on a military runway in rural Pennsylvania, in the lee of a grim low mountain dotted with skeletal trees.

The big airliner landed of its own accord, guided by an unknown pilot flying it remotely.

It rolled to a halt in the darkness.

Floodlights lit up the runway all around it, illuminating a bunker-like concrete tunnel that delved into the heart of the mountain.

The floodlights also revealed the forces waiting for the plane: ten armed Delta Force commandos and a formation of at least two hundred bronzemen, all standing to attention.

At the head of the regiment of bronzemen was a Knight of the Golden Eight.

Pooh Bear, Stretch, Tracy and Lynda looked out at them nervously from the airliner's cockpit.

Suddenly a voice barked from their radio: '*Send out Sir John! Then come out with your hands up or you will be fired upon!*'

They did as they were told.

They cut the royal banker's flex cuffs and opened the forward door for him to leave.

As he stopped in the doorway, massaging his wrists, Sir John Marren said, 'I do hope you all remember what I told you earlier. Screaming and begging.'

With a final snort, he exited the plane, joining the armed commandos on the floodlit tarmac.

Then, with deep breaths, Pooh, Stretch, Tracy and Lynda disembarked behind him, stepping out into the chilly night air with their hands raised above their heads.

As he stepped out of the plane and stood atop the airstairs that had been rolled up to it, Stretch gazed at the landscape around them.

The stark mountain rose above the airstrip, a bulky shadow against the night sky. The trees on it were leafless and bare. The concrete tunnel disappeared into its base.

They'd been brought to Raven Rock, as he'd suspected.

Raven Rock—or Site R as it was known in government circles—was part of America's 'Continuity of Government' plan in the event of war, a terrorist attack or a nuclear strike.

Like Cheyenne Mountain in Colorado, it could operate as a remote version of the Pentagon, controlling and coordinating U.S. forces all around the world, while also accommodating over three thousand people in its vast underground complex.

Rumour had it that a network of road tunnels connected Raven Rock to nearby Camp David and from there reached all the way to the Pentagon down in D.C.

The four heroes descended the airstairs, walking slowly toward the ring of Delta Force commandos.

Stretch eyed the Golden Knight in front of the rows of bronzemen, noting the ring of command that he wore on his right hand.

'Well, I just gotta say it,' Lynda said to Stretch, 'you were right. The Mossad taught you well, Benjamin, made you a good predicter of human behaviour.'

Stretch kept scanning the area, especially one thing.

'Thanks Lynda, although I was kind of hoping I'd be wrong. What do you say, Pooh?'

Pooh Bear turned to face him. 'Benjamin, my friend, you called it. You figured Marren would have some kind of panic button on his person and that they'd hack our plane to retrieve him. And also that they'd bring him here.'

'You ready to rock?' Stretch asked.

'Oh, hell, yes,' Pooh said.

'The explosives are all set?'

'Affirmative.'

'Then let's get this party started,' Stretch said. 'Do it.'

At those words, Pooh Bear flicked the remote concealed in the palm of his left hand and—

BOOOOOM!

—a terrific explosion ripped apart the airliner behind them!

So powerful was the blast that the whole 737 was lifted momentarily off the ground. It cracked in its middle as a star-shaped burst of fire wrenched it open from within.

The ten Delta commandos recoiled from the blast, instinctively turning their bodies away . . .

. . . as Pooh, Stretch, Tracy and Lynda whipped out the guns they had hidden in the backs of their waistbands, raised them and started firing as they initiated one last-ditch plan.

THE RED SEA COAST
29 DECEMBER, 0330 HOURS

While all this was happening in America, another battle was taking place in Egypt: a surprise attack on the temporary airstrip that Jaeger Eins's forces had set up on the Red Sea coast a short distance from where the Life Throne had risen up from the sea.

The attack was both brutal and one-sided.

A Russian Werewolf attack chopper—flown by Rufus and Sky Monster—rained hell down on the various trucks, jeeps and aircraft at the airstrip.

Anything parked in sight was destroyed, blown to smithereens.

Aloysius Knight and Easton sat behind Rufus and Sky Monster in the Werewolf.

'Yee-ha!' Aloysius yelled as he blazed away with a cannon.

With the Knights' main force over on the oil rig now gone, the men back here at the base were leaderless and they fled into the desert, some in cars, others on foot.

By the time the smoke cleared, everything at the base was on fire.

There were so many plumes of smoke and they were so dense, that the sooty black haze blotted out the stars in the sky.

Aloysius nodded with satisfaction. 'Take that, motherfuckers.'

He turned to the others.

'I just hope Jack's still alive inside the Labyrinth.'

Sky Monster scanned the wreckage of the airstrip and nodded to himself.

'I've known Jack a long time,' he said. 'Met him in a really nasty part of the world. The first thing he ever did for me was save my ass. If I could pick anyone to step up now and save us all, it'd be Jack West Jr.'

A MAN NAMED JACK

PART IV

BASRA, 1991

'Well, would you look at that? If it isn't Jack West . . .'
[Kallis] said. 'I haven't seen you since Iraq in '91. You
know, West, my superiors still don't know how you got
away from that SCUD base outside Basra. There musta
been three hundred Republican Guards at that facility
and yet you got away . . .'

THE SEVEN ANCIENT WONDERS P. 72
(MACMILLAN, SYDNEY, 2005)

Jack's Message from the Other Side continued:

For many years now, I've worn my trusty helmet.

I got it in unusual circumstances: saw some guys in New York impersonating a firetruck crew and one of them dropped it. I kept it—at least at first—as a reminder not to trust anyone at first glance.

But as time went by, I came to love my battered FDNY helmet. It's accompanied me on many adventures and saved my head numerous times.

I've also grown to see it in a new and, I think, better light.

You see, the professionals who put on helmets like mine—the real firefighters of this world—wear them for the sole purpose of protecting others. There is no other use for it.

It is worn by those who run toward the danger with the sole goal of helping regular people.

This, in the end, is what has driven me my whole life.

I don't seek fame or fortune, promotion or power. I just want to see the regular people of the world—mums and dads, kids and grandparents—be able to live their lives, love their families and chase their dreams without some entitled king or emperor or whatever ruling over them.

That's what my helmet means to me.

BASRA, IRAQ
OPERATION DESERT STORM
MARCH 1991

The mission had gone to hell in a handcart.

Deep behind enemy lines, having just taken out a SCUD base, Jack had been separated from his American Delta Force teammates.

He was on foot and fleeing for his life from three hundred members of the Republican Guard, the only part of the Iraqi Army worth anything.

They were killers and they desperately wanted to capture a Western special ops soldier and drag his body behind a jeep through the streets of Basra, preferably while he was still alive.

Two hundred metres ahead of him, he could see his American colleagues running for the LZ. Beyond them, in the sky, he saw two inbound rescue choppers.

Fucking Delta, he thought.

Missions with Americans were always a toss-up.

The Marines and Rangers were great: they were reliable.

But not Delta. Delta guys were only ever in it for themselves. If there was credit to be taken, they grabbed it. But if a mission went to shit, they left you for dead to take care of yourself and also to take the blame.

And this Delta team had been led by the biggest and most selfish asshole of them all, a dead-eyed operator named Cal Kallis.

When it turned out that the SCUD base had been guarded by a heretofore unknown battalion of Republican Guards, Kallis and his

Delta shits had bolted, leaving Jack—their forward scout—alone.

Fuck, fuck, fuck.

Jack was due west of Basra, in undulating scrubland on the edge of the open desert.

To his left was an abandoned Iraqi airfield, covered in decades of sand and rust.

Jack raced after the Delta team. He might still catch up to them before the choppers lifted off.

Bullets from his pursuers zinged past his head and he dived to the ground, getting a mouthful of sand for his trouble.

When he looked up, he heard the *whump-whump-whump* of helicopter rotors, close now.

The first rescue chopper landed and Kallis and his Delta shit-heads boarded it. The second chopper hovered overhead, covering the first.

Jack knew it was a long shot to get there in time but he forced himself to get up and run—

—just as a shoulder-launched missile shoomed low over his head, fired from somewhere on the desert plain behind him, and slammed into the second hovering helicopter!

Explosion.

Smoke.

The chopper lurched in the air, engines screaming, trailing a death-plume of black smoke, and it crashed in a heap at the end of the abandoned airfield's runway only fifty metres from Jack.

Jack looked from the crashed chopper to the other one and his eyes met those of Cal Kallis, standing in its side door.

Kallis just turned away and ordered his pilot to leave.

The door slid shut and the rescue chopper lifted off, departing into the glare of the rising sun.

Fucking Delta.

His pursuers then crested the horizon behind him: three hundred furious enemy troops.

Jack dashed over to the crashed chopper.

It was crumpled and burning.

The lead pilot was dead, impaled on the spiked edge of the broken windshield's frame.

The only other crew member groaned. The copilot. He was bleeding badly, but alive.

Jack grabbed him, threw him into a fireman's carry and hauled ass to the only place he could go: the hangars of the abandoned Iraqi airfield.

He grunted as he ran.

The copilot was a big guy, heavy as shit.

Jack kicked open the door to the hangar, peered inside and halted in surprise.

In addition to the usual rats, cockroaches and spiders, there was something else in here.

A plane.

A big plane.

A glistening white, brand-spanking-new, perfectly clean Boeing 747 with ISLAMIC REPUBLIC OF IRAQ emblazoned on its side.

It was a beautiful thing and totally out of place here in the scrub-land wastes outside Basra.

'Okay, I wasn't expecting that,' Jack said aloud.

It turned out that this was a very secret place, known only to an elite few in Saddam Hussein's inner circle, and this was a very secret plane: one of Saddam's own personal escape planes.

It's my escape plane now, Jack thought.

The aircrew stationed here—like most of the Iraqi Army—must have fled as the U.S. tanks rumbled into Basra.

As he climbed the airstairs, heaving under the weight of the chubby helicopter copilot, the unconscious man woke.

'What the—where am I?' he said.

The accent was unmistakable. New Zealand.

Jack put the Kiwi copilot down in the doorway of the plane.

The guy had a big beard, a round face and wide kind eyes.

Jack said, 'You got shot down covering some Delta pricks who then left without you.'

'What about my—'

'He didn't make it. I'm sorry. Do you know how to fly a 747?'

'If it's got wings, I can fly it,' the chubby copilot said determinedly.

Minutes later, as the three hundred–strong force of Republican Guards charged into the hangar with their guns blazing, the giant plane rumbled out of it, blasting right through its flimsy hangar doors.

It raced out into the twilight, powered up and took to the air, safe and away.

In the cockpit, the Kiwi pilot turned to Jack.

'Hey, thanks for the rescue, especially since it was supposed to be us rescuing you.'

'Don't mention it,' Jack said. 'What's your name?'

'The name's Ernie. Ernie Shepherd. But most people call me Sky Monster.'

'Jack West. Huntsman.'

'Nice to meet you, bro. Gotta say, this is a pretty sweet plane.'

It certainly was. It had offices, meeting rooms, a state-of-the-art communications centre, and even a plush bedroom at the back with its own bathroom and a gold toilet.

'I know,' Jack said. 'I think I'll keep it.'

Jack and Sky Monster would remain friends for the next twenty-five years.

Jack would also encounter Cal Kallis again, during his search for the Seven Wonders of the Ancient World.

Their final meeting would be a bloody hand-to-hand fight on a platform erected on the summit of the Great Pyramid during the almost cataclysmic Tartarus Rotation.

Jack would kill Kallis by hurling him off the top of the pyramid and through the blurring blades of a helicopter circling below them, dicing him into a thousand pieces.

A fitting end, all things considered.

**THE FINAL SECTION
OF THE
FOUR-SIDED MAZE**

THE FOUR-SIDED MAZE
29 DECEMBER, 0330 HOURS
96 MINUTES TILL OMEGA

After an entire day of nerve-jangling travel through the rotating maze, at last the end of it came into view for Jack and his team.

As they made their way down the superlong maze, they had kept pace with their rivals: Rastor and his last two men, and Sphinx with Cardinal Mendoza.

Rastor's group maintained their lead, staying about a hundred metres ahead of Jack's team the whole time.

It was different with Sphinx: Jack's team steadily gained on Sphinx and as the end of the maze came into sight, Jack's team was moving level with Sphinx's, albeit on opposite walls.

From his position on the right-hand wall, Jack gazed out at the end of the gargantuan maze.

At first it was just a hazy, darker section, but as he and the others came closer to it, Jack could see that the maze ended at a high pyramid-shaped hill of ornate steps that rose up the face of a sheer stone wall.

A single arched doorway stood at the summit of the hill right in the middle of the wall.

The only exit.

Importantly, Jack noted, as the maze rotated, this end section with the hill of stairs did not.

'Finally, solid ground,' he whispered.

Then suddenly he saw three figures race out of the final trenches of the maze and onto the open space in front of the pyramidal step-hill, and begin bounding up the stairs.

'It's Rastor!' Zoe exclaimed. 'Damn it, he's through the maze.'

Jack swore.

His team, up on the right-hand wall, still had a solid hundred metres of maze to go. And they needed to get onto the flat ground.

'We gotta pick up the pace,' he urged.

He looked out across the maze and saw Sphinx and Mendoza making their way along the opposite wall, level with him and his team.

'Lily, which way will the maze rotate next?'

'To the right,' Lily called from behind him. 'Clockwise.'

'That's better for us and worse for Sphinx,' Jack yelled. 'His wall will go upside down, so he'll have to take cover in a blockhouse, while ours will become the floor—we can stay in this trench and keep pressing onward. We'll be in front of him and right behind Rastor!'

They took off, racing as fast as they could through their wall-trench. They were twenty metres short of the next blockhouse when the giant maze groaned loudly, the precursor to a rotation.

'Move, everybody! Move, move!' Jack yelled.

They leapt headlong down a vertical trench of their wall-maze just as the maze began its colossal rotation—but then a huge gushing wave of sloshing water that none of them saw coming poured out of the flat section of the maze, leaping over the rim of the trenches as if searching for someone to drown, and it came smashing down in between them all, the force of the water sending Jack tumbling forward down one trench, toward the exit, while Zoe, Lily and Alby were hurled back down another, away from the exit.

Jack rolled to a stop and looked up.

He had been swept all the way down the last trench of the rotating maze and suddenly he was out of the infernal thing and standing at the base of the pyramidal hill of stairs rising up to the exit.

But he was alone again, out in front of his team.

He glimpsed Rastor reaching the summit of the hill and racing away through the archway there.

I can't let Rastor reach the second throne first, Jack thought. *He'll destroy it.*

He spun to check on the others, calling out, 'Zoe, you guys all right?'

'We're all okay! But we're gonna need a minute or two to get through these last few twists and turns,' Zoe shouted back.

'Rastor's getting away. I gotta go after him.'

'Go! We'll catch up!'

Jack took a deep breath.

Then, gasping and panting once again, he charged up the steep hill of stairs, determinedly chasing after the mad general.

As he arrived at the archway at the top of the hill, Zoe, Lily and Alby emerged from the maze.

'We're through, Jack!' Zoe called up to him. 'Coming up behind you.'

Jack took in the archway.

It yawned before him, high and dark. Every corner on it was sharp. Spikes rose from it like menacing horns.

He stepped through it . . .

. . . and found himself inside a short tunnel with a dim light coming from its far end.

Cautious, he ventured down the tunnel . . .

. . . and emerged in a high space—far higher than the rotating maze—and not for the first time inside the Supreme Labyrinth, Jack's breath caught in his throat at what he saw.

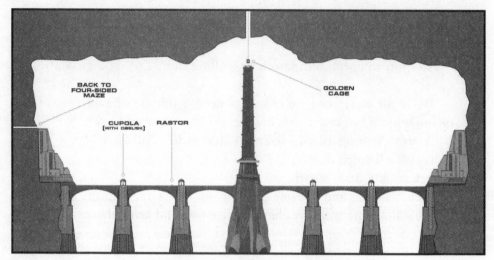

THE TOWER OF JUDGEMENT

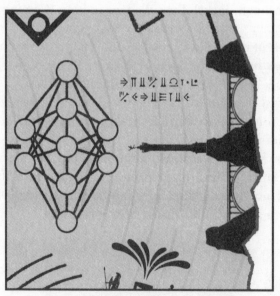

**THE TOWER OF JUDGEMENT
AS DEPICTED ON IMHOTEP'S SKULL**

THE BRIDGE TO THE TOWER OF JUDGEMENT
29 DECEMBER, 0400 HOURS
66 MINUTES TILL OMEGA

Jack gazed out over a broad and spectacular cavern.

A steep set of stairs led down to a superlong, superhigh and very slender bridge that stretched away from him for what seemed like half a kilometre.

This bridge extended out to a gigantic black spire-like tower that stood in the exact centre of the cavern.

Jack immediately noticed that there was something at the top of the tower: a cage suspended from a cable that rose up into a round hole in the ceiling.

The goal of this maze seemed clear: you crossed the bridge, scaled the tower and exited inside the cage.

The superlong bridge at Jack's end of the cavern was supported by two building-sized pylons.

Each pylon must have been four hundred feet high and they both rose up out of a pool of inky-black liquid that covered the floor far below like a moat. The liquid gave off a dull reflective sheen, like mercury or oil. Jack was pretty sure he didn't want to fall into it.

Where each pylon met the long, high bridge, there was an ancient temple-like structure made of greystone: a cupola of some kind, with a domed stone roof mounted on four decorative columns.

Jack looked out over the cavern, desperate to see how far ahead of him Rastor had got.

Beyond the first cupola, he glimpsed him: Rastor was arriving at the second one.

Jack bolted after him, racing out onto the slender bridge.

He came to the first cupola and paused.

Inside it was what could only be described as an ancient fountain.

A greystone obelisk about nine feet tall stood in the middle of a shallow circular pool of water that was maybe two feet deep. Water gurgled out of the pyramidion at the top of the obelisk and trickled down into the pool.

Jack stepped around the fountain and started down the next section of bridge—

—where he stopped.

Rastor stood at the other end of this section, staring back at Jack.

He was no longer running, no longer fleeing.

He just stood in front of the second cupola, his feet planted wide, blocking the way.

'Captain West!' his deep voice boomed. 'It is time we settled our differences.'

Jack swallowed.

'I have to stop you, Rastor.'

'I know you do. It is in your nature. Just as it is in mine to destroy everything in existence.'

Jack took a step forward, out of the first cupola and onto the soaring bridge, never taking his eyes off Rastor.

He'd forgotten how big he was. The man was huge, at least a foot taller than Jack.

Rastor called again, 'Do you know why the four kingdoms feared me, Captain?'

Jack said nothing.

'Because I can happily kill anyone without hesitation. Men, women, children, I care not. And I can do this for a simple reason: I enjoy it, take pleasure in it. Screams of agony do not stir me. In fact, I delight in them.'

So it had come to this, Jack thought. A fight between Rastor and him.

Then Jack glimpsed a grey-clad commando lurking behind Rastor, half-hidden behind the big general. The man was hopping quickly on the spot, like a boxer warming up for a fight.

Rastor said, 'They also feared me because I was smarter than they were, more adept at strategy and tactics. And finally, it was because I inspired loyalty in my troops. The men who joined me here in the Labyrinth are commandos from Serbia who are *total* in their devotion to me. They will do whatever I ask of them. Such a combination proved too frightening for the four kings, so they had me drugged and taken away to a special cell in Erebus.'

As Rastor spoke, Zoe, Lily and Alby emerged from the entry archway and saw the standoff going on far below them.

Rastor grinned again at Jack.

'I left you a gift before, a Vandal with a special something taped to his back. Consider this another gift, only bigger.'

Jack never saw him coming.

A *second* grey-clad commando—who had been hiding on the domed roof of Jack's cupola and who, as Rastor had been speaking, had snuck up on Jack from above and behind.

The commando leapt down onto Jack's back, knocking his fire helmet off his head and hurling Jack to the ground.

Jack's helmet went tumbling a short distance along the bridge while Jack landed heavily on his chest.

He rolled immediately, turning face-up just as the commando slashed at him with a KA-BAR knife.

Jack caught the killer's wrist and was holding the knife at bay when he heard Rastor call, 'Run, my loyal soldier! Finish him! Have faith that all life in the universe will be joining you in the hereafter very, very soon!'

From his awkward position on the ground, Jack glanced up at Rastor and saw the other Serbian commando—the one who had been hopping up and down behind the general—race out from behind Rastor and come running at full speed down the bridge toward Jack.

The man cried out as he ran, a yell of crazed fervour.

He held no weapon, yet when Jack saw what was attached to the crazed runner's chest, he swallowed in terror.

A cluster of twelve red orbs.

Taped across the commando's chest with duct tape.

The Vandal before had had only *one* orb attached to his body and that explosion had been huge.

This guy had *twelve*.

Jack's eyes boggled.

This commando was a berserker, a kamikaze, a fanatical suicide bomber running unstoppably at Jack, coming to obliterate himself, Jack and the other commando.

Zoe, Lily and Alby watched the scene with horrified eyes.

They had seen Jack emerge on the other side of the cupola and exchange words with Rastor.

Then they saw the first commando surprise Jack, saw them both tumble out of view.

And then they saw the second one come running down the superhigh bridge, screaming like a maniac and wearing something on his chest.

There was nothing they could do.

They were two hundred metres away, way too far to help, and they could only watch in dismay as the second grey-clad commando arrived at the cupola.

The second Serbian commando arrived at the cupola at a full-tilt run, and with crazed eyes and a cry of victory, he drew a knife and began stabbing wildly at the orbs taped to his chest, puncturing them.

The result was instantaneous.

Three of the red orbs exploded, and their explosions set off all the others . . .

. . . causing a fireball of unimaginable ferocity—twelve times stronger than the previous one—to blast out from the cupola, shattering its four columns in an instant and cracking its domed roof.

Destroying the interior of the cupola completely, along with anyone inside it, including Jack.

Zoe's jaw dropped.

Lily's eyes filled with tears.

Alby gasped.

There was no way anyone could survive such a blast. Anybody made of flesh and blood would be melted in an instant, blasted apart, vaporised.

They stared in horror at the destroyed cupola.

Small fires licked out from its ruins. Smoke billowed from it. A flaming crimson liquid trickled down one wall of the pylon below it.

And as the echoes of the explosion receded away into the cavernous space, a new sound could be heard.

Rastor's cackling laugh.

What happened next happened in a blur.

Rastor spun on his heel and dashed away, heading for the high central tower.

Lily raced down onto the first bridge, toward the destroyed cupola.

Zoe and Alby took off after her.

But as they came to the cupola, the extent of the damage became clear.

It had been completely shattered by the blast.

Its columns had been blown apart, causing the roof to crash down on some kind of ceremonial obelisk that had been inside it. Landing on the obelisk had both cracked the roof in half and crushed most of the obelisk.

Blood was everywhere.

Grisly chunks of raw human flesh covered the debris. Whether it was Jack's or the commandos' or from all three of them didn't seem to matter.

Sobbing and hyperventilating, Lily slid to her knees and started digging into the pile, hurling the shattered pieces of the cupola away, searching for her father.

But there was no sign of Jack.

Nothing at all.

The only remnant of his presence was his fire helmet lying askew on the ground a short way along the next bridge.

Her fingers smeared with dust and blood, Lily desperately snatched rocks and stone chunks from the pile and threw them clear.

Beside her, Alby could see the truth of the situation. It was beyond hopeless.

The look on Zoe's pale, shocked face said that she knew it, too.

Alby touched Lily's shoulder gently.

'Lily. Stop. It's no use. He's . . . *gone*.'

On her knees, amid the charred and still-burning ruins, in the last place she had seen her beloved father alive, Lily dropped her

head against her chest and began sobbing uncontrollably.

Alby could only hold her.

Zoe just stared at the scene, speechless.

And then the gunfire started.

A fusillade of bullets sparked off the rocky chunks all around them.

Zoe spun and saw the source of the gunfire.

It had come from behind them, from . . .

. . . Sphinx and Mendoza. The two men were standing at the entry archway, two hundred metres away, firing assault rifles.

Zoe hauled Lily off the ground. 'We gotta keep this mission alive! Even if we have to do it without Jack! Move!'

Zoe dragged the despondent Lily down the next two bridges with Alby bringing up the rear.

They had no guns anymore, so all they could do was run.

They reached the base of the black tower in the centre of the superhigh cavern—just as Sphinx and Mendoza hastened across the soaring bridge.

Sphinx and Mendoza hurried through the crumpled ruins of the first cupola, ignoring the large amounts of blood and gore on its shattered pieces.

Then suddenly Sphinx stopped.

And bent down.

And picked up something from the ground.

It was Jack's fire helmet, covered with blood.

Some liquid fire had landed on it and the left edge of its brim was, even now, sizzling and melting, the hard black fibreglass bubbling.

The utility box on its right side near the flashlight had come open and, sticking out from it, Sphinx saw a note.

Curious, he opened it.

> *Dear Everyone,*
>   *Well, I guess that's it. I'm gone.*
>   *God, so much has happened over the last twenty years,*
> *I don't know where to start.*

'Oh, Captain West,' Sphinx said. 'You had courage, I'll grant you that. But you were weak. Weak and sentimental. Motivated by all the wrong reasons. Look where that got you.'

He snorted and said again, 'Look where that got you.'

Then he tossed the helmet back to the ground and hurried onward, racing down the remainder of the bridge.

From the base of the black tower, Zoe saw them coming.

'Quick, this way,' she said, guiding Alby and Lily around the *back* of the tower, away from the exceedingly steep stairs cut into its front face. 'We can't outrun those guns, so we have to hide.'

Clinging to the rocky exterior of the ancient tower, they climbed around it, hanging on by their fingertips and toes, disappearing from view just as Sphinx and Mendoza burst through the last cupola with their assault rifles up.

Sphinx and Mendoza passed by their spot without seeing them and began climbing the steep stairs of the tower, heading for its lofty summit, consumed by their race against Rastor.

When she felt the coast was clear, Zoe crept out from the rear of the tower.

Lily and Alby came out behind her.

'What do we do now?' Alby asked.

Lily just stared into space.

Zoe's mind was a mess. She was literally trying to hold herself together.

She pursed her lips, trying to snap out of it.

'We have to keep going without him,' she said. 'We have to keep trying. That's what Jack would want us to do. Come on, while we're still breathing, we still have a chance.'

And so they climbed the black tower, ascending its ultra-steep stairs. Indeed, the stairs were so steep, it was more like climbing a slippery stone ladder.

At last, they came to the summit of the tower, where they found an open-sided temple made of a dozen sturdy trilithons formed into a circle with no roof.

Far above them they saw the golden cage again, now lowering on its cable from a round hole in the cavern's ceiling high, high above, returning from whatever was up there.

Alby stared in awe at the trilithons ringing the space. 'This is just like Stonehenge. Or, rather, Stonehenge is like this.'

Zoe was gazing up at the returning gold cage. 'Sphinx and Mendoza must have just left—'

'No, only Lord Sphinx left,' a voice said from behind her. 'I had to stay.'

Zoe spun, as did Lily and Alby . . .

. . . to see a lone man emerge from behind one of the huge trilithons, gripping a Steyr AUG assault rifle in his hands.

Cardinal Ricardo Mendoza.

'What happened? Did your boss leave you behind?' Zoe said contemptuously.

Mendoza snorted. 'You really know nothing about this place, do you?' He pointed up. 'My master has a keen sense of history, and that up there is the most crucial examination in this labyrinth. For it is in that cage that one faces the ultimate judge and discovers if they are truly worthy.'

He uncocked the safety on his rifle—

—just as the golden cage lowered fully into the temple and with a subtle but heavy *boom*, touched down in the centre of the stone circle.

It was a breathtakingly beautiful thing.

Made entirely of gold, it was twenty feet high, with a gold pyramidal roof, four gold pillars and a thick gold floor. It hung from a superthick golden chain that reached straight up for two hundred feet before delving into the hole in the ceiling.

The arrival of the striking gold cage had made Mendoza pause.

He went on. 'But you need not concern yourself with such matters, because you will not live to—'

'You know,' another voice said, cutting Mendoza off. 'I'm really tired of the way you assholes give speeches.'

Mendoza whirled.

So did Zoe, Lily and Alby.

And each of their eyes widened in shock at who they saw standing there at the edge of the tower, at the top of its supersteep stairway.

Jack West Jr.
Wearing his helmet and back from the dead.

Mendoza swung his gun around but Jack was already moving.

He leapt forward, snatched the rifle by its barrel and used it to yank Mendoza around, causing the cardinal to go stumbling onto the floor of the golden cage.

Quick as a whip, Jack unleashed a blow with the butt of the rifle, knocking the cardinal out. Mendoza lay unconscious on the floor of the cage, bloody and still.

Alby just stood there, speechless.

But Zoe and Lily raced over to Jack and embraced him simultaneously.

Jack sagged in their joint grip, still breathless from scaling the steep staircase.

His helmet was a wreck: half-melted on one side, its shield streaked with dried fibreglass and splattered all over with blood.

And yet Jack was okay.

Still alive.

And *back*.

Near the destroyed cupola. Minutes earlier.

With a snort, Sphinx tosses Jack's helmet to the ground and he and Mendoza hurry off toward the tall black tower, away from the cupola.

Like Zoe, Lily and Alby, they do not notice the broad round stone podium with the broken obelisk on it.

Mounted on its grey podium of stone, they have dismissed it as simply a nameless shrine that has been smashed by the falling of the cupola's domed roof following the devastating explosion of the orbs.

They do not know that this 'podium' was until recently a shallow pool of water.

So Sphinx and Mendoza don't hear the muffled *whump* come from *within* the podium under the obelisk.

Whump.

Whump.

They do not see the subtle but distinct vibrations come from inside it.

As the second crazed commando had raced toward Jack on his suicidal berserker-kamikaze run, Jack had hurled the first commando off him—banging the man's head against one of the cupola's pillars—and then he'd done something totally unexpected.

Something crazy, even by his standards.

He'd raced back into the cupola and, obscured by the obelisk, he'd thrown himself into the shallow pool with a splash. Then he lay face-up—with his Maghook pointed up as well.

Then he cracked the hourglass of greystone powder he'd taken from the dead Omega monk earlier and upended it into the pool.

After that, he held his breath.

As the berserker commando reached the cupola, the water in the pool beneath the obelisk turned grey, then black and then, with a crack, it hardened completely . . .

. . . and the commando arrived with a crazed shout, stabbing the explosive orbs on his chest . . .

. . . and blew himself to pieces.

Blood sprayed everywhere. Both his blood and that of the dazed first commando, who was also torn apart by the explosion.

It splattered against everything: the obelisk, the floor and Jack's helmet on the bridge.

The columns were turned to dust and the cupola's cracked

domed roof fell onto the obelisk and the fountain, only now the pool at the base of the fountain was solid greystone.

And inside a form-fitting tomb within that new slab of grey-stone—having successfully shielded himself from the terrible blast with the layer of stone—was Jack West Jr.

At that point, Jack was essentially buried alive.

Inside the now solid greystone, it was totally dark and terrify-ingly claustrophobic. Solid rock encased him.

The only thing Jack could hear was his own close breathing. He didn't have much time: he would suffocate soon, especially if he kept panting so hard.

But he did have one thing.

He had his Maghook *pointed upward*.

And so he fired it.

Whump!

It slammed into the greystone slab above him, only travelling a couple of inches, not even fully escaping its launcher, but creating a few minor cracks.

He reeled it in with a press of his trigger finger, and fired it again.

Whump!

The cracks got bigger.

Whump! Bigger again.

And on the fourth powerful blow from the Maghook, it broke through . . .

. . . and Jack peeked through a slit in the greystone slab.

A few more shots from the Maghook and some careful wriggling got him out—he was fortunate that the obelisk had not crumpled completely, and had thus left him some room to slither out from under the fallen roof—and suddenly he was standing there in the crumpled cupola, alive.

He ran out of the ruins, heading for the black tower, stopping, of course, to scoop up his fire helmet on the way.

Zoe and Lily released Jack from their embrace and they all looked at the golden cage in the centre of the stone circle.

It was a truly gorgeous thing and quite obviously not made by humans. Its mighty chain stretched up to the dark round hole up in the ceiling of the cavern.

Zoe said, 'When a culture builds beautiful things, they do so for a reason. This thing is important. Ceremonial.'

'I agree,' Jack said. 'This was constructed with reverence. But for what?'

Alby looked up the length of the cage's stout gold chain.

'By the look of it, it's the only way out of this part of the Labyrinth,' he observed.

'What do you think, Lily?' Jack asked.

Till that moment, Lily had been silent. She had been scanning the cage's four gold columns and its floor.

Jack watched as she stepped back, to get a fuller view of the floor of the cage.

As she did that, Jack realised what she was looking at.

One large but very precise engraving covered the centre of the cage's floor:

'The eye of Horus,' Lily breathed. 'The Eye of Providence. Or . . .'

'. . . the All-Seeing Eye,' Jack finished.

'Yes,' Lily said.

Jack frowned. 'So what does it mean here, kiddo?'

Lily seemed almost entranced as she gazed at the enormous engraving in the golden floor.

She looked up at Jack and the others.

'This marking has been reproduced many times in the course of human history. The Egyptians put it on the capstones of pyramids. The Freemasons used it. The United States has it on their one-dollar bill. But no matter where it appeared, it always had the same meaning: that we are being watched, observed, *evaluated* by a higher power.'

Lily looked seriously at each member of the group.

'This whole Labyrinth has been a series of trials, evaluations, tests of worth,' she said. 'Each maze so far has tested something about us. Nerve got us through the first entry maze. Knowledge got us into the Endless Tunnel and through it. Humility got us past the goldmen statues. And endurance got us through the rotating maze. This cage, however, is a different kind of test. A test you can't overcome with courage or determination, wisdom or even action.'

'What is it, then?' Jack asked.

'It's the ultimate test of worth,' Lily said. 'An examination of our innermost intent.'

'So how does it work?' Alby asked.

'It's simple,' Lily said. 'You step inside the cage and rise into that hole up there in the ceiling. And then you are judged.'

The group was silent for a long moment.

Jack looked at the chain reaching up to the high ceiling of the cavern, unsure.

'The ultimate judgement. I mean, what else did we expect?'

He checked his watch.

4:31 a.m.

Thirty-five minutes to Omega.

He pursed his lips. 'There's no knowing what's up there, so we do this one at a time, in case something goes wrong. We can't lose all of us at once.'

He swallowed deeply.

'And this time I'm definitely going first.'

Zoe, Lily and Alby edged back while Jack stepped onto the golden cage, gripping Mendoza's assault rifle.

Cardinal Mendoza still lay slumped to one side of the cage, groaning, unconscious.

Jack wasn't sure how the cage operated, but after years of encountering ancient tunnel systems and booby traps, he had an idea.

He stepped onto the image of the All-Seeing Eye in its centre . . .

. . . and the cage rose.

Against the immensity of that cavern, the gold cage looked tiny as it was lifted by its chain off the top of the black tower and up toward the hole in the ceiling.

And then, with Jack West Jr standing on it, the golden cage passed into the ceiling.

FIFTH TEST OF WORTH

THE COLOSSUS

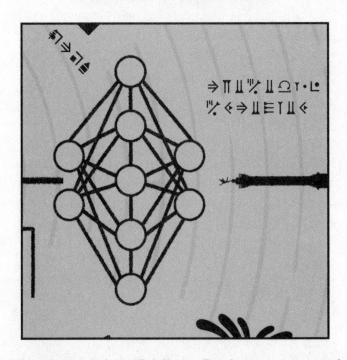

If life was seeded artificially on Earth, one may wonder
whether the seeders are checking on the outcome. And if so,
the fact that we have not heard from them may indicate that
they are disappointed.

SCIENTIFIC AMERICAN MAGAZINE, 2019

Jack rose into a truly splendid space.

It was a slim, narrow cavern but unbelievably high.

And dominating one wall of it was an enormous—*enormous*—statue of a goldman.

Jesus, Jack thought. *It must be as tall as a forty-storey building.*

His cage kept rising, infinitesimally small against the gigantic scale of the statue.

It rose past the statue's mighty golden legs.

It was, quite literally, a colossus.

Jack found himself thinking of the Colossus of Rhodes, one of the Seven Wonders of the Ancient World; indeed, it was the first of the Wonders that he had found. He remembered discovering its giant head inside a booby-trapped cavern in Sudan.

He wondered if, like many of the ancient objects he had found whose original reasons-for-being had been lost, the Colossus of Rhodes had been built in honour of this statue.

Only this colossus was an order of magnitude larger.

Jack's cage kept ascending, slowly and ominously.

It rose past the huge golden statue's waist and chest and neck until finally the cage came level with the colossus's shining gold head . . .

. . . where it stopped.

★ ★ ★

There was no sound.

Jack West Jr stood before the gargantuan golden head, gripping his rifle, dwarfed by its sheer massiveness. The eyeless head, with its fearsome bird-like beak, must have been four storeys tall.

Aware of what had happened to others who had looked at a goldman, Jack kept his eyes downcast.

He had never felt so small—

Suddenly a piercing sensation shot through his head and he reeled, dropping the gun.

He couldn't tell if it was some kind of ultra-high-frequency soundwave or a shot of electricity. He winced in pain and clutched at his ears.

At his feet, Cardinal Mendoza also evidently experienced the same sensation, because he suddenly lurched awake with a shout, wailing as he grabbed his ears.

Jack heard a rising, intensifying noise and abruptly there came a blinding flash of light and he squeezed his eyes shut as the noise reached a crescendo and—

Silence.

Total silence. No more soundwave or electric shock or intensifying noise.

Just . . . *nothing*.

Jack opened his eyes and found that he was *somewhere else*.

He still stood before the giant golden statue inside his hanging golden cage, still with his eyes downcast, but now he was in some kind of borderless void with infinite blackness all around him.

And he couldn't move.

He just stood there, stock-still, his muscles unresponsive, his whole body frozen, his eyes locked on the golden colossus's throat as its eyeless face loomed over him.

And then a voice, impossibly commanding and loud, penetrated his consciousness.

Who comes here seeking to face Omega?

Jack instinctively tried to speak in reply, but when he answered, it was without his voice.

My name is Jack West Jr, he conveyed.

Even in this strange place, this alternate realm of existence, his mind marvelled in wonder.

This was communication from mind to mind: from his fragile human brain to that of the ultra-ancient entity encased in the golden colossus in front of him.

The reply was as harsh as it was instant.

The unworthy may not pass through here.
You are not worthy.
You must die now.

A cry of unfathomable pain echoed out from beside Jack and he turned to see Cardinal Mendoza—also here in the infinite black void, still on his knees, just as Jack had last seen him in the 'real' world—clutch at his head and wail in pure agony.

Then Mendoza's eyes exploded from their sockets and gouts of blood burst out of his ears and the cardinal collapsed to the ground, deader than dead.

Jack was speechless.

He'd thought *he* had been done for. But the golden colossus hadn't been addressing him.

It had been addressing Mendoza.

The unworthy may not pass through here. He was unworthy. Raise your eyes. In this place, you may look upon me.

Jack peered up cautiously, looking directly at the face of the giant gold colossus.

In what way was he unworthy? he asked.

His intent was impure. His life was about deceit and giving others false hope. He tried to conceal his thoughts.

Is my intent impure?

Your intent is pure.

Am I worthy?

You are worthy.

Why?

In response, an array of images suddenly swirled through Jack's mind.

He saw himself inside the volcano in Uganda on the day of Lily's birth, saw himself thrust his real left arm through a waterfall of lava so that he, Lily and Wizard could escape—then he was atop the Great Pyramid at Giza, battling Marshall Judah and placing a jar of red dirt under the Golden Capstone before the beam of light lanced out from the sun and struck the pyramid—then he was inside the Sixth Vertex of the Machine inside a stadium-like cavern underneath Easter Island with Lily, fighting his father, Wolf, for the final Pillar—then he was on the final fighting stage of the Great Games, facing a man dressed as Cerberus—then he was swimming in front of the submerged city of Atlas, heading inside its vault—and then he was on his knees inside the Rock of Gibraltar, sobbing for what he thought was the loss of Lily.

You once possessed great power, yet you did not use it. Why?

I don't want power, Jack replied.

What do you want?

I just want people to be able to live their lives.

The answer came from Jack perfectly naturally, with uninhibited honesty.

And it struck him that he actually had no choice in the matter.

This colossus—whatever it was—could see right *into* him, right *through* him, to his core, to the very heart of his character, his beliefs, his being.

This was indeed a whole new kind of test, the ultimate examination.

There was nowhere to hide here, no concealing your thoughts, your desires, your intentions.

And abruptly a line from Imhotep's skull came to him:

But there is no escaping the ultimate choice.

In the face of Omega, you cannot conceal your desires.

Jack wondered if he could pass such a test.

He also found himself wondering how long this was taking back in the real world. It could be taking seconds, minutes or, worse, longer, and he had no way of knowing.

He was running out of time to save the universe.

What a fucking trip.

He also found himself questioning how the colossus was 'speaking' to him in English.

Unbidden, it answered. There was truly no hiding here.

I am merely communicating with you. It is you who interprets my messages in the form of language.

In the face of this strange being, Jack was beginning to regather himself.

Somehow he managed to convey a question to the colossus.

The two men who came through here before me, were they pure or impure?

Their intentions were not like yours, yet their intentions were pure. The first's intention was to see everything end.

That was Rastor, Jack thought.

The second intends to rule.

That was Sphinx.

How can such intentions be pure? Jack asked.

I judge not in terms of benevolence or malevolence, only purity. Their intentions were as pure as yours.

What are you? And what is all this—the Tartarus Rotation, the Machine, the Great Games, this Labyrinth—what is this all about?

I am the consciousness of the ones who built the universe and who seeded complex life on this planet with the Lifestone five hundred million years ago.

There are seven planets in the universe that we seeded with Lifestones and that we monitor. The seven sentient worlds.

Your planet is one of these.

The universe can only continue to exist if life advances, grows, evolves; if it understands its own value.

Each of the challenges you faced were ways of telling us that your species had advanced to a sufficient level to warrant the continuation of your existence.

All the other chosen planets have successfully fulfilled the requirements of Omega.

Only yours has not.

We sent you everything you needed—the Word of Thoth and the Oracles who can read it; the six Pillars of the Machine, inlaid with knowledge that would have advanced your species exponentially.

All your kind needed to do was safeguard that wisdom and use it when required.

But over time, your species—squabbling and petty, fighting among yourselves, desirous of power over each other—lost many of them, retaining only fragments of the larger body of wisdom.

Now Omega is upon you and with it your reckoning.

What has all this been for?

It has been a test. A test of worth.

Your intent is pure and thus you are worthy.

You may continue.

Suddenly everything around Jack flashed white and he squeezed his eyes shut and—

—Jack blinked and found himself back in the real world, back in the high cavern inside the cage in front of the golden colossus— except that the cage had started rising again, toward another hole in the ceiling here.

On the floor of the cage beside Jack was the dead body of Cardinal Mendoza. Mendoza's head was a gruesome mess of exploded eyeballs and bloodied ears.

Jack shook his head as he picked up the rifle. 'Too bad, Mendoza. You should've been worthier.'

The cage lifted away from the faceless golden colossus and disappeared through the hole in the ceiling, into the final part of the Supreme Labyrinth where only those with total purity of intent could enter.

Thirty seconds later, Jack's cage rose up into a small stone chamber that looked like an ancient chapel . . .

. . . where Jack was instantly assailed by a wave of automatic gunfire.

FINAL TEST OF WORTH

THE THRONE
OF THE TREE OF DEATH

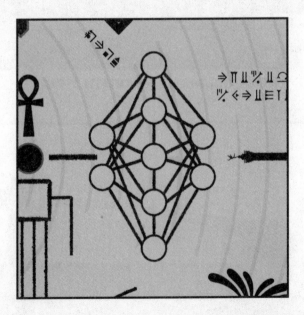

Christianity is premised on the idea of resurrection and rebirth. But it is not about the resurrection and rebirth of a man, but rather the rebirth of existence itself.

AN INTERTEXTUAL ANALYSIS OF THE GOSPELS
DIANE FALLOON
(W.M. LAWRY & CO., SYDNEY, 2012)

THE STADIUM OF THE DEATH THRONE

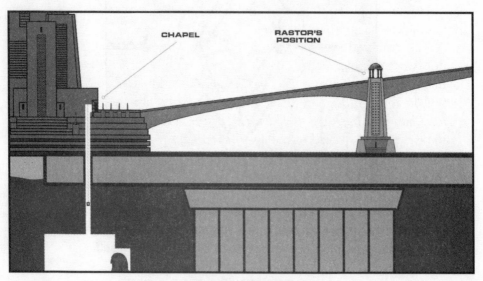

CHAPEL

RASTOR'S
POSITION

JACK'S CHAPEL
(CLOSER VIEW)

THE THRONE OF THE TREE OF DEATH
29 DECEMBER, 0447 HOURS
19 MINUTES TILL OMEGA

As bullets impacted all around him, Jack dived to the floor of the cage, instinctively taking cover behind the only thing he *could* take cover behind: Mendoza's dead body.

A volley of tracer rounds came in through the only apparent doorway and smacked into the corpse, thudding into it with loud fleshy slaps.

Huddled behind the corpse, Jack saw that he was indeed inside an ancient chapel-like chamber.

The rear wall of the place had a doorway set into it, but the doorway was entirely filled with a thick slab of metal that shone dully. It was a slab of metal, Jack realised, that he had seen before.

This is the other end of the Emperor's Route, he thought. *If the way had not been shut off earlier, this is where that tunnel after the entry cavern would have eventually led.*

On the opposite side of the chapel was a square stone doorway that led outside: the only way out. To Jack's surprise, dim sunlight seeped in through it.

Unfortunately, another wave of bullets came fizzing in through the doorway and Jack lay flat behind Mendoza's corpse as it took more sickening impacts.

But then it happened.

The golden cage shuddered . . . and began to lower back down into the hole through which it had entered the chapel.

And suddenly Jack had no choice but to get off it.

Amid a hail of bullet sparks, he leapt away from the corpse, firing Mendoza's assault rifle as he jumped off the lowering golden cage. The gun fired four shots before it clicked, empty, as Jack slid behind an altar a few feet away . . .

. . . only to slam into someone else already taking cover behind that altar, trying to avoid the same incoming fusillade of gunfire.

Sphinx.

In his wildest imaginings, Jack never thought he'd find himself taking cover from a hail of gunfire with his mortal rival and bitter enemy, Hardin Lancaster XII, the Sphinx.

Cruel yet shrewd, Sphinx was the man who had made Jack's life a living hell during the trials of the secret cities and the iron mountains.

He was the one who had forced Jack to conquer the flooded city of Atlantis while he'd kept Lily captive in a drowning cell and then made Jack think that Lily had been sacrificed at the Rock of Gibraltar.

Sphinx had variously beheaded nuns or fed them to Vandals. And in his insatiable desire to create a new world order that he alone would rule as an unchallenged tyrant, he had unleashed the Siren bells on the world, putting the populations of entire cities to sleep—many of which he did not intend to wake; he would just let them starve in their comas.

Right now, Sphinx was huddled behind the little stone altar as bullets sparked and ricocheted off its front face. He held an assault rifle of his own that was also evidently dry.

'It's him!' Sphinx yelled above the din. 'Fucking maniac!'

Jack didn't need to be told who the problem was.

It was their *other* rival in this deadly race, the one who had got here first—ahead of both Sphinx and him—and who didn't want to see anyone sit on the throne and thus avert Omega.

Jack checked his watch.

4:48 a.m.

Eighteen minutes till Omega.

He'd only been inside the colossus's chamber—and the strange void—for a few minutes.

During a brief pause in the gunfire, Jack peered over the altar and saw a figure a hundred metres away, on a tower of some kind in the centre of an upwardly sloping bridge, with an assault rifle of his own aimed back at the chapel and unleashing a torrent of tracer fire with it.

It was a classic sniper's position, perfect for holding off anyone coming out of the chapel, with a clear field of fire over the narrow slanted bridge.

'Nice to see you again, Captain!' Sphinx shouted above the gunfire. 'Welcome to the end of all things!'

'You're such an asshole.' Jack glanced around the altar, trying to take in their full predicament.

Out through the doorway, he saw a vast round space, one that was almost identical to the one he had encountered at the first throne, the Throne of the Tree of Life.

Only this was the home of its sinister sibling: the Throne of the Tree of Death.

A magnificent many-spired castle—mounted on a sturdy stone pedestal and with a pinnacle stretching skyward from its topmost level—stood out in the middle of a superwide circular area that, like the earlier megastadium, was itself ringed by an eight-hundred-foot-high wall of greystone.

But there were distinct differences.

While the previous castle had been white and silver, this one was black and gold.

It was also crafted in a different style: it was more severe, with sharper angles and a fiercer aspect.

It also had, Jack saw with his trained eyes, *one less window-balcony* than the earlier castle.

This, he knew, was the subtle but important difference between the Tree of Life and the Tree of Death: while otherwise similar in their designs, the Tree of Death possessed one less 'node' than the Tree of Life did.

Another major difference was that the broad round space

around this castle had *no* maze in it; no city-sized tangle of buildings, temples and obelisks.

It just had one long ascending bridge of stairs that extended out from Jack's chamber to meet the base of the castle.

This bridge, with its rising stone stairs, passed through a towering greystone pylon before it reached the all-important castle.

On this pylon was the temple on which Rastor had entrenched himself with his assault rifle.

It was the ideal spot for him to make his last stand.

Because it was a perfect bottleneck.

Neither Jack nor Sphinx could reach the castle without going up the narrow bridge and through that temple.

All Rastor had to do was run out the clock and hold them off till 5:06 a.m., now only sixteen minutes away.

As more bullets slammed into the altar beside him, Jack assessed the space around the castle and below Rastor's position.

Far below the castle, the bridge and the pylon, he saw sandy yellow ground, which heaved and rolled with barely perceptible waves, like windblown ripples on a lake.

Jack had seen this before. Quicksand.

Don't fall in, he thought grimly.

One other thing of note was happening as Jack arrived at the site of the second throne.

The cavern's soaring domed roof was opening.

Jack hadn't seen this occur at the other throne and it was quite a sight.

The huge hemispherical greystone ceiling above the black castle was retracting in eight gigantic pieces. Those pieces withdrew down into the rim of the space's high circular wall.

As the roof retracted ever further, the brilliant pre-dawn sky could be seen outside, purple-pink in colour and shot through with high-altitude clouds.

Seen underneath the eerie discoloured sky, the dark and angular castle somehow seemed even more fearsome.

If Jack had been outside the dome, up on the desert floor, the sight would have been perhaps even more amazing.

Just as the previous dome had risen up from the seabed, this dome had, moments before, risen up from beneath the sandy desert floor.

Located about ten miles due east of the Labyrinth's entrance gates, the great grey dome had pushed up through the desert soil like some kind of subterranean leviathan.

Sand and rocks had fallen off it, tumbling to the ground as the mighty greystone dome emerged from the Earth and rose to a colossal height until it stood there on the barren plain like an over-sized sports stadium, unimaginably huge and magnificent.

As the dome opened fully to the sky and Rastor's tracer rounds impacted all around them, Sphinx shouted to Jack: 'Well! We're out of ammo and pinned down! Got a clever solution for *this*, Captain?'

Jack looked from Sphinx to the wide-open roof and the dawn sky above it to Rastor in his sniper's nest and then back to Sphinx.

He checked the time: 4:51.

Fifteen minutes.

'No!' he called back.

No, he didn't have a solution, and time was running out.

NEW YORK CITY, U.S.A.

Iolanthe and Nobody roared through the night-time canyons of New York City in their chopper, chased by the two military attack helicopters that had arrived above Central Park just after Iolanthe had snatched the Blue Bell from within the fallen obelisk.

Nobody gunned the throttle, guiding their Jet Ranger at crazy speed through the empty city streets.

In the passenger seat, Iolanthe gripped the Blue Bell—the unique and precious Siren bell that could wake millions from their slumber—while peering anxiously back at their pursuers.

Those pursuers—Chloe Carnarvon and her men in the two gunships—swooped after them, flying fast and low, their side-cannons blazing.

Nobody swept his chopper down 42nd Street and into Times Square just as two huge digital billboards exploded in a zillion sparks, ripped apart by the first pursuing chopper's storm of gunfire.

Rotors booming, Nobody banked their chopper left, rocketing low over Times Square and blasting away down Broadway.

'I can't shake 'em!' he yelled.

'Whoever holds this bell holds the fate of whole populations in their hands!' Iolanthe called back. 'We can't let Chloe get it! We have to think of some way out of this!'

RAVEN ROCK MOUNTAIN COMPLEX (SITE R)
BLUE RIDGE SUMMIT, PENNSYLVANIA
SAME TIME

The Air France 737 exploded on the runway.

The Delta commandos guarding Pooh Bear and Stretch—and the Knight of the Golden Eight commanding the legion of bronzemen behind them—had been caught completely unawares by the sudden blast.

But Pooh and Stretch had been ready.

As had Sister Lynda and Dr Tracy Smith.

This had been their daring plan.

They all whipped out their guns and opened fire, blasting the Delta commandos to hell and—most importantly—nailing the Knight at the front of the legion of bronzemen.

It was Stretch, former sniper and deadeye marksman, who hit the Knight squarely in the forehead, dropping him.

Pooh was on the man in an instant, taking the striking ancient ring off the man's finger and putting it on his own . . .

. . . and suddenly, he had command of all the bronzemen.

The royal banker, Sir John Marren, grabbed a gun off the ground and was whirling around to fire on Pooh Bear when Tracy Smith shot him—three quick expert shots—and Marren's chest burst open with three bloody wounds and he fell.

Covered by Tracy, Pooh ordered the bronzemen into action immediately, while Stretch—covered by Sister Lynda—got started on his part, the final part, of their plan.

THE THRONE OF THE TREE OF DEATH
29 DECEMBER, 0454 HOURS
12 MINUTES TILL OMEGA

Jack and Sphinx were still pinned down by Rastor's heavy gunfire inside the chapel at the edge of the round space surrounding the Throne of Death.

And suddenly it hit Jack.

'I do have a solution,' he said to himself as the realisation dawned.

He turned to Sphinx. 'We both have the same solution. Didn't you have some kind of electromagnetic shield before? A Warbler of some kind?'

'I lost the damn thing inside the rotating maze!' Sphinx shouted. 'It doesn't matter, he's firing high-velocity tracer rounds! There's no knowing if a Warbler could deflect those rounds! Would take a hell of a device to deflect them!'

Jack gritted his teeth.

'*My* Warbler was designed by Max Epper. He wouldn't let me down.'

And with those words, Jack sprang out from behind the little stone altar and raced out of the chapel, out into the open, onto the slender ascending bridge, and into Rastor's deadly field of fire.

Head bent, arms pumping, legs driving, Jack raced up the bridge.

Crouched in his sniper's nest inside the temple, Rastor frowned.

West again.

Determined as ever. But this? This was madness.

Rastor shrugged.

And opened fire.

As he ran up the bridge, Jack found himself thinking of a bunch of things: Lily, Zoe, and, oddly, his old friend and mentor, Wizard, Professor Max T. Epper.

It had been Wizard who had invented the Warbler and the little device had saved Jack earlier inside this very Labyrinth and also, eight years ago, in the Israeli desert after Jack had found the tomb of Jesus Christ in an abandoned Roman mine.

But on both of those occasions, the Warbler had protected Jack from *pistol* shots.

Jack didn't know if it would work against an assault rifle firing heavy-bore high-velocity rounds.

Help me now, Wizard. One last time, he thought.

And so Jack ran upward.

While Rastor fired downward . . .

. . . and the withering burst of tracer fire rained down on Jack as a swarm of sizzling-hot streaks . . .

. . . only to bend around him as they reached him!

It was a fucking astonishing sight: the figure of Jack racing up the stone bridge, into the rain of visible gunfire, only for the bullets to part in a V-shape—pushed away by the invisible electromagnetic field created by the Warbler—and whiz by Jack on both sides.

'Thanks Wizard,' Jack whispered as the white-hot streaks slashed past him and he bounded upward.

Rastor roared in pure rage as he saw his bullets diverge around Jack and then his clip ran dry and suddenly Jack was *there*, with him, inside the temple on the gigantic pylon.

Rastor threw his gun to the ground.

And rose to his full height. He still wore his black tactical vest over his grey uniform and he towered a full foot taller than Jack.

'And so it comes to this,' Rastor said. 'The two of us. No weapons. No allies. Just one final hand-to-hand fight.'

'I guess it does.'

'You know you can't beat me,' Rastor said. 'You can't win this.'

'I know,' Jack said. 'But I've been in fights like this going all the way back to my schooldays. So I'm gonna do it anyway.'

And with those words, they fought.

With a roar, Rastor came at Jack with a flurry of martial arts moves.

For a big man, he moved with incredible speed and precision and it was all Jack could do to avoid his blows.

Jack ducked and bobbed as Rastor's fists and boots whistled by his ears or missed his face by millimetres.

And suddenly, deep in his heart, Jack knew.

He couldn't beat this man.

He'd fought many warriors over the years—including several instances of brutal mortal combat during the final stages of the Great Games—but in every one of those cases, he'd known he had a chance.

Not so here.

Rastor was too big, too strong, and quite simply too good.

And then one of Rastor's blows hit home and Jack's vision blurred.

And a flashing memory of that schoolyard fight whipped across his mind: a succession of vicious blows from those three bigger boys—*bam, bam, bam!*—slamming into his face, while Sumil stood helplessly behind him.

Jack had lost that fight. And in that moment of blurred vision, he knew he was going to lose this one, too.

But he fought anyway, doggedly dodging Rastor's swings, and even landing a couple of punches of his own, not that they did much.

Then another of Rastor's terrible blows landed, smashing into Jack's cheekbone.

Jack heard the bone break and he staggered, close to the edge of the temple, high above the drop.

He felt dizzy, saw stars.

Stay conscious! his mind screamed. *You must stay conscious or else he'll throw you off this tower into the quicksand!*

It was no use.

Rastor's next blow broke Jack's nose and Jack collapsed like a sack of shit to the floor.

Jack lay on his stomach, gasping.

Blood poured from his nose, mixing with spittle dribbling from his mouth.

Pain shot through him, from his broken cheekbone, from his busted nose.

Aw, damn . . . he thought. *I didn't want to go out like this.*

And then Rastor stomped on Jack's titanium left hand.

Once, twice, three times, till he had dented its thinner struts and broken its fingers.

Jack lay with his face against the ground, groaning.

Broken and beaten, he tried to crawl away from Rastor.

'You might have been one of the five greatest warriors, West, yet I am in every measurable way a better warrior than you are.'

Rastor stood over him as Jack tried pathetically to get away from the giant general.

Then Rastor picked him up by his collar and carried him like a rag doll to the edge of the temple and held him over the drop.

Jack's feet dangled above the edge.

His cut and bloodied face stared dazedly back at Rastor.

His hands hung uselessly by his sides—the real right one, dirty and bloodied; the artificial left one a bent and broken mess of titanium and steel rods.

'You know the strength of my conviction,' Rastor said. 'Indeed, I couldn't have reached this innermost sanctum of the Labyrinth if my intentions were not pure. The colossus told me so.

'We are opposite sides of the same coin, Captain. The ardour of your conviction is equally strong, but my *passion* is greater than yours. *I want more than anything to see everything end.* But take solace. While you will die now, the rest of the universe will join you in the afterlife in a matter of minutes.'

As Rastor spoke, Jack's boots—dangling above the edge of the polished floor—had been silently reaching for the ground and now they touched it, their soles searching for grip.

And as they found that grip, with his last ounce of strength and his one good hand, Jack suddenly grabbed Rastor's utility vest tightly and, clutching it with fierce determination, he launched himself backwards, off the edge of the temple, pulling the shocked general with him, and they both fell off the high platform into space.

Jack and Rastor plummeted down the side of the enormous stone pylon.

The various windows, balconies and ledges of the pylon rushed past them as streaking blurs.

As he fell, Jack released the shocked Rastor and reached out with his good hand.

He caught a balcony and his fall was instantly arrested while Rastor kept falling, screaming with rage as he plunged toward the quicksand far, far below.

Gasping for air, struggling to stay conscious, his face a bleeding mess, his artificial left hand bent and useless, Jack didn't care what happened to Rastor.

He just hauled himself over the balcony's stone rail and tumbled, breathless, to its floor. He lay there on his back for a moment, chest heaving, sucking in oxygen.

Which was when he saw Sphinx far above him, peering down from the temple at the top of the pylon, maybe forty feet away.

Sphinx gave Jack a disdainful salute and then raced away up the next ascending bridge toward the castle and the throne on its peak.

Won't this ever end? Jack thought.

And so, slowly and painfully, he hauled himself to his feet. To his relief, a tight spiralling staircase ran up the inside of this pylon.

With a deep breath, Jack began to hurry up that staircase, chasing after Sphinx one final time.

THE CASTLE OF THE THRONE OF DEATH
29 DECEMBER, 0457 HOURS
NINE MINUTES TILL OMEGA

Sphinx raced into the castle that supported the Throne of the Tree of Death.

Like the previous castle before it, its interior was a high and airy space. Inside that space—also like the earlier castle—was a criss-crossing array of soaring stair-bridges, each leading to a ceremonial archway.

Sphinx had a map with the correct path traced onto it and he followed it.

As Sphinx passed through the first archway, Jack entered the castle behind him and—since he had no map—he bounded up the same stairway Sphinx had taken.

Up they ran, back and forth, hurrying up the interior of the spectacular castle.

Three minutes later, Sphinx burst out onto the summit of the castle—springing into daylight—and found himself standing at the base of the black-and-gold pinnacle there.

He gazed up its towering height and immediately started climbing it.

Jack emerged on the roof of the ancient castle seconds later and looked up at the pinnacle.

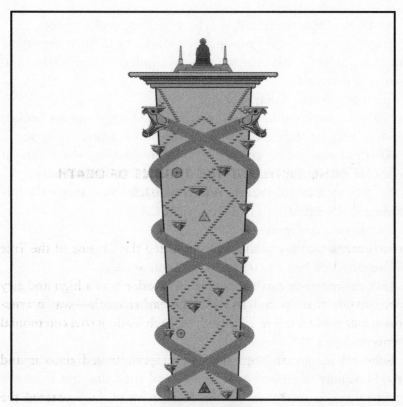

THE PINNACLE

Seen up close, it was actually quite a complicated and intricate thing.

It was essentially a supertall cylinder, covered with irregularly shaped protrusions, ledges and indentations.

The protrusions took the form of two huge serpents, each five feet in diameter, that wrapped around the pinnacle, as if climbing it themselves, before ending at snarling snake heads that jutted out from the upper reaches of the pinnacle like massive gargoyles on a cathedral.

Hand- and footholds were carved into it for one to climb yet they rose in bending and diverging pathways that wended their way past all the snake bodies and ledges.

And it was tall, really tall, maybe a hundred and fifty feet.

Standing atop the already massive black castle, high above the quicksand floor of this mighty space, to climb it was a dizzying and terrifying prospect.

Yet that's exactly what Jack did.

With his one good hand and the crumpled fingers of his broken artificial one, he started climbing up the pinnacle after Sphinx.

After all the secret cities, the iron mountains, the altars at Gibraltar and on the moon, it was a simple flat-out race now.

A 150-foot dash to the top of this pinnacle, high above the forbidding black castle.

Six minutes to Omega . . .

Sphinx gripped every handhold firmly.

One hundred feet to go and he was still ahead.

Jack gasped as he pushed himself upward.

Seventy feet to go and Jack was getting closer, only a few feet below him now.

Five minutes to Omega . . .

Fifty feet to go and Sphinx took a fork going right, moving toward a huge silver-and-gold snake head springing out from the pinnacle.

Jack went left, around the other way, running briefly across a silver-floored ledge indented into the pinnacle.

Four minutes to Omega . . .

Forty feet to go and Jack came level with Sphinx—they were on opposite sides of the slender shaft now, almost level with the fierce snake heads—and for the first time, Jack saw the underside of the peak of the pinnacle: a cleanly cut squared-off ledge.

Three minutes . . .

Energised, he increased his speed, grabbing the next handhold, and for a moment he saw Sphinx, off to his right . . . a couple of metres *below* him.

He had pulled ahead!

Twenty feet . . .

. . . and Jack stepped out onto a final silver ledge that lay on top of the giant snake head that jutted out from his side of the pinnacle. He looked up at the summit.

'Oh, damn . . .' he breathed when he saw it.

The squared-off edge of the pinnacle's peak was an *overhang*.

Hand-rungs had been carved into it, allowing the worthy candidate to climb up and around the overhang . . .

. . . if he had two good hands.

Two minutes . . .

Jack stared in dismay at his broken artificial hand, its titanium and steel fingers all bent and mangled.

And he froze.

He couldn't scale the overhang with one hand. It was physically impossible.

He'd come all this way—through all the challenges and difficulties, deaths and heartache, victories and losses—and he was going to fail here because of his one weakness, his left hand.

'Oh, damn,' he said again.

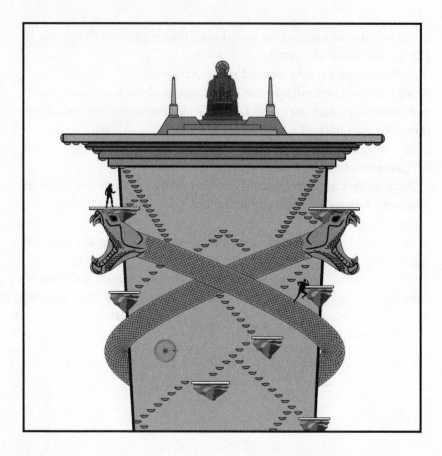

And in that moment of absolute despair, of all things, Jack heard laughter.

Someone nearby was laughing.

Sphinx.

Jack spun to see his rival over on a ledge on the other side of the pinnacle, about forty feet away and a little below him, chuckling.

'How fitting, Captain!' Sphinx called. 'After all your dashing heroics, you can't overcome the final simple obstacle!'

Jack swore in outright frustration. He couldn't believe it.

Couldn't.

Fucking.

Believe it.

Sphinx snorted coldly. 'I told you, Captain, but you didn't listen! The poet Robert Browning was wrong! A man's reach *shouldn't* exceed his grasp! You should never have tried to do this! You should have *remembered your place!* This throne—this moment, this test—*it is literally out of your reach!* Your grasp isn't long enough!'

His face bloody, his metal hand twisted and broken, Jack could have wept.

Because Sphinx was right. There was nothing Jack could do to overcome this situation. He was finally, truly, out of options.

And then Jack heard a voice.
  'Dad! Incoming!'

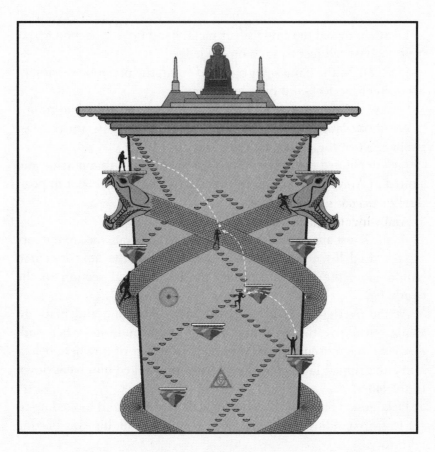

It was Lily's voice, calling from below him.

Jack looked down and saw a short distance beneath him . . .

. . . Zoe and Lily, both clinging to the side of the pinnacle, and on a ledge further below them, Alby.

They'd all evidently entered this vast space, run up through the castle and then climbed the pinnacle, too.

One minute . . .

'Alby!' Lily called. 'Toss it up!'

And then Jack saw Alby do something and his eyes widened in total shocked surprise.

Alby unclipped his own artificial left hand at the wrist, separating it from the forearm mount, and threw it up to Lily.

Lily then tossed the shiny silver metal hand up to Zoe who threw it up the last ten feet to Jack on his ledge.

Jack caught the hand—*his own old hand*, the previous version of his current model—and his eyes lit up.

Sphinx saw him catch it and instantly knew what he had to do.

No more laughing or gloating. Sphinx hauled ass up the last twenty feet of the pinnacle on his side.

Jack unclipped his bent and broken metal hand, cast it aside and slotted in Alby's in its place. It fit perfectly and he locked it in position with a satisfying click.

And suddenly Jack was whole again.

And still just ahead of Sphinx in this final desperate race to the top.

Jack used his newly attached hand to grab the next indented handhold in the wall and scaled the last vertical section to the overhang.

At the overhang, he gripped the first hand-rung and made to swing out above the drop and get up and around it—when suddenly a large muscular hand appeared from out of nowhere below him and gripped Jack's foot like a vice and yanked him back down to the ledge.

Jack landed back on the ledge in a clumsy heap and looked up to see Rastor standing over him, back from the dead, his eyes blazing with fury.

50 seconds . . .

Rastor picked Jack up by his lapels, lifting him fully off the ground again and holding him up to his massive face.

The giant general growled, 'As I fell I managed to clutch a balcony further down that pylon. Like you, I don't die easily.'

Jack couldn't believe this.

He was so close!

Over Rastor's shoulder, he could see Sphinx, climbing upward, about to take on the overhang.

He didn't have time for this.

'I see that, General,' he said. 'So you'll just have to die *hard*. This is my gift to you for killing my mother, you rat bastard son of a bitch.'

And with those words, Jack—still hanging from Rastor's mighty fists—pulled something from his jacket pocket and jammed it into Rastor's mouth.

Rastor never expected the move, never saw it coming, and his eyes sprang open in surprise.

Jack took that split-second opening to punch away Rastor's forearms, forcing the big man to release his grip on Jack's lapels.

Jack dropped to the ledge, landing like a cat, and he unleashed a withering uppercut with his new titanium fist, a blow that smashed up into Rastor's chin, causing his teeth to clamp together . . .

. . . and puncture the small red orb that Jack had stuffed into his mouth.

Jack dived away as Rastor's head exploded, blown apart from within by the blast of the ancient orb—the one Jack had removed from the ceiling of the Endless Tunnel to examine.

Liquid fire splattered outward and Rastor's whole head just vanished, vaporised in a burst of red, and suddenly the big general's body was standing there stupidly without a head.

It wobbled unsteadily for a moment before its legs buckled and the headless body fell with a *whump* to the ledge before rolling off it and falling down the side of the pinnacle.

General Rastor—commander of the royal forces, escapee from Erebus, nihilist who wanted to see the end of the universe—was finally dead.

40 seconds . . .

Jack was moving before Rastor's headless body landed.

Now, it was just him and Sphinx and he sprang upward, leaping for the handholds on the underside of the overhang, just as on the

other side of the pinnacle, Sphinx did the same.

30 seconds . . .

Jack swung hand-over-hand and then hauled himself around and over the lip of the overhang.

20 seconds . . .

Then he rose to his feet on the summit of the pinnacle, right in front of the Throne of Death.

At that moment, Sphinx appeared on the opposite side of the wide silver-floored platform.

The pink sky above them was suddenly shot through with celestial lightning. The very fabric of the universe was cracking, about to rush inward in a cataclysmic singularity.

10 seconds . . .

Between Jack and Sphinx stood the Throne of the Tree of Death.

It was both stunning and frightening.

It sat on a podium of three broad steps and was made of the same black-and-gold stonework as the castle.

It was high and wide, with broad armrests. Its backrest had been carved in the shape of a goldman: his faceless beaked head poised above it, the armrests fashioned in the shape of his arms.

The effect was that whoever sat on the throne would be sitting in the embrace of the fearsome alien being.

Sit in the embrace of Death . . .

Jack was fractionally closer to the throne, maybe a metre.

Sphinx shook his head at the sight of him: at his broken nose, his bloodied face.

'Do you even know what sitting on that throne will do to you?' he called.

Jack frowned. Had he missed something? Something he'd needed to do before ascending this throne?

8 seconds . . .

'Life is rule and death is life, so death is rule, too!' Sphinx shouted. 'I am ready for that! Are you? How about this? I will make you a prince in my new regime. I will give you a whole continent to rule as your own. You've done enough, Jack. It's time to stop. Let me take my place on the throne and do what I was born to do.'

6 seconds . . .

Through his bloodstained teeth, Jack gave Sphinx a crooked smile.

'You clearly don't know me, do you? I didn't come this far, just to come *this* far.'

4 seconds . . .

Sphinx bolted off the mark, diving for the throne.

Jack sprang forward, too, with his metre head start.

He bounded up the three broad steps with Sphinx lunging close behind him, crying, 'No!'

3 . . .

But Jack got there first and with two seconds till the end of all things, he hurled himself onto the Throne of the Tree of Death, into the embrace of the goldman carved into it.

A blaze of blinding light sprang up all around the throne, engulfing Jack and throwing Sphinx back to the floor.

A hurricane of wind whipped all around Jack as a deep resonating *thrum* began to grow within the castle structure beneath him.

The thrumming grew and grew and grew, intensifying to a mighty crescendo until with a resounding *boom* of ungodly scale . . .

. . . a bolt of incandescent white light shot up from the pinnacle and lanced away into the sky at many times the speed of light.

It was a stunning thing to behold.

As he saw it shoot skyward, Jack realised that this was Einstein's quantum pulse: informing the advanced beings who had built this place that the inhabitants of Earth were worthy of continued existence.

But then, as he sat on the throne, enveloped in the raging wind and looking up at the spectacular quantum pulse, Jack felt the light shoot *through* him.

His body spasmed.

His teeth clenched.

It felt like every fibre of his being was being disassembled and then reassembled by the light: ripped, wrenched, jerked, pulled, yanked, torn apart and then put back together, when suddenly—

—silence.

He was in the black void again, soundless and empty, the alternate plane of existence or whatever it was.

The roar of the wind was gone.

The blazing whiteness of the light was gone.

The electrifying of his body was gone.

And in a distant corner of his mind, Jack wondered if Sphinx had been telling him the truth, that he had overlooked something, something important he'd been supposed to do before he'd sat on the Throne of the Tree of Death.

He wondered: Am I dead? Did I just die?

Life is rule. Death is life.

It was the same voice as before, deep and authoritative.

Tell me, am I dead?

You are being reborn.

Reborn as what?

As you but different.

How will I be different?

All will obey you.

There came another flash of light and everything went white and . . .

. . . Jack blinked . . .

. . . and suddenly he was back in the real world, on the summit of the pinnacle, sitting on the throne in the sculpted arms of the goldman, underneath the purple desert sky.

The wind stopped blowing.

The otherworldly light went out.

Sphinx lay on the silver floor in front of the throne, staring up at Jack in wide-eyed, absolute, petrified horror.

'Oh, my God . . .' he stammered. 'You . . . you did it. You stopped Omega.'

Jack breathed in hard and deep.

'Bet your ass I did it,' he said.

Sphinx was still gaping at him in awe.

'Please, I must know, do you *feel* it? The power? Do you feel it?'

To be honest, Jack didn't feel any different, at least not from how he'd felt before he'd sat on the throne. His broken nose and cheekbone still hurt like hell.

All will obey you, the disembodied voice had said in the black void.

Jack thought about that.

Then he said to Sphinx, 'Stand up.'

And Sphinx, to his own evident surprise, instantly stood.

'Put your hands by your sides,' Jack said.

Sphinx immediately did so, his eyes bulging with astonishment.

He has no choice, Jack thought in wonder. *He has to obey me . . .*

Holy. Shit.

This was the power Sphinx had sought. Total obedience to his every command. When combined with the power of the Siren bells to immobilise entire populations, it would indeed have made him the undisputed ruler of the world.

And now Jack had that power.

Sphinx made to step toward Jack.

'Don't move,' Jack ordered and Sphinx froze on the spot, no longer able to command his own muscles, unable to take another step.

Jack's eyes fell on the gold signet ring on Sphinx's finger with its giant red gem.

The ring of the emperor, the ring that commanded *all* of the bronzeman armies, that overrode every other ring of command. Another awesome tool.

'I think I'd better take that.'

He stepped forward and, as Sphinx watched—unable to move, helpless to resist—Jack slid the powerful ring off Sphinx's finger and put it on his own hand.

Jack felt dizzy, sick even.

More than that, he felt unworthy, unsure he could handle all this power.

He was still reeling from those thoughts when Zoe and Lily scrambled up onto the platform and ran over to him. Alby, with his one hand, had of course remained below.

Zoe stared at Sphinx, immobilised in mid-stride.

'Okay, what's with him?' she asked.

'You're not gonna believe me when I tell you,' Jack said.

NEW YORK CITY, U.S.A.

Nobody and Iolanthe were still racing through the night-time streets of New York City in their Jet Ranger helicopter, fleeing from Chloe's two attack choppers with the all-important Blue Bell in their possession.

As they roared through the urban canyons, banking and bending, Iolanthe suddenly had an idea.

She started shaking the Blue Bell.

It immediately issued a piercing, ethereal chime. If the song of the other Siren bells was ecstatic, this sound was of a higher order still: it cut through the air like an aural laser beam, like a glorious, all-encompassing call to life.

And suddenly the citizens of New York City—lying on the sidewalks, slumped in their cars—began to stir and rouse and stand, blinking in confusion, rubbing their heads and eyes.

'It's working!' Iolanthe yelled.

'Nice,' Nobody said, yanking on his control stick, guiding the chopper around another corner, bullets from their pursuers slicing through the air all around it.

'All right,' he said. 'I've just about had enough of this. I grew up in Jersey, across the river from this town. Let's see if these assholes know New York City as well as I do.'

He gunned the chopper south—shooming downtown as people on the streets below rose from their collective slumber like a giant

Mexican Wave—before he cut left, out of view.

The two pursuing choppers followed, banking in the same direction just in time to see Nobody's and Iolanthe's chopper cut right at the next narrow canyon-intersection and ascend.

The two chase choppers swept around the turn, also going up—

—to suddenly see the cables of the Brooklyn Bridge right in front of them, too close to avoid!

Nobody had known this was coming, and had swept nimbly under them, but these pilots hadn't.

The first attack chopper went ploughing right into the cables, disappearing into them and twisting awkwardly.

The second chopper, with Chloe Carnarvon in it, ploughed right into the first one and the two military choppers exploded together.

The fireball caused all the bridge's cables to wobble and vibrate as flames and rotor blades flew out in every direction.

Nobody and Iolanthe hovered in their helicopter a short distance away, watching the two enemy choppers burn.

'See you later, Chloe,' Iolanthe said softly. 'You picked the wrong team.'

SINAI DESERT, EGYPT
29 DECEMBER, 0525 HOURS

Twenty minutes after averting the end of the universe—and having helped Alby scale the overhang—Jack sat with Zoe, Lily and Alby on top of the pinnacle of the Throne of Death, staring up at the sky.

The spiderweb of cataclysmic white cracks had faded, replaced by a serene morning glow.

The gargantuan stadium-like space that had risen up out of the desert floor simply remained in its new place, a colossal new feature on the landscape.

After all the mayhem with the pulse and Sphinx—who still stood motionless nearby—Jack had put out a call on his radio, hoping that Sky Monster or Aloysius Knight might respond.

To his pleasant surprise, both answered.

'We're just over at the Red Sea coast, boss. Been dealing out a bit of death and destruction. On our way.'

As he waited for them to arrive, Jack turned to the others.

'So, I guess we were all worthy, huh?' he said. 'I had a hell of a conversation with that gold colossus. What did he say to all of you?'

'Apparently, I'm pure loyalty,' Zoe said.

'Pure love,' Lily said. 'And a "most holy and wise Oracle".'

'Courage,' Alby said. 'Pure courage.'

Jack smiled at the three of them. 'Loyalty, love and courage. Couldn't have put it better myself.'

Eventually, two helicopters arrived above the massive grey megastadium: a skinny attack chopper and a larger transport helicopter.

Rufus and Aloysius Knight were in the cockpit of the attack chopper, while Sky Monster, Easton and Smiley could be seen inside the transport bird.

Sky Monster brought his helicopter in low over the pinnacle and, high above the megastadium, Jack and the others boarded it.

Jack grabbed some handcuffs from the chopper, bound Sphinx with them, and ordered him inside.

Sphinx obeyed.

Then the two choppers lifted off and headed west, leaving the gargantuan open-air megastadium behind them.

The team returned to the temporary airstrip at the Red Sea coast, where there was some communications gear that hadn't been destroyed.

They called the other teams—Iolanthe and Nobody in New York; and Pooh, Stretch, Tracy and Sister Lynda in D.C.—desperate to know how they had fared in their missions.

Pooh Bear answered immediately. 'We're at Raven Rock, north of Washington, D.C. and we have full lists of all the members of the royal world who were gathering at the three rendezvous points for the Omega Event.'

'How are they all reacting to this?' Jack asked. 'Not well, I imagine.'

Stretch answered. 'Oh, no, they're fine. After they sprang their trap and hacked our plane, we sprang ours, took control of their bronzemen and then rolled a Siren bell into their underground living quarters and put them all to sleep.'

Iolanthe's voice came over their earpieces next.

'And Nobody and I have the Blue Bell,' she said. 'We're flying it down from New York City to D.C. right now, ringing it as we go, waking up the population. We'll be sure to hold off when we get close to you, though, Stretch—wouldn't want to wake up any of those royals you put to sleep.'

Jack sighed. 'There's gonna be a lot of things to clean up after this. Entire populations to wake and a whole world to put right. Our work has just begun.'

A MAN NAMED JACK

PART V

THE WORLD AFTER OMEGA

Heroes come and go, but legends are forever.

KOBE BRYANT

In the months that followed the Omega Event, Jack's story slowly became known.

On 29 December, the whole world—at least those people who had been awake—had seen the sky fill with dreadful cracks and then seen the colossal quantum pulse of energy shoot up into it.

Television networks, released from Sphinx's emergency broadcast signal, showed footage of the event, captured on cell phones.

And then, gradually, word seeped out about an event that had occurred in the Sinai Desert in Egypt, and in the Red Sea near it . . .

. . . and suddenly, the news channels were filled with aerial images of the massive megastadium in the Red Sea—filled to the brim with seawater—and the newly risen stadium in the Sinai Desert.

Something historic had happened—something not just on a human scale but on a universal scale—and the world wanted to know all about it.

Heads of state called each other, searching for answers, and soon it became apparent that a small team of soldiers hailing from several minnow nations had been working on this mission for twenty years, a team led by a crack Australian trooper by the name of Jack West Jr.

The first thing to do was wake everyone up.

Under Sky Monster's command, flanked by escort planes, the Blue Bell was flown over all the cities that had been afflicted by Sphinx's ringing of the Siren bells.

Most of the populations awoke, groggy and hungry, but alive.

A small few fared worse than others: Moscow, for instance, as the first city to succumb to a bell, saw several thousand of its citizens die of exposure or starvation during their week of unnatural slumber.

And so the world woke to tales of white-cracked skies and quantum pulses and the story of a man named West who had saved the world and seen off the end of the universe.

Discussions were held at the highest levels.

It was decided that hearings would be held in the Security Council chamber at the United Nations Building in New York.

When the leaders of the world's most powerful countries gathered there, they called on Captain West and his associates to address them.

As the details unfolded over the course of weeks, it became clear to the world that this man and his team had saved *everyone*.

Many people remembered when the TV airwaves had been hacked a week previously and Captain West had been cast as a villain to be assassinated.

But now they knew the truth.

He told them of ancient prophecies and the expansion of the universe and a celestial phenomenon called the Omega Event.

He also told them about the secret royal system that had been pulling the strings of governments around the world for centuries.

This revelation, naturally, caused a worldwide sensation.

Judicial commissions were established in countries worldwide to investigate 'the hidden royals' within their governments, courts and military forces.

Captain West and his associates assisted them.

The lists that had been obtained from Sir John Marren's briefcase helped immensely in this task.

But Jack had a knack, people said, of getting royal sympathisers to talk and thus he helped weed out members of the royal world who had infiltrated all kinds of national and international institutions, parliaments, spy agencies and armies.

Some exposures caused uproars, especially in Britain and Europe, where many members of prominent aristocratic families were revealed to be part of this secret cabal. They were put on trial, shamed, and sent to prison.

The entire Russian Army was disbanded, given how hopelessly riddled it was with royal agents.

Likewise, certain special forces units, like the British Royal Marines and America's Delta Force underwent full-scale purges.

The Catholic Church was completely restructured. Given the roles its most senior figures had played in the whole affair, for a time the Church became the target of worldwide hostility and anger. A special commission was created just to investigate the full extent of its actions.

Captain West suggested a person to lead that commission: Sister Lynda Fadel of the Order of Serene Maidens of Novodevichy Convent in Moscow.

She turned out to be a wise and compassionate investigator, insisting that despite the flaws of some in its senior leadership, the Church still had much to offer the world in terms of charity, spiritual care and—when it came to the many artefacts and artworks at the Vatican—history.

And so, with Jack's assistance—and his uncanny way of getting the truth out of even the most stubborn witness; it was said that at his questioning, witnesses went to water and instantly offered up the truth—Sister Lynda purged the Church of its corrupt elements.

And then there was the man named Sphinx, Hardin Lancaster XII, the man who, in his lust for world domination, had ordered the ringing of the bells that had felled millions and killed thousands.

He was sentenced to life in prison, to be served in an old royal jail named Erebus whose location was, and would remain, unknown.

There was also the issue of the bronzemen and silvermen. Several thousand of them were still out in the world.

An investigation was conducted into the locations of the four rings of command, the rings that enabled their wearers to command particular battalions of bronzemen.

Two of the rings had vanished with the deaths of Dion and Jaeger Eins. Pooh had the third and Easton retained the fourth.

In the end, Jack had the ring of the emperor and it overrode all of the others, allowing him to command *all* the automatons.

So, to kill two birds with one stone, Jack sent all of the automatons—bronze and silver—to Erebus as well. There they stood, stock still, in countless rows, absolutely filling the place.

Their one order: to make sure that Sphinx never, ever escaped.

Naturally, historians and archaeologists descended upon the super-ancient sites that Jack and his team had uncovered over the course of their twenty-year mission.

The Fall shaft within Mont Saint-Michel in France.

And the one within Mont Blanc.

And a third inside the blasted-open Temple Mount in Jerusalem.

The megastadium in the Red Sea was drained and its walls repaired so that it could be studied. Like many of the other sites, after a year or so, it soon became a must-see tourist destination.

Cruise ships would sail to it, allowing their passengers to peer down into the round city-sized space and take photos of the magnificent white-and-silver castle in its middle with the broken pinnacle atop it—the one Jack West had shot with the main cannon of the destroyer mounted on the aircraft carrier, both of which were still there, left in their positions for history's sake.

It was the same with the second megastadium in the Sinai Desert. While its inner sanctums and chambers were secured, tourists were permitted to flock to it, to stand at a respectful distance near its mighty walls and look down at the spot where Jack West Jr had saved the universe.

In the years following the Omega Event, normal life resumed.

As humans do, people went back to their jobs and their lives and their regular everyday issues.

Jack, of course, became the most famous person on the planet.

Others might have revelled in such monumental fame, but not Jack.

He declined invitations from presidents and prime ministers, even one from Oprah.

His fame, it could be said, was like that of Neil Armstrong, the first person to set foot on the moon: he had not accomplished what he'd done to be famous. He'd done it because he had been the right person for the job.

Jack treated his fame in the same way Armstrong had: he largely retreated from public view, spending most of his time at his farm in the Australian desert.

The Australian government, ever thankful for his efforts over the course of twenty years, helped him by providing a no-fly zone over a thousand-square-kilometre-wide space around his property.

Plus conferring on him the nation's highest military honour.

Plus a lifetime unlimited pension.

But Jack didn't really care for any of that. He lived in glorious isolation on his farm with Zoe, his aging falcon Horus and his beloved dogs.

He was not seen in public often.

When he was, it caused something of a sensation, like the time he arrived, without warning, at Easter Island, to explore a deep shaft beneath the Vertex there, to retrieve, he said, a Pillar that had fallen into it some years before.

The wisdom etched into it, he said, would be important in the future.

He retrieved the Pillar and then retreated back into obscurity.

Life went on. The world went on.

The Olympic Games were held. Hurricanes hit coastlines. Wildfire seasons came and went. Governments were voted in and out.

Of course, nations squabbled, although every now and then, Jack would be asked to mediate some international dispute somewhere and he would go.

And he would always—*always*—walk away from those summits with the matter settled and the parties acting as he asked them to.

It was strange. It was as if everyone just wanted to do what he told them.

Lily would complete her medical studies at Stanford and became an accomplished cardiac surgeon based in Los Angeles.

Of course, after all the Omega stuff, she too became well known around the world.

Her fame, however, was more like that of a First Daughter, which meant—sadly—that it was often focused on her looks or hairstyle or what she wore.

For a while, being young, Lily didn't mind it, but once she had completed her studies and begun working full-time at the hospital, she figured out ways to avoid the cameras and soon the media lost interest in her and found standard celebrities to follow.

Oh, and on the day after she graduated from med school, she married Alby Calvin.

★ ★ ★

Alby would go on to become one of the world's foremost physicists, mentioned in the same breath as Stephen Hawking, Richard Feynman and his hero, Albert Einstein.

His early involvement in the Omega Event gave him insights into the subject matter that few others could even hope to emulate, to the extent that his work furthering the Friedmann Equation—the mathematical model of the expanding universe—and Einstein's work on it where k was greater than zero was seen as groundbreaking.

He became a professor of astrophysics at the California Institute of Technology, a position he would hold for the rest of his life.

But for all his accomplishments, all his scholarly work, he was most proud of his family.

Alby and Lily would have four children. First, twin girls, then a boy and then another girl.

The twin girls, of course, were born with the ability to read the Word of Thoth, but Lily and Alby quickly realised that the other two were also very adept at picking up languages, so Lily taught it to them as well.

This was something that, in the months after the Omega Event, Lily and Alby had spoken about with Jack and Zoe.

They needed to ensure that Earth did not lose the knowledge required to avert Omega again, and as the ones who held that knowledge—the Capstone of the Great Pyramid, the six Pillars of the Machine, the locations of the Three Secret Cities, the Altar of the Cosmos inside the Rock of Gibraltar, the four remaining iron mountains, and of course, the Throne of the Tree of Death inside the Supreme Labyrinth—it was their responsibility to make sure this knowledge was not lost.

The first step was teaching Lily's children the Word of Thoth and also enhancing the Church's computer programs that could decode it.

They also set about analysing the Altar of the Cosmos inside the Rock of Gibraltar and the sacrificial pool within it. They did this with a team of the world's finest geneticists and DNA experts

and after a few years, it was deduced how the terrible ritual at that chamber could be performed with only the blood of an Oracle and not require anyone to be killed for the ritual to work.

Nobody and Iolanthe went on their date and it went very well.

They lived together at Nobody's estate in Jamaica.

Iolanthe never let her hair grow back.

In fact, she lived the rest of her life with her head shaved. She said she preferred herself that way.

Pooh Bear and Dr Tracy Smith would also go on a date, and then more dates, and then, a year or so later, they got married in a glittering ceremony in a palace in the United Arab Emirates while Pooh Bear's beaming mother cried with joy.

The best man, of course, was Stretch.

Jack attended as the second groomsman.

The media went nuts about that: that someone could have Jack West in his wedding party was amazing, but that he was the *second*-best man was simply out of this world.

Aloysius Knight and Rufus returned to the business of bounty hunting.

It turned out that hunting down fugitive royals and their sympathisers was both dangerous and particularly lucrative, which meant it was right up their alley.

They visited Jack whenever they happened to be nearby.

Easton returned to the minotaur kingdom in the Underworld in India as an out-and-out hero on a par with the great Asterion.

As the personal friend of Jack West Jr, he was offered the leadership there, to be the next king.

He politely declined.

Instead, he asked Jack a single question and Jack had answered, 'Why, of course.'

And so Easton lived out his days in a small standalone cottage on Jack's farm, happily tending to and playing with Jack's two dogs.

Easton actually had a companion living with him in that cottage, albeit a silent one, with a partially melted back.

Despite his wounds, Smiley, the bronze automaton who had stepped in front of a blast of liquid fire to shield Jack and his team, still functioned, and he happily helped Easton and Jack with various duties around the farm.

He was great for heavy lifting and a particularly good scarecrow.

He was also very useful as a messenger who could carry packages and messages to Jack's new next-door neighbour and owner of the enormous adjoining station, Sky Monster.

And finally, Jack.

He and Zoe lived happily on the farm, content and in love.

Jack thought often about his adventures, about the time he saved the world and stopped the collapse of the universe.

And while, of course, he'd told his team about it, he never told the world about the power that had been bestowed on him when he'd sat on the Throne of Death during Omega.

All will obey you.

Zoe and Lily kidded him about it, especially when it came to household chores.

'Don't you ever tell me to take out the rubbish or do the laundry, Jack West Jr!' Zoe joked.

Of course, he might have used the power sometimes, subtly of course, like at those international mediations, but that was only ever in the pursuit of peace.

★ ★ ★

More than anything, though, Jack loved sitting on his porch in the morning, sipping his coffee as he looked out at the view.

One day, a couple of years after Omega, he was doing just that, enjoying a mug of coffee and gazing out at the rising sun. Horus was perched on his chair back, grey-feathered with age but ever watchful.

Zoe was still inside, asleep.

Easton was in his cottage, also asleep, with Roxy the poodle sleeping on her back at the foot of his bed while Smiley stood in the corner like a statue.

Jack's other dog, Ash, the placid labrador, was with Jack. She always joined him for this morning ritual on the porch, happily curling up at his feet.

Jack looked down at the dog and saw a faded old tennis ball nearby, the ball that Ash famously refused to fetch for anyone.

Jack thought about that day on the pinnacle and shrugged to himself.

He picked up the ball.

'Hey, Ash.'

The dog looked up at him.

He tossed the ball a short distance off the porch.

'Fetch the ball, Ash,' he said gently.

The dog gave him her usual unimpressed look . . .

. . . but then she stood, trotted off the porch, picked up the ball in her teeth, brought it back and dropped it at Jack's feet.

And at that Jack West Jr smiled and took a deep satisfied sip of his coffee.

THE END

ACKNOWLEDGEMENTS

Well, I guess we've reached the end, so I think it's appropriate for me to mention those people who've helped it all happen.

First, my thanks to Cate Paterson, my longtime publisher at Pan Macmillan. She was the one who discovered a copy of *Contest* way back in 1996 and signed me up to a two-book deal. She was there again in 2004 when I said I was writing a non-Scarecrow book that would feature a new hero, an adventurer named Jack West Jr who would go in search of ancient artefacts in ancient places. That book would be called *Seven Ancient Wonders*. It came out in 2005. Cate has supported every book of mine and has been a champion of me since the beginning.

This is no small thing. In Australia, I think it's fair to say, the literary world kind of looks down its nose at big blockbuster fiction, and yet Cate—like me—has always just pressed on publishing it because, well, those are the kinds of books she enjoys reading! I would not be here without her.

My editor, Alex Lloyd, has done a superb job with the Jack West Jr books (and quite a few of my standalone novels, too), with his encyclopaedic knowledge of the series, detailed mind, and tireless work ethic. Seriously, it's very hard work keeping up with me, especially with all the diagrams, but he has done that admirably!

Speaking of the diagrams, Gavin Tyrrell deserves a shout-out. As the books became more complex, so did the pictures, and Gavin does them all so well. He has also created all the Jack West cover

art since *The Four Legendary Kingdoms* and those awesome covers speak for themselves. I don't think any series has had such a wonderful and consistent theme to its covers (Gavin even did the recent special edition of *The Seven Ancient Wonders* so that it matched all the other books).

My publicist at Pan Macmillan, Tracey Cheetham, organises all the touring and media, and is unmatched in Australian publishing, maybe even in world publishing.

On the home front, Kate Freeman is my biggest supporter and loving companion. She encourages me, and that's worth more than all the gold in the world. And she loves Dido, too (that's my seventeen-year-old dog). Kate is always one of the first people to read my books—sometimes over a year before the rest of the world—and she always reads them with enthusiasm.

My brother, Stephen Reilly, is also one of the first to read my stuff, yet he does so with a more technical, story-based, critical eye. His advice is always constructive and kind, helpful, never negative. Every writer needs readers like this. Thank you, brother.

Beyond that, let me send out a huge thank-you to all my readers who have joined me on this journey with Jack and his team for sixteen years. Jack's story was always meant to be about friendship and family—about how a hardbitten team of soldiers could become a family because of this sweet little girl in their midst, and how they could bring out the best in each other—and I like to think readers liked that about it. It's fun to read about acts of heroism, but when it's done for family, it's, just, well, better! I've always enjoyed that side of the series and I confess I had tears in my eyes as I wrote the final chapters.

I'm glad you enjoyed the ride.

AN INTERVIEW WITH MATTHEW REILLY

SPOILER WARNING!

The following interview contains SPOILERS from *The One Impossible Labyrinth*. Readers who have not yet read the novel are advised to avoid reading this interview as it does give away major plot moments in the book.

So, it's over! You've ended the Jack West Jr series! Tell us your thoughts on this series, ending it, and whether, just maybe, there could ever be The Zero Something Something.

Ha! I don't think there will be a *Zero Something Something*. I think I'm done. I don't have any more ancient places or myths to write about and I feel that the characters have all reached places where we can let them literally live happily ever after.

I very much enjoyed writing this book, especially the extended epilogue. In fact, that epilogue was one of those rare pieces of writing that pretty much wrote itself: I just gave each character what I felt they deserved, after all their trials and efforts.

(I particularly like Pooh Bear's wedding: how he's found a great girl and his mother is overjoyed; but most of all, I love that Stretch is his best man and Jack—the world-famous Jack West—is the *second*-best man! Stretch and Pooh's friendship is one of my favourite things in this whole series and it has lasted since they both dived from cover at the same time in *Seven Ancient Wonders* to rescue Lily. That friendship is really emblematic of the whole series.)

Because really, when I think about it, this series is about friends and family and love, and how your friends lift you up and help you reach further than you could reach by yourself. In the climax, for instance, Jack, with the help of those who love him—Lily, Zoe and Alby—literally reaches further than he could have by himself.

And over the course of seven novels, that's been a consistent theme. Having Lachlan Adamson carry his brother, Julius, to safety in *The Five Greatest Warriors,* and when he's asked if he needs assistance because Julius must be heavy, he says, 'He's not heavy, he's my brother.' (This also made their deaths in *The Three Secret Cities*, especially Julius's when he confronts the Knights of the Golden Eight, more tragic.)

I should also add that I enjoyed writing about Jack's fame. He has always acted in obscurity, out of the world's eye, and I felt that after all he did, over twenty years, he deserved recognition! That said, I was always intrigued by how Neil Armstrong handled his massive global fame—with quiet dignity. So I modelled Jack's reaction to his fame on Armstrong's.

Ultimately, this book is an ending. It's a send-off for a bunch of characters we have known for sixteen years and a chance for readers to say goodbye to them. It's very rare to end a series. Indeed, it's not something I've ever done before, so it's all rather new to me, too.

But I'm happy to do it here.

I wrote 'THE END' and I felt very content.

We start this book seconds after The Two Lost Mountains, *which ended with Jack West's ingenious Russian Doll plan. You don't waste time getting right into the action for this last book!*

Essentially, *The Two Lost Mountains* and *The One Impossible Labyrinth* are one story. They were designed to flow right into each other. (Truth be told, the last four books of this series are essentially one single story: once I decided to write *The Four Legendary Kingdoms* I actually planned out the last three books in the series. Indeed, you can see many things mentioned in *4LK* coming to life in the later books: things like the two sacred trees and the Lifestone were mentioned way back in *4LK*.)

And, hey, I like a book to start quickly! Always have.

The tattoos on Imhotep's skullcap were featured at the end of 2LM. *Did you plan how the whole Labyrinth would unfold while writing the previous book?*

Mostly, yes, I did. The idea that the skullcap's tattoo was arranged in a spiral was always there, as were the two trees with their thrones being placed on either side, the notion of the Emperor's Route, and the Endless Tunnel. Beyond that, I left myself a little room to come up with some new mazes, like the rotating maze.

You make the stakes feel very real for the characters early on—we all thought Zoe really was a goner!

I wanted to give readers a real shock right from the start. That opening scene is designed to be an out-of-control blitz of wild action and I wanted it to end with a jarring and unexpected emotional loss.

And since I do have a history of killing off nice characters, I felt readers might think—even if only for a moment—that I'd done it again.

In the end, the stakes are everything. And while the fate of the universe is ultimately at stake in this book, for Jack, the wellbeing of his close-knit team and family is what matters most to him.

In my novels, I've often pondered the *idea* of a hero. In *Scarecrow*, where Shane Schofield loses a loved one, he asks if the world even cares about what he's doing; if the millions of people he saves actually recognise what *he* sacrifices in doing so. It was similar here: I wanted Jack to contemplate if it's worth saving humanity when you have to see your loved ones die.

But it's not just bottomless caverns and endless tunnels our heroes have to worry about. The Bronze and Silvermen were menacing enough, and in The One Impossible Labyrinth you finally introduce the Goldmen.

Yes, once we had bronzemen and silvermen, we had to have goldmen! I like the idea that each one is slightly better and more capable than the previous model.

With the bronzemen, Jack figured out a way to beat them. And in this book, he finds out that you can defeat a silverman, almost.

For the goldmen, I just wanted them to be something totally dangerous. So dangerous, you can't even look them in the face.

And yet, I still got to have a little fun and create Smiley, a bronzeman who is totally loyal and will defend whoever he is told to defend. Some of my favourite moments in this book involve Smiley stepping in front of danger!

While Jack and his group battle their way through the Labyrinth, some of our other heroes are discovering the true location of one of the most famous cities in the world—Troy!

One of my goals with the Jack West series has always been to link all the cool ancient places around the world and also to retell many of our most famous and enduring myths in interesting and modern new ways.

And of those myths, Troy and the Trojan War has long been on my mind. And it's such a famous tale—alongside the tale of Theseus and the minotaur—that I decided to keep it (and the Theseus legend) till the final book.

I love the idea that the horse was a ramming ship, rather than some kind of large statue. It seemed more 'real' to me.

Poor Bertie . . .

Not everyone can survive.

Then there are those other pesky Shadow Royals causing trouble on the surface, including a new character, the royal banker.

I loved introducing Sir John Marren in this book—although eagle-eyed readers will remember that he was named in *4LK*, when he was elevated to the position of Duke.

Part of the fun of this series is building the shadow royal world, figuring out what mechanisms and bureaucracies it would need to function, and a banker/treasurer seemed likely to me way back when I introduced the idea of the shadow royals in *4LK*.

I must mention that there is actually a real fellow named John Marren! He's a lovely man and a great friend of mine! Not anything like the dastardly royal banker we meet in this book.

You draw from all the previous Jack West books for this one, from Jack's sister to conversations with Wolf to flashing back to when Jack was in the military. You dedicated this book to your loyal fans for a reason!

Yes, the dedication was for exactly that reason: as a thank-you to my readers for following the story for so long. I'm very aware that

my readers pay close attention to *all* the details in my books, so I tried to reward that in this book with many detailed references to the previous ones.

When I sat down to plan this final book, I thought readers of the series would really appreciate references to earlier books: to things like the Warblers and Wizard.

The reference to Jack's sister is a unique one. That mention of Lauren, his sister, was something I put into *The Six Sacred Stones* way back in 2007. To be honest, I had planned to use it for a plot twist back then (it was going to be something like: Jack was meant to be on that plane with Lauren but for some reason, he didn't catch the flight; the whole airliner was crashed in an attempt to kill him and so she was killed instead), but I decided not to follow that plot strand. But I still left the mention of Lauren in *6SS* just in case I decided to use it at some point in the future.

When I decided that the final book would be all about Jack and his character and how he became the hero we know, I felt it was the perfect time to refer to her again.

The quadrilateral maze has to be one of your most brilliant, complex creations, Matthew. How did you come up with it?

I just wanted the Supreme Labyrinth to have one totally wild maze and the rotating maze was it.

Coming up with it wasn't so hard. It was describing it that was tough! Figuring out how to describe a wall becoming a floor, or a blockhouse going upside down took many, many rewrites.

Then we finally get the answers we've been waiting for when Jack meets the Gold Colossus and learn the secret of the Lifestone, the seven worlds . . . how satisfying was it to finally write this scene, to reveal everything?

Yes, this was a very satisfying scene to write. It was something I'd thought about back when I wrote *The Six Sacred Stones*. (It's funny, the whole series really began with that book. *Seven Ancient Wonders* gave me a taste of the world I was creating, but it was really while writing *6SS* that I truly sat down and contemplated the question: *who built all these ancient sites and why?*)

I love all the mysterious ancient places in our world and I've visited many of them. The inexplicable nature of them just intrigues me. The Great Pyramid. Stonehenge. Chichen Itza.

It's this kind of inherent mysteriousness that gave rise to the Gold Colossus's words and the idea that we humans, with all our tribalism and wars, are failing at some kind of celestial test that was left here for us.

It's a close fight right until the end, and the odds are never in our heroes' favour—but they are triumphant. How did you go about deciding fitting ends for Ezekiel, Dion, Rastor, Mendoza and Sphinx?

This is a good question. It's all about comeuppance. About these villains getting what they deserved.

Ezekiel, the woman-hating monk, of course, had to be killed by a woman, and so that honour went to Zoe.

Dion—who had been doing dastardly things since *4LK*—had to meet his match in Lily. And Lily had to defeat him *without* Jack's help. This was always going to be her moment, her triumph over him.

Cardinal Mendoza was always going to die at the hands of the Gold Colossus. He's a snivelling toady, a conniving manipulator, and thus unworthy. He was always going to be there for the shocking moment where it seems that the colossus has condemned Jack to die.

Sphinx and Rastor were both such big villains that their fates had to be meted out by Jack, our main hero. Sphinx, because he and Jack had been battling each other for three novels, since *The Three Secret Cities*. And Rastor because he was just so much fun! When you're writing a story about the end of the universe, trust me, you need a bad guy like Rastor who *wants* everything to end. It just makes it more interesting. Having him be this big, strong guy meant he was always going to break Jack's artificial hand, requiring Jack's family to throw him Alby's hand, and as a team, defeat Rastor and Sphinx and win the day.

'Life is rule, Death is life.' Jack earning the power to 'rule' was quite a twist! He is basically a superhero now. Was killing Jack off ever on the cards for you?

No. Never.

Call me a softy, but I'm still, at heart, a storyteller who likes to see the good guys win and the bad guys get what's coming to them. Jack was always going to survive and triumph.

Quite literally at the end of this book, I think, everyone gets what they deserve, and that includes Jack. I mean, hell, he worked his ass off for seven books! He deserved to sit on that throne and, perhaps more importantly, *to find out what would happen to whoever did*! What makes Jack different from, say, Shane Schofield, is that he *wants to know*. He's curious about these things. (Like Scarecrow, he doesn't give up. Ever.)

I like it that the person who gets this awesome power—to be obeyed—is the one guy who won't use it to his own advantage. He will use it to settle international disputes—and to get his obstinate dog to fetch a ball—but otherwise, he just won't use it. That's a real hero.

Stepping away from Jack West for a moment, while you were writing this book you had another major project in the works. Talk to us about Interceptor, *Mr Director!*

Yes, this year I directed an action movie, *Interceptor*, starring Elsa Pataky. It's not from a novel. It's an original screenplay that I wrote with my friend, the great screenwriter, Stuart Beattie.

As many of my fans know, I've wanted to direct movies for a long, long time, and I wrote *Interceptor* in such a way that I would have a shot at directing it. How? By making it take place largely in one location, an interceptor missile facility. By doing that, I kept the cost of the movie down to under $20 million and because of that, I was given the nod to direct it.

I had a blast! I love the movie—it's a wild, out-of-control romp—and, as someone who for years has worked alone, I loved the experience of working with talented and creative people. I very much want to do it again!

It must be a dream come true. Will you be back in the director's chair any time soon? Turning one of your own novels into a movie, perhaps?

Two words. *Ice Station.*

Have we lost you to Hollywood? Are you writing your next book yet?

Ha! No, you haven't lost me to Hollywood. Writings novels is still something that I love doing very much and I don't think I'll ever stop doing that! I'm 46 now, and I've been writing novels professionally for 23 years. The idea of moving into a new phase of storytelling appeals a lot. Making movies would be a nice thing to do in between the books. Maybe that's what I'll do: make a movie, write a book, make another movie. That'd work for me.

While I have started a new novel—a standalone—after this last year with *The One Impossible Labyrinth* and *Interceptor*, I need a bit of a break, so it'll be a while till I finish it.

Any final words?

I always say at this point that I just hope readers enjoyed the book. For this one, let me add that I hope they found some closure and satisfaction.

I dedicated it to my fans because they read my books with a sense of fun and enjoyment and yet also with deep attention to the details: for that reason, this book had a lot of detail in it, detail that readers of the whole series would appreciate. So for this one, let me say, I hope you enjoyed *the whole series* and its conclusion.

But I will return . . .

Matthew Reilly
Sydney
July 2021

MORE BESTSELLING TITLES FROM MATTHEW REILLY

Ice Station

THE DISCOVERY OF A LIFETIME

At a remote ice station in Antarctica, a team of US scientists has found something buried deep within a 100-million-year-old layer of ice. Something made of *metal*.

THE LAW OF SURVIVAL

In a land without boundaries, there are no rules. Every country would kill for this prize.

A LEADER OF MEN

A team of crack United States marines is sent to the station to secure the discovery. Their leader – Lieutenant Shane Schofield, call-sign: SCARECROW. They are a tight unit, tough and fearless. They would follow their leader into hell. They just did . . .

Area 7

A HIDDEN LOCATION

It is America's most secret base, a remote installation known only as Area 7.

THE VISITOR

And today it has a guest: the President of the United States. But he's going to get more than he bargained for on this trip. Because hostile forces are waiting inside . . .

HIS SAVIOUR

Among the President's helicopter crew, however, is a young marine. His name is Schofield. Call-sign: SCARECROW. Rumour has it, he's a good man in a storm. Judging by what the President has just walked into, he'd better be . . .

Scarecrow

IT IS THE GREATEST BOUNTY HUNT IN HISTORY

There are 15 targets. And they must all be dead by 12 noon, today. The price on their heads: $20 million each.

ONE HERO

Among the names on the target list, one stands out. An enigmatic Marine named Shane Schofield, call-sign: SCARECROW.

NO LIMITS

And so Schofield is hunted by gangs of international bounty hunters, including the 'Black Knight', a ruthless hunter who seems intent on eliminating only him.

He led his men into hell in *Ice Station*. He protected the President against all odds in *Area 7*. This time it's different. Because this time SCARECROW is the target.

Hell Island

It is an island that doesn't appear on any maps. A secret place, where classified experiments have been carried out. Experiments that have gone horribly wrong . . .

Four crack special forces units are dropped in. One of them is a team of Marines, led by Captain Shane Schofield, call-sign: SCARECROW.

Nothing can prepare Schofield's team for what they find there.

You could say they've just entered hell. But that would be wrong.

This is much, much worse.

Scarecrow and the Army of Thieves

THE SECRET BASE

It is a former Soviet base known only as Dragon Island. It houses a weapon of terrible destructive force . . . that has just been re-activated.

A RENEGADE ARMY

The island has been seized by a brutal terrorist force calling itself the Army of Thieves, and the fate of the world hangs in the balance.

ONE SMALL TEAM

There is an equipment-testing team up in the Arctic. It does not have the weaponry or strength to attack a fortified island held by a vicious army. But it is led by a Marine captain named Schofield, call-sign: SCARECROW. And Scarecrow will lead the team in anyway, because someone has to.